AND THEN THERE WERE TWO

A Dani Ross Mystery

AND THEN THERE WERE TWO

GILBERT MORRIS

CROSSWAY BOOKS • WHEATON, ILLINOIS
A DIVISION OF GOOD NEWS PUBLISHERS

And Then There Were Two

Copyright © 2000 by Gilbert Morris

Published by Crossway Books
 A division of Good News Publishers
 1300 Crescent Street
 Wheaton, Illinois 60187

Unless otherwise noted, Scripture is taken from *Holy Bible: New International Version*®. Copyright © 1973, 1978, 1984 by International Bible Society. Used by permission of Zondervan Publishing House. All rights reserved.

The "NIV" and "New International Version" trademarks are registered in the United States Patent and Trademark Office by International Bible Society. Use of either trademark requires the permission of International Bible Society.

First Crossway printing, 2000

Cover design: Cindy Kiple

Printed in the United States of America

Library of Congress Cataloging-in-Publication Data
Morris, Gilbert.
   And then there were two / Gilbert Morris.
      p. cm. — (A Dani Ross mystery ; bk. 2)
   ISBN 1-58134-193-8 (alk. paper)
   1. Private investigators—Louisiana—New Orleans—Fiction.
2. Women detectives—Louisiana—New Orleans—Fiction.
3. New Orleans (La.)—Fiction. I. Title.
PS3563.O8742 T44   2000
813'.54—dc21   00-008983
                                                           CIP

15	14	13	12	11	10	09	08	07	06	05	04	03	02
15	14	13	12	11	10	9	8	7	6	5	4	3	2

To Rick and Karen Long

*This is a dark world, but from time to time
I encounter those whose shining light
shatters the darkness. You two have been
a joy and a light on my path.*

CONTENTS

One

GENTLE PERSUASION

From the confines of a heavy gilt frame, Colonel Daniel Monroe Ross stared down at the couple who faced each other squarely. Bars of pale April sunlight filtering through the high window to the colonel's right highlighted his aristocratic features, giving a richer texture to the gray Confederate uniform complete with red sash and gleaming saber hilt. The colonel had been resting peaceably in the family graveyard since ten years after the War of Northern Aggression ended. However, a vividness caught by the artist in the eyes and firm lips gave animation to the lean features.

A man and a woman, definitely not composed of dead pigment but of flesh and blood and nerves, faced each other under the stern eyes of the Confederate officer. The colonel's great-great-granddaughter, Dani Ross, was holding herself upright, her backbone stiff as a ramrod. She was a young woman of twenty-six, and something about her features were faintly reminiscent of the colonel. Her gray-green eyes were deeply set in her squarish face. Her mouth was too large and her nose too short for classic beauty, but the coloring and fine texture of her skin offset that, and the deep tones of the auburn hair cut just over her collar were the envy of most women. Her 134 pounds were trim but womanly, and the dress she wore accentuated her femininity. It was a simple black piqué, a two-piece dress with large white buttons on a striped jacket. The jacket fitted tightly at the waist, accenting her figure. She wore two pairs of black and white drop earrings joined by gold rings. It was a simple costume that only a woman confident of her appearance could wear.

In the awkward silence that filled the office, Dani shot an involuntary glance up toward the colonel. She had formed a habit of talking to him when she was alone, for he had been a man much to be admired. Her father had told her many times, *He never quit, Dani. He may have had the wrong cause, but he gave it all he had.*

"Your report won't do, Ben." Dani broke the silence with the terse statement. "I'm not happy with it at all."

"Sorry to hear that."

The speaker, Ben Savage, was exactly five-ten, and his weight was so well distributed that he seemed smaller than he actually was. He looked more like a finely-tuned middleweight boxer than a detective. His Slavic face, square with a shelf of bone over his eyes and a short nose that had been broken at least once, revealed his European ancestry. His hair and eyebrows, coarse and unruly, were as black as anything in nature. Savage was wearing a pair of light tan chinos, a gray sweatshirt, and a Texas Ranger baseball cap shoved back on his head. He wore a pair of black Nike's, scuffed and well worn. As he stood slouching before her, Dani thought he should dress better.

As the two of them stood examining each other warily, Dani reviewed their history in her mind. She hadn't wanted to hire Savage in the first place; but after her father's heart attack, she had taken charge of the Ross Investigation Agency. From the beginning she had discovered that some jobs required a hooligan, and she had set out to hire one. Savage, whom she had disliked on sight, had been an ex-aerialist with a circus, an ex-Marine, an ex-homicide detective, and ex-several other things. The two of them, however, had been thrown together in a bizarre case that had become known as the Silo Adventure. Dani and Savage, along with eleven other people, had been captured and kept in an empty grain silo. The maniac who had accomplished all this was a wealthy man named Maxwell Stone, and it had required all of Dani's intelligence and Ben's acrobatic and physical ability to make their escape from the silo.

Since that episode Dani and Ben had fallen into a strange partnership—a love-hate relationship that neither liked, but for some reason neither of them could walk away from. Most of their vitriolic arguments centered around Dani's character. Savage insisted that she was trying to be a man, while Dani countered with the charge that he was threatened by her ability.

The present argument had begun over something as trivial as the newly decorated offices that housed the agency. The Ross Investigation Agency was located on Bourbon Street in New Orleans. Once the setting had seemed romantic to Dani, but parking was a nightmare, and the tourists flocked like lemmings to the area hoping to get involved in sinful pursuits. But after the publicity of the Silo Adventure, many clients had sought the agency out, and Dani had decided to redecorate the offices instead of moving to a more reputable section of the city.

Savage had been absent for almost a week, prowling around doing his usual sleuthing. When he had come in and first saw the newly decorated offices he said brusquely, "I don't like it. It's too fancy." Dani had been stung by this since she herself had overseen the decorations.

She said between gritted teeth, "You never had any taste! If you had liked the redecoration, I would have had it all ripped out!"

Savage lifted one raven-black eyebrow in a quizzical expression. "I think you should."

"What's *wrong* with it?"

"Poor clients will feel inhibited."

"They'll be impressed."

"No, they won't. They'll feel out of place. But then maybe you don't want any poor clients."

"What kind of crack is that, Ben?" Dani demanded, her eyes turning more green as they tended to do when she grew angry. "What's wrong with a few trappings of success?"

"It's like restaurants," Savage said abruptly.

"Restaurants! *What's* like restaurants? You have a mind like a blasted butterfly! It flits all over the place!"

"Well, when you go out to eat, you can either have good food or you can have fancy decor."

"You can have both."

"No, you can't."

Dani glared at Savage and shook her head. "It's impossible to get any culture into you, Ben Savage, so I'm going to stop trying."

"Good," Ben said cheerfully. "Now, down to business."

"What about the Anderson case?"

Savage shrugged and said, "I think I've about got that nailed down."

Dani waited for him to go on, but when he said nothing she exclaimed, "What do you mean *nailed down*? What have you done?"

The James Anderson case involved a middle-aged man who had been injured in an industrial accident. He was a family man with four young children and had been, perhaps, permanently crippled. His insurance company insisted it was the fault of the company Anderson worked for, claiming they had not observed safety precautions. The company, of course, denied this, and the insurance company retained the Ross Agency to prove their claim. Dani had little hope of uncovering the truth, for it had been quickly discovered that, as always, employees were not quick to speak out. Most were afraid for their jobs, and some just didn't care.

Going back to her desk, Dani sat down and put her hands flat on the glass surface. She wore a beautiful turquoise ring on the middle finger of her right hand, and she examined it for a moment and then looked up. "What are we going to do? We can't go to court without more evidence."

"I have a witness," Ben said. "He works at the Brady Company where the accident occurred. I think with a little encouragement he'd be willing to testify."

"He'd be afraid of losing his job."

"Not this one. He's not crazy about his work."

"Give me his name, Ben. I want to talk to him myself. I'm particularly interested in this case."

"Why's that?"

"Because James Anderson may never work again, and it's not fair that the Brady Company gets off without paying for that. They can afford it."

"The companies that can afford it hate paying the worst. You know what the Brady Company's like. They're big here in Louisiana. Lots of people have gone after them, and no one has won."

"Just give me the name, Ben. I'll see that the man testifies."

Savage reached up and ran his hand through his coarse, black hair, displeasure in his angry eyes. "Better not, Dani," he said quietly. "I think I'd better handle it."

Dani stood up and walked around the desk. "Oh, you think it's too hard for me! What is it—a *man* thing?"

"More or less."

The silence ran on, growing almost palpable. Finally, seeing that his boss was not going to let the matter go, Savage said evenly, "You're like this office, Dani—too good-looking and too dainty to handle Joe Bob Redd."

Dani snapped, "I said I'd handle it!" Her eyes flashed, and she leaned forward as if about to attack Savage.

Grinning suddenly Ben said, "You know, like they say in the movies, 'You're beautiful when you're angry.'"

"Where do I find him?"

"He'll be at the Blue Crab Festival today."

"And where's that?"

"Over at Lacombe."

"I want you to write up all the reports you've been working on. How will I know this man?"

"Oh, you'll know him all right. He's a member of a motorcycle gang. Just pick out the biggest, ugliest, hairiest, most tattooed troglodyte," Savage said cheerfully. "That'll be Joe Bob."

Dani nodded and said, "Get those reports typed up—and I want them neat this time. You hear me?"

"Sure. I think the people in the next office heard you."

Dani stepped outside into the outer office, where she found Angie Park hammering away at her computer. Angie was a rather attractive woman of twenty-seven with blonde hair and blue eyes. She appeared very fragile, but she always seemed to attack the keyboard as if it were a personal enemy. She looked up briefly and said, "You have an appointment with Judge Clemson tomorrow at three o'clock."

"All right. I'll take care of it, Angie. I'm going out to make a call, but I should be back by this afternoon." Even as she spoke, she caught a glimpse of Ben coming out of the office. As he stopped and looked at her innocently, she glared at him, daring him to speak. He said in the blandest of tones, "Have a good day, boss." He plucked a delicious apple from the fruit bowl on Angie's desk and stood chomping it loudly.

"Go on, Ben." Dani's eyes glinted as she stared at him.

"Go on with what?"

"Try to talk me out of it. I know you're going to."

Ben chewed for a moment, swallowed, then shook his head. "Nope. I believe in letting people do what they want to do."

"Good!"

Changing into a snowy-white, three-quarter-length jacket, Dani left the office. *Why do I let him get to me? I should have learned by this time that he just has to play his macho games!* Ignoring the crude comments of a pair of overweight tourists wearing garish Hawaiian shirts, she went to the parking lot. Getting into her Cougar, she was grimly happy at the thought of doing something to prove Ben Savage wrong. It had become irritating to her, for some reason, how he uncannily saw through people. She had fancied herself quite an expert in pop psychology, but more than once in his brief tenure Savage had proved that he was better at that art than she.

Traffic was relatively light in New Orleans that day, and without losing her temper more than once or twice at tourists, she threaded her way down narrow streets barely wide enough for two cars to pass until she made her turn on 610. Turning west she drove quickly,

changing lanes past Metairie, then took the causeway that spanned
Lake Pontchartrain.

A feeling of relief washed over her as she stepped on the accel-
erator, leaving the city behind. New Orleans was a fascinating place,
an international city, but something about the city depressed her.
It was as if all of the evil that had taken place for so many years
had penetrated the entire metropolitan area, soaking into the very
stones. Dani was wise enough to know that stones can't be evil
any more than they can be good, but put enough people with a
depraved lifestyle close together for a hundred years or so and what
they are seeps into the very nature of the city. Ben had said once,
"The Saints are never going to win anything. People don't go to
watch them play football—they go to get drunk." Dani had argued,
but to her chagrin the Saints wound up every season with records
like 3-13 or worse.

The causeway reached straight across Lake Pontchartrain like a
white arrow made of concrete, and the small toll was insignificant
when compared to the difficulties faced in driving around. As the
Cougar covered the miles over the causeway, Dani took her eyes
away from the long, narrow, white strip long enough to watch a
flight of pelicans skimming over the surface of the water. She'd
never learned why they sometimes flew so close to the water that
the smallest waves could touch their gray undersides. They made
comic figures with their protruding beaks and short tails, but something in their group flight was pleasing to Dani. She had often
wondered how they decided which bird would lead in the V for-
mations and what signals they gave to turn the whole formation
right or left.

Overhead, seagulls' white undersides flashed in the clear morning air, and she heard their raucous cries over the noise of the
Cougar's engine.

Slowing down, she paid the toll and flashed a smile. "Hello,
Harry."

"Hello, Miss Ross." Harry smiled back and waved her on saying, "Watch your speed. The cops are thick today."

"Thanks, Harry."

Leaving the causeway, she thought about stopping by her home in Mandeville, but she was anxious to nail down Joe Bob Redd's testimony. Turning right on Interstate 12, she sped along thinking of how to handle a tough biker. She knew deep down Ben would have been a better choice for this task, just as she would have been better dealing with the president of a large company. Being a CPA was always an asset with those people, but with the lower elements a CPA did not win much respect.

Turning off at the Lacombe exit she saw at once that the festival was set up as close to the interstate as possible. She pulled the Cougar into the parking lot, which was mostly filled with pickup trucks and older cars. Getting out, she locked the Cougar, then noted the bumper sticker on the red Dodge Ram with a jacked-up body—*Just keep honking. I'm reloading.* A smile touched her lips, and she noted that the owner also had plastered Confederate flags on the back windshield and another on the antenna. Inside, a pair of large foam dice dangled from the rearview mirror.

Leaving the parking lot, she made her way toward the activities. The smell of Cajun cooking came to her, rich and spicy—fried shrimp, crab bisque, jambalaya, and gumbo. Passing by an open space, she studied the dancers moving briskly to the music of a zydeco band, and more than once a man asked her, "Hey, baby, you wanna dance?"

Shaking them all off, Dani walked quickly around and almost at once spotted her quarry. At one of the tables at the edge of the activities, a group of bikers was washing down huge plates of food with bottles of beer.

As Dani moved forward, she thought, *They all dress alike. Not an original outfit in the bunch!*

The "uniform" was, for the most part, skintight jeans, half boots with steel on the toe and the heel, black leather jackets open with no shirt beneath, and motorcycle caps shoved back. Most of them had long hair in ponytails, and all were tattooed. A flicker of memory touched Dani as she approached. One of her clients, a middle-

aged woman, had been forced to accept a female biker as a daugh-
ter-in-law. "The best thing about her," the woman had moaned,
"is that all her tattoos are spelled right."

As Dani stopped at the edge of the group, the acrid odor of
marijuana drifted to her. When most of the bikers turned to stare
at her, she said clearly and precisely, "I'm looking for Joe Bob Redd."

A howl went up, then raucous words and lascivious whistles. A
huge man stepped off the saddle of a black Harley. He must have
weighed over 250 pounds, a great deal of it in his stomach, which
poked out hairily past his vest, sagging over his huge, leather belt.

"Here I am, honey bunch," he grinned. As he came closer, Dani
had an impulse to step back from the odor of raw alcohol, sweat,
and other primal odors. *I should have let Ben handle this . . .* Dani
pushed the thought away; it was too late for that now.

"Are you Mr. Redd?"

"Aw, honey, you can call me Joe Bob." His smile was marred
by a missing tooth, and his whiskers were tangled. He was probably somewhere in his forties, but his dark brown hair was streaked
with silver. Coming closer, he loomed over her like a mountain.
Winking lewdly he said, "What's a purty little thang like you doin'
here? I bet you wanted to see whut a *real* man was like."

Catcalls and whistles came from the group, and a voice said,
"Why don't you show her, Redd?"

Dani said hurriedly, "Could I speak with you privately?"

"Private as you like, darlin'. Come right along."

Dani felt her upper arm seized by a powerful hand, and she
was piloted away from the group. She wanted to dig her heels in, but
she was pulled along relentlessly. "There's a nice place right over
there. Won't nobody bother us, doll."

An alarm went off in Dani's head, and she said quickly, "I don't
think—" But Joe Bob broke in, "Don't you worry none, baby. You
come to the right place. I been plannin' to upgrade my women for
a little while, and I believe you're about right for me."

Apart from screaming and throwing herself to the ground, Dani
could think of no way to extricate herself. She found herself pulled

behind a line of trees, where underbrush and vines hid them from the others' sight. She could hear the sounds of the rock music and laughter, but fear overwhelmed her.

"Please! This is far enough!"

"I reckon so." Red turned around and, reaching into his back pocket, pulled out a bottle. "Have a drank."

"No, thank you, Mr. Redd. What I want to talk about is—"

She had no chance to explain her mission, for suddenly she was held tight by a pair of arms with gorilla-like strength. She found herself being pulled to the ground, and Joe Bob's hands were pulling at her clothes. Opening her mouth to scream, she felt a huge paw cover it. She tried desperately to scratch the man's face, but his strength was too much for her. Redd laughed insanely as he said, "Now, doll, you gonna find out what a real man is like."

During all the time trapped in the silo at the mercy of a madman, Dani Ross had known fear, but this was different, and for the first time she knew real terror. Kicking futilely at the huge man and trying to reach his face with her one free hand, the other pinned beneath her, the fear she felt was brutal and ugly and unclean.

Clunk!

Dani heard the sound that came sharply and clearly to her ears, and immediately Redd's body went totally limp. His full weight was on her, but she felt the huge man pulled aside, and a voice said, "Well, boss, how's it going?"

Dani stared up at Savage, who was looking down at her, his face expressionless. Her face colored. She always hated it when she blushed! She got to her feet and pulled her torn blouse together. "How—how did you get here?"

"Followed you." Ben Savage nodded cheerfully.

For a moment Dani almost lost it. She had been proven wrong again, and somehow that was almost worse than what had nearly happened to her! Well, not really, but . . . She searched Savage's square face for a sign of laughter. If she had seen it, she suspected she would have screamed. But his face was as innocent as a newborn child as he glanced down and said, "He's a mean one, but he's coming around."

Quickly Ben reached down and pulled up one of Redd's pants legs but found nothing, then the other one. He jerked a small automatic out of the biker's ankle holster and glared at it. "Nice piece," he observed, then watched as Redd stared at him.

Redd rolled back and forth and groaned; then his eyes opened and he looked around wildly. He came to his hands and knees and then rose. He stared at Savage and ignored Dani. "Whatcha hit me with?" he growled.

"Didn't hit you with anything. I kicked you in the neck."

Redd took a step forward but stopped as abruptly as if he had run into a wall when Savage lifted the 9mm and chambered a shell. The sound made a sharp clicking noise that registered on the biker's ears, and his eyes narrowed. "Hey, I know you!"

"Sure you do, Joe Bob. We talked a couple of days ago. You remember? It was about your testimony."

"Ain't testifyin'. Give me my piece back."

Dani had nothing to say. The world into which she had suddenly stepped was as alien to her as Mars or Venus. But it was not, as she had known before, an uncomfortable world for Savage. She saw the almost pleased expression on his face.

"You know, Joe Bob," Savage said mildly, "your parole officer's going to be real disappointed when we give him this gun and Miss Ross and I testify that you were carrying it."

The words seemed to penetrate quickly, and Redd's eyes grew small. "What would that get you?"

"It would put you back behind bars in Angola."

"Why do you want me there? I ain't never done nothin' to you."

"You disappointed me, Joe Bob. I wanted you to testify. Now you know in your heart that Anderson got hurt because of bad safety in the plant."

"What are you talking about? I already told you I'd testify."

"But you wanted money. That would not do at all. The jury

would not like it, nor would the judge. Makes your testimony less believable, you know what I mean?"

"Whut do you want then?" Suspicion narrowed Joe Bob's red eyes, and he leaned forward as if he would throw himself on the smaller man even though the gun was pointed directly at his heart.

"I just want you to testify to the truth like a good, upstanding citizen. You are a law-abiding citizen now, aren't you?"

Something stirred in Redd's eyes, and he muttered, "I got to get somethin' out of it."

"Well, you get to stay out of Angola. That's a bonus. But no money." Ben Savage hesitated for one moment and then added, "Of course, after the case is settled and Mr. Anderson gets his settlement, I think it's highly probable he would show his appreciation for your assistance."

Redd grinned abruptly as the light broke through. "Oh, I gotcha! Sure, man, I'd be glad to testify. You just never explained it like that."

"That's good, Joe Bob. You remember that. You remember how mean those guards can be at Angola, let alone the more immoral inmates. You be at Miss Ross's office tomorrow at nine o'clock, and we'll take your statement."

"Okay. You're sure about that 'preciation?"

"Very sure." Ben turned and said, "Come along, Miss Ross. I think we've accomplished our mission."

"Hey, what about my piece?"

"You can pick it up tomorrow at our office."

As Dani walked away in her high heels, stumbling over the broken ground, Ben reached out and took her arm. When she looked up at him, he said, "Always good to see justice and truth prevail, isn't it, Miss Ross?"

Dani glared at him as she stalked back past the zydeco dancers.

Two

MONEY IS *ALWAYS* THE ANSWER

Pulling up into the driveway that circled the front of the two-story house, Dani stomped on the brakes, got out, and slammed the door viciously. Slamming things seemed to give her pleasure. She had tried to lose Ben on the way back from Lacombe, but every time she looked in her rearview mirror the '66 Pinto with fading paint was right behind her. She hated everything about the Pinto, but Ben had bought it for junk, overhauled its engine, and totally ignored the nicer things such as window crank handles. As he pulled up beside her and got out, she ignored him and stalked toward the house. Usually just the sight of the house pleased her. Set back off the road, it was sheltered by towering oaks bearing loads of Spanish moss. A split-rail fence ran parallel to the house. A rust-colored quarter horse came galloping up, throwing his head up at the sight of her.

"Not now, Biscuit," Dani said grimly as she marched up the steps. She was aware that Ben was right behind her as she entered the house. As soon as she stepped inside, she saw her mother and father who had evidently been in the living room off to the left of the foyer. Taking one startled look at her dirty attire, her father exclaimed, "Dani, what happened?" He was a tall man of sixty with a patrician look, including prematurely silver hair and a long, aristocratic nose. His heart attack had given him a pale color but had not reduced his good looks.

An impish mood came on Dani then, and she said loudly, "Ben assaulted me!"

A startled look swept across the face of Ellen Anne Ross, Dani's mother. A tall, ash-blonde beauty from Texas, she was usually able to take Dani's statements, no matter how wild, without shock. But this time she blinked and whispered, "Ben!"

Dani felt an immense satisfaction. For once she had managed to shake up Benjamin Davis Savage! His jaw was actually sagging, and he was staring at her wildly. "Well, go on! Tell them what you did, Ben. You're a fiend. Admit it!"

Suddenly Ellen began giggling, and Dani whirled to see merriment dancing in her blue eyes. "Well, fine! You think it's funny that a thug would attack your daughter!"

By this time Daniel Ross was smiling also. "Come on, out with it. What's the truth?"

"I take it I have no credibility here," Dani pouted. Holding her head high, she stalked down the foyer, followed by her mother, leaving the two men alone. Dani climbed the stairs, and as soon as she was in her room her mother inquired, "What really happened?"

Dani turned and began pulling her ruined blouse off. "I told you what happened. Why don't you believe me?"

"Oh, don't be silly! Ben wouldn't do a thing like that."

"Are you infatuated with that man or something, Mother? It's a shame and a disgrace at your age!" Dani snapped, her eyes flashing. She slipped out of her blouse and skirt, then announced, "I'm going to take a shower." She scurried into the bathroom and got into a hot shower. The scuffle with Joe Bob Redd had left her feeling somehow unclean on the inside, but a good hot shower with lots of soap would at least cleanse the outside. Knowing her mother would not leave, she stayed in the shower a long time, taking a perverse delight in making her wait. Finally Dani turned the water off, stepped outside, and dried off, then moved into the bedroom.

She said with resignation, "All right, all right, it wasn't Ben—though I don't know why you're always on his side."

"Dani, what really happened?" Ellen listened quietly as Dani related the incident, but her eyes showed alarm. "You shouldn't have done that, Dani. That's what you hired Ben for."

Simply because she knew her mother was right and she had been wrong, Dani refused to say anything more. Moving over to the closet, she began to riffle through her outfits and selected one of her favorite business suits. She slipped into the slim skirt, then into the fitted jacket. Moving over to her shoe closet, she selected a pair of braid-webbed, white shoes and slipped them on.

"I have to go back to the office, Mother," she said.

Knowing better than to talk to Dani when she was in such a mood, Ellen sighed and followed Dani back into the kitchen. "I want to eat first," Dani said. "I don't want to stop at a restaurant."

"I'll heat up something," her mother said. Soon she served Dani's favorite—red beans and dirty rice. She set the steaming bowl on the table along with a bowl of gumbo and freshly baked Mexican cornbread, her husband's favorite. The others sat down for lunch as well.

Sitting down at the table, Daniel took his wife and daughter's hands. Ben silently took Dani's other hand and bowed his head. "Lord, we thank You for this food, and we thank You for the safety that You provided. Thank You for Your constant care. In Jesus' name, Amen."

Daniel took a generous helping of the gumbo, but Ellen at once seized it and poured half of it back. "You're not supposed to have this. We're trying to get those arteries of yours clear."

"Well, *my* arteries are wide open," Ben said firmly and at once threw himself into consuming the gumbo, along with generous portions of red beans and rice. He picked up the Tabasco sauce that Ellen had put out for him.

"I don't see how you have any taste buds left," Ellen said, a grimace on her face. "It seems like you would have burnt—" She was cut off as the phone on the wall rang.

"I'll get it," Dani said. She rose and picked up the receiver. "Hello? Yes, it's me, Angie. Go ahead."

The others went ahead with the meal, Daniel speaking with Ben about the chances of the Texas Rangers winning the pennant, a small miracle, he thought.

When Dani returned to the table, she didn't sit down. "Well," she said in a strange tone, "we're moving up in the world."

"What do you mean by that, Dani?" Daniel Ross asked.

"Good news, Dad. We just got a call from J.T. Denver. He wants to see us. He wants to do business with the agency."

Interest flickered in her father's eyes. "Well, if you have a client like J.T. Denver, you don't need another one."

The name of J.T. Denver was known in practically every household in America, especially those interested in tycoons. Denver was a self-made man who got his first big start by taking over a floundering tractor factory in New Jersey and putting it on its feet. In the process he made a lot of money, but his big break came when he invented a device to dig ditches under sidewalks and streets without tearing them up. Every construction company in America and overseas just had to have one. Denver then moved onto bigger things such as shipping, stocks, and electronics. But the one thing everybody knew about J.T. Denver was that he was a ruthless competitor. He was often compared to a killer shark.

"He wants to see us right now, and I don't intend to keep J.T. Denver waiting." She turned, her gaze on Savage who had gone back to eating with his large spoon. "You have to come too, Ben."

"Me? What for?" Ben was surprised because Dani always did the preliminary work with clients. She was good at it, and he was not, being too outspoken. He sat there for a moment, then rose saying, "I don't know why he'd want another thug. He has plenty of them working for him already."

"We'll find out. Hurry up."

Savage followed Dani to the Cougar outside. "You want to take my car?"

"No. I don't want to be seen in that thing! Get in."

With a shrug Savage got into the Cougar and said nothing as Dani roared out of the driveway, then quickly headed back toward the causeway. When they were halfway across, he took his eyes off the gulls that were circling a fishing boat and said, "Where's his office?"

"He's in the Sacre Coeur Hospital."

"Funny place for an office. Why is he . . . ?"

Dani didn't answer, her mind busy with exciting possibilities. *Dad's right. If we can get J.T. Denver in our corner, the agency will be home free!* She didn't say another word until she pulled up in front of the hospital. As she got out of the car, a mockingbird perched on a branch in an azalea bush puffed his chest out and anthemed the day.

"That fellow's got something to sing about," Ben said idly. He had to hurry to keep up with Dani as she rushed into the building. She went up to a receptionist sitting at a desk, a nun dressed in black, and said, "I need to see Mr. J.T. Denver."

"He's on the second floor. Room 232."

As they marched down the hall, Ben looked around with interest. Old crucifixes and faded religious paintings decorated the wall. "I hope the equipment's better than the pictures."

"I like them," Dani said firmly. "This is the oldest hospital in New Orleans. The nuns put up tents for the wounded when Bienville was storming around the swamps trying to find out exactly what he was claiming for France."

"Before my time," Ben grinned.

The automatic door slid open, and they turned left. "Most of the interns here come from LSU and Tulane Medical School. They're pretty tough and hard-nosed—you know, fresh interns."

"They all look pretty young," Ben said. "I wouldn't trust some of these doctors to change a tire."

They were stopped by a tall nurse in a nun's habit. Suspicion lurked in her sharp, gray eyes. "May I help you?"

"We need to see Mr. Denver."

"You can go into the waiting room. His family's in there."

Following the nurse's gesture, the two made their way into a large, airy waiting room with windows flanking one side. Pale, yellow sunlight flooded through, splashing on the walls and spreading out over the floor.

Two women and a man looked up as they came in. One woman, somewhat older, was sitting, and the other two persons were standing beside a window and talking in a hushed voice. They stopped as soon as Dani and Ben entered the room.

"My name is Danielle Ross from Ross Investigation Agency. This is my associate Mr. Savage."

The older woman reminded Dani of Bette Davis after her prime. She was thin and smoked with short, nervous puffs on a long cigarette. Her voice was unpleasantly shrill as she said, "I don't know why J.T. sent for detectives. We can get all the police we want."

The younger woman said, "This is my mother Vivian Sanderson. My name is Loreen Franz, and this is my husband Bobby." She was tall and dressed expensively. "I work for my father, and my husband is his accountant."

"What's happened?" Dani asked quickly. "Is your father ill?"

"He was in an accident," Vivian said. She got to her feet, took three quick puffs on the cigarette, then waved it around, pointing it at Dani. "I told him not to buy that stupid car—that he'd kill himself in it."

Bobby Franz said quickly, "I don't think it was his fault, Vivian." He looked like a man whose name would be Bobby instead of Robert. He was tall, painfully thin, and there was a shy awkwardness about him that probably reminded everybody he met of a younger Jimmy Stewart. There was trouble in his light blue eyes, and he ran his hands nervously over his light brown hair. "I don't know what J.T. wants to see you about. He wouldn't tell *us*."

Dani stood there hesitantly for a moment. "Hasn't he said *anything*?"

"Not to us," Vivian said. "And I'm his wife. It seems like he would talk to me."

"You *were* his wife, mother," Loreen said. She squared her shoulders, and a hardness glinted in her dark eyes. "I think you'd better go in and see him, Miss Ross, then come out and tell us what in the world he's thinking."

"Will he see us?"

"Yes," Bobby said quickly. "He left orders for you to come in. It's down the hall. Room 232."

"I'll get back to you as soon as I talk with him."

The two detectives made their way down the hall and knocked on the door. "Come in," a voice said, and Dani walked inside followed closely by Savage. She recognized the man in the bed from the pictures she'd seen of him. J.T. Denver was forty-five, and she could tell he was rather tall. He had a tapered face with a broad forehead and a rather narrow chin. The most noticeable features were the brown eyes that seemed to bore into her. He had crisp, brown hair prematurely gray at the temples.

"You Ross?"

"Yes, I'm Danielle Ross. This is my associate Mr. Ben Savage."

"Let's see some ID."

Dani smiled but pulled her license from her purse. She watched as the broad mouth of J.T. Denver tightened. He nodded. "All right. I'm going to hire you."

Both Dani and Ben noticed that he didn't say, "I'd like to hire you" or "Will you take my case?" He simply announced, "I'm going to hire you," and both had the impression this was not an unusual approach for the man.

"To do what?"

"To find out who tried to kill me."

Dani's eyes narrowed. "Perhaps you'd better tell us all about it, Mr. Denver."

Denver didn't speak for a moment. He finally said, "I read about you two being imprisoned in that silo. The way I read it, you were the brains, Ross, and you were the brawn, Savage."

"Beauty and the beast, our close friends call us," Ben said. He had a pleasant smile on his face and was studying the figure of the man lying on the bed. He saw something rash come into Denver's eyes, as if he were not used to being spoken to so lightly, but the look passed.

"I'm laid up and can't take care of myself for a while. That's what I want you two for."

"What actually happened? And how badly are you hurt?"

"One arm is pulled out of joint, though not broken." He held up his right arm. "And the other one is so bruised I can't bend it. I can't even wipe my nose. I have internal injuries and a gash in my scalp." He started to gesture toward his head, then winced. "It could have been worse," Denver said, speaking as calmly as if he were addressing a board of directors. "I was driving down—"

The door opened, and a heavyset nurse with a no-nonsense air walked purposefully toward the bed. "I have to give you something for the pain."

"Not now!" Denver snapped.

"It's important."

"Step outside, ma'am—or nurse or sister or whatever they call you."

"Sister will do. But I have orders from your doctor. You must be in severe pain by now."

"I'll call you when I'm ready. Shut the door on your way out."

Dani frowned, not liking the demanding tone in the man's voice.

"As I was saying, I need help. Somebody is trying to finish me off."

"You said that. What makes you think so?"

"I drive the same route every day to my office. Yesterday I was on an open stretch, and a semi was coming from the other direction. He let me get within fifty yards and then left his lane and headed straight for me." Denver's eyes clouded, and his lips grew tense. Finally he said, "No question—it was deliberate."

"You didn't collide head-on, did you?" Savage asked quickly. "You wouldn't be here if that were the case."

"No. I was driving a BMW convertible, but the truck would still have wiped me out. They knew that, whoever it was. I drive the same car every day on the same stretch. Anyway, I swerved, and he missed me, but I ran through a steel guardrail. I flipped the car and rolled over half a dozen times."

"You're sure it was deliberate?"

"Look, Miss Ross, I don't have time for small talk. When I tell you it was deliberate, you just have to take my word for it."

Dani had an impulse to turn and walk out of the room. Denver's rudeness irritated her. He was a man used to being obeyed instantly, and he did not take opposition lightly. "Perhaps we'd better get something straight, Mr. Denver. I'm going to give you every courtesy. In return," she said slowly, locking her eyes on his, "I will expect the same courtesy."

For a moment the room was still, and Dani expected that Denver would begin to shout. Instead he laughed. "All right, Miss Ross," he said cheerfully. "I stand rebuked. I had to claw my way up from nothing, and I didn't get to the top by being polite. But you're right. I forgot my manners. Sorry."

Dani was almost astonished at the sudden change in the man. When he smiled he was altogether pleasant. Changing gears, she said, "So who would want to kill you, Mr. Denver?"

"You pay your money, you take your choice. Any of several folks I've crossed in the past."

Dani half smiled, for Denver's battles with his competitors were notorious. "But just because you had a run-in with a business associate doesn't mean he'd try to kill you."

"Somebody did. My money's on Jack Byron."

"Mad Jack Byron?" Savage spoke up, his eyes lighting with interest.

"That's the one. He's tough enough to do it and ornery enough too. Totally depraved."

Dani quickly ran over what she remembered about Mad Jack Byron. He had been given the nickname while playing linebacker for the Chicago Bears. On every play he seemed totally dedicated to killing somebody. He'd gone into oil using his earnings from football and made several more fortunes. Aloud she murmured, "I've heard he's a man who succeeds any way he can."

"So I've heard. In with the Mob. Well, we're competing on a big deal. High-speed ferries. Big money is involved, and the winner gets the big contracts from the Orient as well as from our own nation."

Dani asked, "Why us, Mr. Denver? You have enough money to hire one of the big firms. You can have anybody you want."

For the first time Dani and Ben both saw embarrassment sweep across Denver's face. He reached up to touch his face but winced and allowed his arm to drop gently back to the bed. "Well," he said finally after considering his words, "here it is. I met up with God a few months ago, and I read in the papers that you're some kind of a minister. Is that right?"

"I'm a Christian believer, but I'm not really a minister. I planned to go to Africa as a missionary, but that's out of the picture now."

"Why?"

"God hasn't told me to do it yet."

Her answer took Denver off guard. His eyes narrowed, and he studied her carefully. "So God tells you things?"

Dani smiled. "Have you read the Gospel of John? Jesus said, 'My sheep hear my voice.'"

"I'm working through the Bible, but I guess I missed that one. You actually hear God talk?"

"Not with an audible voice, of course. But I think the Lord speaks to us through His Word and sometimes through other people. It's a still, small voice in our heart."

"Write down for me where that is in the Bible. There's a notebook right there."

Dani was amused but intrigued too. As she wrote the reference down and put the notebook back, she said, "I would have thought the newspapers would mention a man as visible as you becoming a Christian."

"I don't tell anybody much. No more than I can help."

"Why not?"

Denver shifted uncomfortably. "It's nobody's business but mine. I don't think much of celebrities riding on God's coattails as if they're doing Him a favor."

"How did you come to know God?" Dani asked curiously.

"I've always thought about God," Denver said, and a thoughtful look passed over his face. "And I've always known I was living in the wrong way. Any man knows that—any woman too, I guess. Well, a few months ago I began thinking about it for some reason, and as I was passing along on the east side of the city a man was preaching. He was just a poor guy wearing running shoes and denims and a jacket. Ordinarily I would have passed him on by, but that day I stopped and began to listen. I'd always been kind of cynical about religion, organized religion anyhow. But he didn't say anything about a church or about money." Denver paused. "He began to talk about Jesus and how all we had to do was call on Him and God would forgive us." He looked up and said quietly, "Well, that's what I did, Miss Ross."

"And that's how you met God?"

"Yes. Do you think I'm crazy?"

"No. People meet God in all sorts of ways. Some in cathedrals, some in churches, some on the lower east side."

"Well, I'm glad you think that. I have a lot to make up for, and I'm going about it the only way I know how—straight on."

"What are you doing?" Dani asked curiously. "To make up to God for what you've done, I mean."

"Well, I'm supporting about half a dozen missionaries that nobody else wanted to support. I'm supporting some colleges that are turning out preachers." Denver went on naming causes he was supporting, and finally he said, "That's what I do. I make money, and I try to use it to help spread the good news."

"What church do you attend?"

"I don't go to any."

"Why not?"

"Don't need one, Miss Ross. I've always been a lone wolf. I don't like crowds. If I went, they'd all want something from me."

Dani shifted uncomfortably. Something was wrong with all this, and she knew she couldn't let it pass. "You can't be a lone ranger, Mr. Denver. Psalm 68:6 says, 'God sets the lonely in families.' And in the New Testament we're directly commanded, 'Let us not give up meeting together.' As a matter of fact, Paul talks about the church as a body. A body has eyes, it has hands, it has feet. All together Christians make up the body of Christ."

"I'll tell you my favorite Scripture," Denver shot back instantly. "It's in Ecclesiastes, the tenth chapter and the nineteenth verse. I bet you don't know this one. It says money will do anything."

It was Savage instead of Dani who answered, "I don't believe that."

"That's what it says. There's a Bible there. Pick it up and read it."

Picking up the Gideon Bible on top of the nightstand, Ben handed it to Dani and said, "Find that. I'd like to see it."

Dani found the verse and read it aloud. "'Money answereth all things.'"

"Well, there you are," Denver said. "It's true enough too."

"But it only answers 'things.'"

"Well, that's what we want, isn't it? Things."

"We want more than that. Money will buy a car. That's a thing. It'll buy any house if you have enough of it. That's a thing too. But it won't buy love. It won't buy respect. It won't buy trust. It only buys things."

"Well, that's enough for me."

"No, it isn't. You need the family of God."

A savage look swept across J.T. Denver's face, and Dani saw the cruelty that lurked there. *He might have found God, but there's still some of his old ways left in him!* "Miss Ross, I have *three* families!" The voice was harsh and the words grating. "And all of them hate me. They only want one thing from me."

Dani was puzzled and confused. "What is it you want us to do, Mr. Denver?"

"I want you, Miss Ross, to find out who tried to kill me. And I want *you* to keep me alive, Savage. What are your terms?"

Dani mentioned the rates of the agency, and Denver nodded his head. "I'll pay that, with a bonus if you do the job. Get anybody you need. For one thing, I want somebody at this door day and night. I don't think they can get in through a window, but they might. Have somebody under the window out on the ground starting right away. Now, tell that nurse to come in and give me some joy juice."

Dani realized that she was being dismissed. "I'll get started on it, Mr. Denver. But I'll want to talk to you more about your Christian life."

"Just call the nurse. God and I will take care of my Christian life."

As they walked outside and shut the door, Dani looked at Ben. "If he's so arrogant now, think of what he must have been like before he met God."

That amused Ben. "I think now would be a good time to slap him on the cheek, while he has two bum arms. Somehow I don't think he would turn the other one."

"This is an odd situation, Ben. You get started on the security here. I'll start the ball rolling on my end."

"What are you going to do?"

"Well, for one thing I'm going to look into Jack Byron. Then I'll start looking for that semi that ran Denver off the road."

"Maybe somebody saw the accident."

"We'd better hope so. That's about the only clue we've got. I'm worried about that man, Ben."

"You're worried about a guy with his dough?"

"Yes. He's headed for a worse crash than he's been through if he thinks he can buy his way into the Kingdom of God."

Savage studied the face of Dani Ross thoughtfully. "Well, that's your department. I'll do my best to see that somebody doesn't send him on to his reward in the sky—or wherever he's headed."

Three

BEN MEETS A SUSPECT

Every time Dani stood next to Luke Sixkiller she felt fragile. It wasn't because she was a small woman—she was five-eight and firmly built. But something about Sixkiller always made other people seem small. He was no more than five feet ten, but he weighed 190 pounds. Somehow to Dani he always seemed more *solid* than other people. Sixkiller had the blackest hair possible, and his obsidian eyes veiled his emotions. At times a flicker of amusement would light them, and she had learned to recognize that. He was a pure Native American untainted by any white blood. He had high cheekbones, a Roman nose, and a wide mouth and looked much like the Sioux who had roamed the plains of America for years before the white man touched the shores.

The word on the street from the criminal element was, "Don't try to buy Sixkiller." Dani had noticed that the toughest members of the street gangs walked around him carefully, just as they would move around a minefield where something was likely to go off at any moment. He had taken three bullet wounds in his career with the police department, and now as Dani spoke with him, she thought that if she were in real trouble and couldn't get in touch with Ben Savage, this would be the man she'd ask for help.

Sixkiller took Dani back into his office. The decor of the New Orleans Police Department held true there as well—cheap battered filing cabinets, a scarred desk, three straight chairs in addition to the green padded one behind the desk. Strangely enough an original painting by Turner hung on the wall. Dani had always been fascinated how a rough, hard-nosed, streetwise cop like Luke Sixkiller could have a delicate, beautiful painting that must have cost at least a year's salary. But when she had asked, he'd merely said, "I like it."

Leaning back now, Sixkiller looked at Dani with his dark eyes and said," So you're working for J.T. Denver. That'll put you in another tax bracket."

"It might, Luke, but I'm at a dead end."

"That's my address most of the time." Sixkiller shrugged and picked up a rubber band. He bent a paper clip into a hook and mounted it on the band, then sent it flying across the room where it struck a picture of President William Jefferson Clinton. Sixkiller grinned and shook his head. "Too bad I don't have the real article here. What kind of a deal is it?"

"If I don't find that semi, Luke, I don't know where to turn."

"No description? No license plate?"

"Nothing. All Denver remembered is that it was light in color. He didn't have much time to think about it."

"Could have been somebody went to sleep at the wheel."

"Denver doesn't think so."

"He wouldn't be paranoid about everybody being out to get him, would he? That's the way it is with those money guys."

"Rich people are only poor people with money."

"That's what Hemingway said, but he was wrong. Having that much money makes people different. They live in a world all their own. The rules don't apply to them. They can buy their way out of trouble."

"That's what Denver said in a way." Dani suddenly remembered the magnate's remark. "He quoted a verse of Scripture from Ecclesiastes: 'Money answereth all things.'"

"Or at least it'll make a down payment on them. What do you want me to do?"

"One situation has possibilities, Luke. Denver and Jack Byron are fighting for a huge contract to build high-speed ferries. Most of them will be sold in the Orient, I think, but it's big. The one that finishes the prototype first will probably get the cream."

"Mad Jack Byron they call him. You ever met him?"

"No. Have you?"

"We don't move in the same circles." Sixkiller grinned suddenly, his teeth startlingly white against his bronze skin. "All I have to deal with here is murderers, embezzlers, and rapists. Of course, Mad Jack Byron's not that nice of a guy from what I hear."

"Will you look into him?"

"Me! I'm too busy giving out parking tickets and citations for jaywalking."

"Luke, you could do it. Check with your friends in the FBI."

"The FBI doesn't have any friends."

Dani stood up, and Luke quickly stood with her. He came over and reaching out squeezed her arm in what was meant to be a gentle gesture. The power of his hand was so tremendous that Dani had the feeling he could have crushed her arm easily.

"Say pretty please."

"Pretty please."

"With sugar on it."

"With sugar on it. And a cherry on top." Dani smiled.

"All right. I can resist anything except sweet talk from a babe like you. How about going out tonight?"

"Not tonight, Luke. I'll be working late at the office."

"Someday you're going to forget to turn me down."

"I know. Good-bye, Luke."

As Dani left the office, she thought about the sometimes ineffective and crooked police officers in many of the cities in America. The pay was pitiful, working conditions were terrible, and it was a miracle that more of them were not on the take. Sixkiller, she knew, was as solid as a rock, although often in trouble with his superior officers. *Insubordination* was the term they usually put on him, but she was glad there were men like him carrying a shield. It occurred to her that Ben Savage had been labeled the same way when he was a policeman.

When she arrived back at the office she found Al Overmile putting the moves on Angie, something the burly detective had been trying for some time. "Al, I want you to see what you can find out about Jack Byron."

"What's to find out? He's got a billion dollars."

"I'll need a little bit more than that. He has a pretty shady background."

"Shady! That's putting it nicely." Overmile was a big, bluff man in his mid-thirties. He had been an interior lineman at Alabama under Bear Bryant, and his battles on the gridiron accounted for his beat-up face. He was too rough in his tactics for Dani's liking, but there was no questioning his ability to move among the underworld of New Orleans. To work there was like swimming in an ocean of barracuda and killer sharks, but Overmile had learned how to survive. He was less effective when it came to dealing with corporation types, but even then he earned his paycheck.

Dani nodded toward Angie. "You may as well go on home. I'm going to be working late tonight."

"Yeah. Come on, Angie. Let's go out and grab a bite."

Angie seemed about to refuse but then said, "All right. I'll see you down at the car."

After Overmile left Dani hesitated. "He's not going to do you much good, you know."

Angie gathered her purse and coat, and as she left the office, there was a rather desperate look in her mild, blue eyes. "I like men. That's my curse. It's a good thing you don't."

After Angie left, Dani went into her office and went over to the fish tank. The biggest tropical fish looked back at her and opened his mouth in a surprised *O*. "Who says I don't like men, Jefferson?" she said.

The question seemed to hang in the air, and Jefferson stared at her as the water made his filmy fins flutter.

Dani moved away from the fish tank and sat down at the desk. Putting everything else aside, she began to work.

◆ ◆ ◆

Ben Savage moved a chair out of the waiting room and placed it in
the hallway so he had a clear view of the door that led to the hospital suite occupied by J.T. Denver. From time to time one of the
sisters would go by, never failing to give him a suspicious look.
Because it was late, the interns, who had filled the corridors all afternoon, were mostly gone. The hospital had gone to sleep more or
less, and as Ben sat on the only slightly padded seat, he fought off
the sleep that threatened to overcome him.

He focused his eyes on the book he was reading and managed
to read a few lines. They made no sense whatsoever, so gritting his
teeth he read them again. He heard footsteps approaching and,
moving his head only slightly, saw a fat intern step off the elevator
and come down the hall. He was whistling the *William Tell Overture*
in a rather professional manner. Stopping beside Savage, he looked
down and said, "How's it going, detective?"

"All quiet on the western front. What about you?"

"I don't lead an exciting life like you do." The intern's name,
Savage knew, was Proctor. He had a round, red face and wide brown
eyes and looked like a weight lifter who had gone to fat. He had
brought Savage coffee and donuts from the cafeteria earlier, and
now he asked, "You need something to eat?"

"No. I'm okay."

Glancing down at the book, Proctor asked, "What are you
reading?"

"A book by Steven Hawking. It's called *A Brief History of Time*."

"What's it about?" Proctor asked idly, shifting his weight from
one foot to the other.

"The cosmos."

"Oh, is that all?" Proctor smiled.

Savage laughed and said, "What are you going to be when you
grow up, Proctor?"

"I'm going to start a combination brain surgery and bait shop
out on the highway to Baton Rouge."

"Ought to be a winner. Everybody either needs bait or their brains worked on."

Proctor stood there talking for a while, then moved on down the hall. He was unaware that Savage was watching him carefully as he passed Denver's door.

Time crawled on for the next hour, and only one sister, Sister Veronica, walked by. She stopped long enough to say, "You may as well go to bed. Nobody's going to get to your man here."

"That's not the way it works, sister."

The nun was a small woman, no more than five two or three, with delicate features and mild blue eyes. "I see you're reading Hawking's book."

"I've read it three times, and every time I understand it a little bit less. Can't figure out whether he believes in God or not."

"He doesn't. Not the right God anyway," she said. Then without a break, she went on, "Do you believe in God, Mr. Savage?"

Ben grinned suddenly, amused at her directness. "Why don't you stop beating around the bush and just come out and say what's on your mind, sister?"

Sister Veronica returned his smile. "You didn't answer my question."

"I believe in God, but I don't do anything about it."

"If you ever decide to make His acquaintance, let me know. I'll be glad to introduce you."

Savage studied the woman as she moved down the hall. She went inside Denver's room, and he waited until she came out. As she passed by him again, she nodded, then disappeared around the corner.

Time crept on slowly, and finally the detective got up and stretched. He bent over and placed his hands flat on the floor. *I wonder how long I'll be able to do this.*

There was no way of knowing, of course. He did a few deep knee bends to get the blood running and stepped back inside the waiting room. It was empty, and he searched the magazine rack for something a little lighter than the history of the cosmos. He found a three-year-old copy of *Field and Stream* and stood there reading a story about how to trap beaver. Since he was relatively certain he would never trap a beaver no matter how old he got, he was having trouble staying awake even standing up and reading. A slight noise caught his attention, and at once he tossed the magazine onto a chair and moved where he could get a clear view of the corridor. As he did, he saw a woman with something in her hand stop beside J.T. Denver's door.

As she moved inside, he ran lightly down the hall. The running shoes he had on made no sound, and when he reached the door he considered pulling his gun but decided against it. The door was closed, and he went in at once. He saw the woman raising something in her hand, and without hesitation he threw one arm around her and struck at the forearm holding the object. It fell to the floor with a clatter, and the woman cried out and began to struggle.

Savage glanced over at Denver, who threw his arm up over his head but did not awaken because he was so heavily sedated.

The only light in the room was dim, and as Savage turned the woman around, still retaining his hold on her arm, he said, "Who are you, and what are you doing here?"

"Who are *you*? And why did you sneak up on me?"

Savage caught the odor of perfume, the same one Dani used. He was no expert in cosmetics, but this was one he liked. Looking down at the floor, he reached over and picked up a small metallic covered camera.

He pulled the woman outside and shut the door. "Funny time of the night to be taking pictures."

The woman before him was no more than nineteen. She had ash-blonde hair and green eyes and wore a dark green pantsuit made of silk. The jacket buttoned up the front to the neckline where it ended in a low-cut V, and the sleeves were long and adorned with the same dark green buttons as the front of the jacket. The slacks were loose-fitting and seemed to almost touch the black leather heels that peeked out.

"I take it you're not a doctor."

"I'm a private investigator hired to protect Mr. Denver."

"Well, you're doing a good job. I'm Tara Franz."

Savage considered the young woman who stood before him. She was looking at him with a rather provocative expression. There was something sensual about her, but he ignored that as he said, "You're Mr. Denver's granddaughter."

"Got it in one guess!" A thought touched the young woman's eyes, and she grinned suddenly. "I'm the black sheep of the family, which considering the competition I have is quite an accomplishment."

Ignoring this, Savage asked, "Why were you taking a picture?"

"I wasn't."

Savage considered what seemed to him to be an obvious lie, then said, "At first I thought you had a gun."

Tara studied him even more closely. "What's going on? What's your name?"

"Ben Savage."

"What's this all about, Savage?"

"Your father thinks somebody tried to kill him. I'm being paid to make sure they don't."

"Do you have any suspects?"

Savage didn't answer, and his silence seemed to amuse the young woman. She stepped closer and said, "I've read all the Philip Marlowe novels. The tough detective always has a beautiful young woman throwing herself against him like—like this."

Ben Savage's reactions were normally phenomenally fast. However, this time he was caught completely off guard. The young woman put her arms around his neck before he realized what she was doing. He stood there almost helpless, and then she kissed him on the lips.

He had been right about the sensuous quality of this young woman. As she pressed against him, he felt himself involuntarily enjoying her touch.

When he heard a sudden sound, he looked up to see Danielle Ross. Her eyes were as cold as polar ice, and Ben quickly pulled the clinging arms from around his neck. Clearing his throat, he said, "Hello, Miss Ross. This is Mr. Denver's granddaughter, Tara Franz."

Tara studied the woman, and when Ben identified her as the head of the agency, she said, "You don't look like a private detective to me. I'll do business with Ben here." Seeing something stir in Dani's eyes, she laughed suddenly and said, "I'm going in to sit beside my grandfather." She hesitated and turned to Ben. "Unless you want to do a strip-search first."

"Uh, no."

When the door closed, Dani stood as stiff as a Marine drill sergeant. When she said nothing, Ben explained lamely, "She caught me off guard."

"I can see that."

Usually Ben Savage won the verbal jousts that he and Dani carried on. But this time he could feel his face burning, and he cleared his throat and said, "I need to have some help on this job. I can't be here twenty-four hours a day."

He waited for her to answer and then shook his head and said, "I haven't felt this guilty since I got sent to the principal's office when I was in the ninth grade."

"If you have the time," Dani said, "come down to the waiting room. We have things to talk about."

As Ben followed her, he knew he had some difficult moments ahead of him. His thoughts went back to Tara Franz, and despite himself he smiled. *She sure knows her detective novels. I wonder . . .*

Four

TOO MANY ACCIDENTS

"Hey, I think I've come up with something on this Denver thing!"

Al Overmile's voice had always irritated Dani, but she was so desperate to find something on her most prominent case that she looked up. Overmile had opened the door without knocking, his big body bulging with muscle overlaid with fat. He was grinning now in a lopsided fashion, knowing he had caught Dani's attention.

"What is it, Al?"

Moving away from the door, Overmile moved forward until he towered over Dani. "Maybe a witness to the wreck."

Instantly Dani lay down the paper she held in her hands and demanded, "A witness! Who is it?"

"I thought you'd be interested in that. It's a woman named Allison St. John."

Dani waited for a moment for Overmile to continue but knew he was teasing her, as he liked to do from time to time. She waited, and finally Overmile shrugged his beefy shoulders. "She called 911. I got her name from the cops."

"Have you talked to her?"

Overmile shifted uncomfortably. "Aw, she wouldn't say much, Dani. I tried to pump her, but she clammed up on me."

"Did she see the accident?"

"She said she didn't, but I think she's lying."

"Give me her address, Al. I'll go have a talk with her." She waited until the big man had fished a notebook out of his shirt pocket, ruffled through it until he found the page, then tore it off. "I think you'll be wastin' your time. According to her story she got there after the wreck, and all she saw was Denver's car."

"Thanks, Al. I'll follow up on it."

"How about I go with you?"

"Not this time, Al. It's about time for you to go and relieve Ben."

Overmile was unhappy with this, but there was little he could do. He turned and left mumbling to himself, and Dani immediately got up. She was wearing light green slacks and a white blouse. Opening the door, she thought about how much she hated guns. Nevertheless, Ben had insisted she wear one, so she clipped a pistol to the back of her belt, then slipped on a single-breasted, light gray jacket and stepped out of the office. "I'll be back when I can, Angie."

Dani made her way to the parking lot and fifteen minutes later was threading through the heavy traffic filtering into New Orleans. Driving in the city was not something she liked, especially when she had to go to places such as the projects. These sections of the city had been noted for high crime rates for years. And now as she kept checking the street signs, she noted the young men standing or walking here and there. They were almost instantly recognizable as gang members. She had learned to live with the fact that some sections of New Orleans were breeding grounds for crime. Still she wished briefly that she'd been more open to Overmile or Ben coming along with her.

Spotting Azalea Street, she turned and found 2306. It proved to be an apartment building in a section that once had been middle-class but now was degenerating into a slum. It was not as bad as the projects yet, but it was headed that way.

Getting out of the car, Dani carefully locked it, glanced around, then walked up the three steps that led to the first story. Reading the list of tenants, she found the name of Carl St. John and entered the building. There was a musty smell of cabbage and dust, and from the back she could hear the shrill cries of children playing. Reaching apartment 3, she knocked and waited for what seemed like a long time. Finally the door opened, and a very young girl no more than four or five stood staring up at her.

"Hi. My name's Barbara."

"Hello. Is your mother home?"

"Yes." The girl had long blonde hair in need of washing and was wearing a pair of blue shorts and a T-shirt with food smeared across the front.

"Could I see her, do you think?"

The girl had no chance to answer, for a woman appeared suddenly. She was in her mid-thirties with blonde hair and dark blue eyes. She would have been attractive except for the exhaustion in her face, and something like fear came to her eyes as she said, "What is it?"

"My name is Danielle Ross. Are you Mrs. St. John?"

"Yes."

"I'd like to talk to you if I could."

"About what?"

"If I could step inside . . . It won't take but a minute."

The woman hesitated, then shrugged wearily. "Come on in," she said.

Stepping inside Dani scanned the low-rent apartment. Most of it was taken up by a combination living room, dining room, and kitchen. Something was cooking on the stove, and a door to the left led to a short hallway where she assumed the bedrooms and the bathroom were located. Some attempt had been made to dress the place up with new curtains, but the building itself was old and worn down. A sudden sympathy moved Dani as she saw that the woman was fighting a losing battle against poverty. She'd seen it often enough before, but there was something noble in the woman's face. She turned to a young boy and said, "Hello. My name's Dani. What's yours?"

"Tony."

Mrs. St. John reached over and touched the boy's dark hair. He had deep, brown eyes that studied Dani as he said, "Do you like milk?"

"Why, I love milk."

"You can have some of mine."

Dani laughed suddenly. "That's very nice of you, Tony, but I wouldn't want to drink your milk."

"I'm a little busy, Miss Ross," Mrs. St. John said.

"I hate to interrupt you, but I won't take long," Dani said quickly.

"If it's about the accident, I told the officers all I knew."

"Would you mind going through it one more time for me?"

"What for?" Suspicion was evident in the woman's eyes, but she shrugged her shoulders. "Okay, I guess so. Would you like some coffee?"

"That would be nice."

Dani sat down, and the woman brought out two large, white mugs. Dani watched as the woman took a glass pitcher, filled the cups, then replaced it on the coffeemaker. "I was driving along the highway . . ." Her voice was tired, and she hurried through her story. Somehow Dani felt, as had Overmile, that the woman was not telling the truth. But how to get her to do so, she did not know.

"So that's all there was to it. I was in a hurry, and there was really nothing I could do. The car was already wrecked, so I just called 911."

"Do you have a job, Mrs. St. John?"

"I have three kids here at home." She saw the questioning look in Dani's face. "Christine's seven. She's next door right now playing with friends. I'm home schooling her." As if in answer to Dani's unasked question, she said, "My husband, Carl, died two years ago. It's been—a little tough."

"I'm so sorry," Dani said quietly. Dani's sympathy seemed to touch Mrs. St. John.

"It's hard being a single mom and trying to make ends meet. I had a job for a year cooking at a bakery, but by the time I paid baby-sitters it wasn't worth it. Now I have a new job. I'm selling Mary Kay cosmetics."

"Are you doing well at it?"

"Well, not too well, but I hope to do better. I have to go all over the city to make sales presentations, and it's hard to get someone to stay with the kids."

Dani listened to the woman, and all the time her mind was telling her, *She knows something that she's not telling.* Finally she said, "You know, Mrs. St. John, anything you tell me will be confidential."

Instantly the woman straightened up. "I'm telling it just like it was," she said stiffly.

There was no point pressing the matter, and Dani sipped her coffee knowing that the interview was over. She noted the woman's cheap, light blue dress and the lack of proper hair care, and an idea came to her. "I'm in the market for some cosmetics. Would you like to show me what you have?"

Instantly Allison brightened up. "Oh, yes!" she said quickly. "Let me get my kit for you."

Soon Dani was looking at the array of cosmetics that the woman brought out. She herself did not use that brand, but she didn't mention that. In the next half hour she bought over a hundred dollars worth of cosmetics including creamy cleanser, revitalizing mask, purifying freshener, balancing moisturizer, liquid foundation with sunscreen, a pink compact housing two eye shadows, one cheek color, black mascara, eyeliner, lipstick, and a lip pencil.

"Thank you so much, Miss Ross! This will help."

Dani, knowing that she would use little of the items she'd purchased but that Angie and her sister Allison would use them, didn't feel she had done much. "I'll call you from time to time."

"I have a card right here! And I'll be glad to deliver them."

Dani took the card and stood up. She reached over and laid her hand on Tony's dark hair. He looked up at her and grinned suddenly. "You smell good," he announced.

"Thank you, Tony. So do you."

"Good-bye, Allison."

"Good-bye."

As Dani left the building, she felt depressed. Poverty always did that to her, and although Allison St. John was not as bad off as some, Dani still tried to imagine taking care of three children with no education and no help. The thought frightened her a little, and she breathed a brief prayer of thanksgiving for the things God had given her. She had told Ben once that she didn't save up prayers and give them to God once a day or whatever but said short prayers as she went along. He had grinned saying, "Kind of an installment plan, eh?"

As Dani headed for Sacre Coeur Hospital, she couldn't get the woman off her mind. She kept thinking about her until she walked into Denver's room, where she found Ben and two visitors.

"This is Miss Shelley Bracken and her son Creighton," Ben said quickly.

"Another one of my exes and her son from Shelley's earlier marriage," Denver said. He was sitting up, and there was more color in his face. He smiled rather sardonically and added, "You'll get to the end of the string one of these days."

"You shouldn't talk like that, J.T." Shelley Bracken was a rather attractive woman somewhere in her late forties. She had red hair that looked real, but Dani knew it was not, and her complexion was very good. She was wearing pricey clothes and had several expensive, large rings that caught the light as she moved her hands nervously.

"You ought to be used to it by now, Mother." The man was tall with dark hair and dark eyes. There was a rough handsomeness about him, and he looked Dani over the way a womanizer usually does. His clothes too were expensive, and Dani wondered briefly how much money this particular ex-wife had won in alimony.

"I think it's *awful* that we're all under suspicion," Shelley pouted as she turned to face J.T. "You know none of us would do anything to hurt you."

J.T. didn't answer but gave her an inexpressive look. "I'll leave all that up to my hired help, Shelley. According to Mr. Savage here, everybody's a suspect."

"Guilty until proven innocent, is that it?" Creighton said.

As the man spoke, Dani saw something flicker in J.T.'s eyes, but he merely answered, "What's this new project of yours, Creighton?"

"It's a good one," the man said eagerly, and his whole face lit up. "And it won't cost over 500,000 to get into it with both feet."

The way he tossed the number around amazed Dani. She knew that to J.T. Denver 500,000 was no more than 50 dollars was to her. *I can't imagine living with so much money.*

Both Dani and Ben listened as Creighton described the project that would involve stocks and bonds and a new product. Neither of them were really interested in that, but they were both fascinated by the way Shelley Bracken kept her eyes fixed either on her son or her ex-husband. There was something rather pathetic about her, and Dani suspected she was a heavy drinker. She didn't smell any alcohol or hear slurred speech, but there were other tell-tale signs.

Creighton turned to Dani. "Maybe you and I could go out and see the sights sometime."

"Maybe." Dani smiled. "But I'm pretty busy working for J.T."

After the two left, Dani gave the report of her interview with the St. John woman. Denver listened to it and said, "Stay on it. Find that truck. I want you—" The phone rang, and he picked it up. "Yes?" He listened for a moment and then issued some strong, harsh language. "Can't you do anything right?" he finally snapped and slammed the phone down.

"That was Bobby, my son-in-law. There's been a screw-up out at the shipyard. It'll slow us up for a week."

Dani studied J.T. Denver and finally she said, "Was it Mr. Franz's fault?"

Surprise washed across Denver's face. "What do you mean?"

"You were pretty hard on him, Mr. Denver."

"That's just my way." Denver shrugged and would have gone on, but Dani interrupted him.

"It's not the way of Jesus."

The bare statement seemed to take Denver by surprise. He blinked and shook his head. Anger came into his voice as he said, "You don't understand. I've been in the jungle for a long time. I can't change what I am."

"Being Christian means change," Dani said quietly. She saw she was irritating him but felt she should continue. "Being a Christian means growing into Christ—becoming like Him."

As she had expected, Denver suddenly grew angry. He covered it badly and waved his hands. "You think you have a better way, go on down to the shipyard and see what you can do."

As they left the room, Ben said, "Well, we won't have to worry about this job for long."

"What do you mean, Ben?"

"You keep on needling the guy like that, he'll show us the door."

"There are other clients."

"Not with a billion dollars." Ben grinned crookedly.

◆ ◆ ◆

When Ben pulled up beside the shipyard on Mobile Bay, they both looked at the framework of the huge ship. "Looks like an ocean liner, not a ferry."

Getting out, the two walked to the gate, where their identification was checked by a short, muscular man with a thin mustache. He grinned saying, "I got a call from Mr. Denver. He says to show you anything you'd like to see." He was wearing a light blue uniform that looked official, and he gave his name as Juan Martinez. "Charlie, you take over while I show these two around."

Neither Ben nor Dani had ever been in a shipyard, and the size of the ferry astonished them. It had three decks and was over 250 feet long. For over an hour Martinez took them into different sections, and by the time he was through, Dani shook her head. "This is a big job."

"It's big all right, and from what I hear, they want to build twenty more just like it."

"Do you know where we can find Mr. Franz?"

"Sure. His office is over on the dock. I'll show you."

The two followed the stubby security officer off the ship. Franz's office was on the shore, an aluminum building with people filling their small offices almost like a beehive.

Martinez led them to the end where he knocked on the door. A voice answered, "Come in."

"I'll leave you here," Martinez said.

"Thanks, Juan," Dani said quickly.

The two of them entered and found Bobby Franz engaged in some sort of argument with a tall, lanky man whose hair seemed to stand straight on end as he pulled it upward. He seemed to be trying to lift himself off the planet by his hair, and finally he said, "It can't be done, Bobby."

"It's got to be done, Thad! Now get out of here and come back with the answer."

As soon as the lanky man had left, Franz smiled wearily. "Glad to see you. I guess you've come down to look the situation over."

"Mr. Martinez has already given us a quick tour," Dani said. "What's the trouble? We were there when you made the call to Mr. Denver."

Bitterness etched itself across Franz's thin face. He shook his head and then with a gesture threw his pencil down on the desk. It rolled off, and he stared at it for a moment. He reluctantly bent over and picked it up. "It's just what we need—another slowdown," he muttered.

"What happened?" Ben asked curiously.

"Somebody let a crane load of heavy steel slip. It crashed down through two floors. That'll set us back at least a week. Maybe more."

"Who was handling the crane?"

"Pete Samuelson. And he says it wasn't his fault. It's never anybody's fault."

"Maybe we can talk to Samuelson."

"I wish you would." Bitterness edged Bobby Franz's lips, and he stood silently for a moment. "I don't know what else to do. I've tried everything, but things keep going wrong."

"We'll talk to a few people if you'll give us a little time."

"Sure. I'm not going anywhere," Franz said. He plumped down in his chair and didn't look up as they left the room.

For over three hours Dani and Ben talked to those in charge of building the ship. It had no name as yet, so they all simply called it *Miss Nameless*. Pete Samuelson proved to be a tough man indeed. He explained in no uncertain terms that it was not his fault the derrick had fallen. "It was a malfunction in the machinery. You can't help that."

Samuelson stared at the two suspiciously. "What are you two trying to do? Find out why there's so many slowdowns?"

"Is that happening often?" Dani asked quickly.

"Too often!" Samuelson growled. "And we can't understand why. There's just too many accidents."

"There are always accidents on a big job like this, aren't there?" Ben inquired softly.

"Not the way they've been happening around here."

After they had finished talking with the men, they went back to Franz, but he couldn't explain it either. As they left his office, Ben said, "I think he can be trusted."

"I don't think he gets along too well with his boss though."

"I'm not sure anyone does."

The two got into the car and headed back toward the office. They talked about the case briefly, and finally Ben said, "We have to put somebody on the inside, Dani."

Dani turned quickly to look at him. "Undercover?"

"Sure."

"It might help, but it would have to be somebody with street smarts, and it has to be done quickly, Ben."

"I know someone who might help and has the time."

"Who is it?"

"An old partner of mine on the police force in Denver—Jamie Cordova."

"You'll stand behind your choice, I guess."

"Jamie can handle it."

"All right. Take care of it." Dani didn't like to hire people sight unseen, but she had learned to trust Ben Savage's judgment. "I hope it works," she said grimly. "Nothing else has."

Five

THE NANCY

The bookstore was crowded, but Dani shouldered her way into the young peoples' section. A redheaded boy with an abundant crop of freckles frowned at her from where he sat on the floor. "Watch where you're steppin', lady!"

"Sorry." Dani smiled apologetically. "Do you like to read?"

"I'm readin', ain't I?" Then the boy's whole expression changed. "Sure. That's all I like to do."

"I was that way when I was your age." Dani engaged the boy in conversation for a few moments, then moved down the shelves. She picked out eight or nine books, then went to check out. Leaving the bookstore, she drove directly to Allison St. John's apartment building. Locking the car door carefully behind her, she went upstairs, and when she knocked the door was opened almost at once by a blonde girl with wide, rather suspicious eyes. "I bet you're Christine."

"How do you know my name?"

"I met your mother the other day, and your brother and sister. You weren't here though. My name is Dani Ross. Is your mother here?"

"She's in the bathroom. You can come in and wait if you want."

Dani stepped inside, and at once Tony and Barbara rose from where they were watching *Sesame Street* and came over to greet her. They were very attractive children, and Dani sat down in the battered chair that Christine offered and spoke with them until Allison came out.

"Oh, hello," Dani said. "Sorry to burst in like this, but I had something to give to the kids."

Allison was wearing a robe, and her hair was damp. "I just got out of the shower," she said. She was more friendly now than she had been on the first visit and said, "I'll pour you some coffee."

"Oh, don't bother," Dani said. "I have to run. I just thought you might enjoy these." She put the sack on the table, and at once all three children began removing the books.

"This one's mine!" Tony said excitedly. "It's about airplanes."

"I remembered seeing you play with some toy airplanes," Dani said. "So I got you a couple of books you might like."

"Is this mine?" Barbara said. Her blonde hair was in her face, and she shoved it back, looking up at Dani curiously.

"Yes. Your mother may have to read some of your books to you."

"What are these?" Christine asked.

"Oh, those are sort of fantasy books. They're called the Narnia Chronicles. I loved them when I was about your age, Christine, but my mother had to read them to me."

As the children sat down and began thumbing through the books, Dani moved over to the kitchen table where she did accept a cup of coffee, seeing that it was already fixed. "And I have something for you, Allison."

"For me? Why, you didn't have to do that."

"It's nothing much. Just a list of friends you might use in your business. I don't know if they're potential customers or not, but they all use makeup."

Dani saw the woman's face flush, and a strange expression came into her eyes. *Not many good things come her way*, Dani thought. She saw that the woman was very close to tears. "I'm sure things will go well for you eventually. It takes a while to build up any business. Believe me, I know."

Allison shook her head. "It's been hard, but I'm going to keep at it."

"I don't want to bother you with this, and I wouldn't want you to think I'm trying to help you just to get information from you. I'm doing it because I believe Jesus wants me to. But I do need some help with my investigation of Mr. Denver's accident. If you think of anything that could help me find the truck that forced him off the road, would you give me a call?"

For a second Allison hesitated, and it seemed to Dani that an answer of some sort trembled on her lips. She sat very still hoping for something, but then the same expression she had noted before—almost abject fear—flashed in the woman's eyes, and she knew better than to push it.

"I was just wondering—are you attending church anywhere, Allison?"

Surprised and somewhat taken aback by the question, Allison shook her head. "No, we don't go to church. We did for a while when my husband was alive. His grandfather was a preacher, but it's so hard to get everybody ready."

"I know it is, but I attend a really fine church, and they have such good programs for children there. I think your kids would really like it. If you want to go, I could come by and pick you up."

For a long moment Allison hesitated. "All right. What time does it start?"

"I'll pick you up at nine o'clock. We'll take the kids to their class-rooms so they'll feel comfortable."

"We'll be ready."

Dani rose and walked over to where the children were poring over the books. "Good-bye, kids," she said. "You're all going to church with me next Sunday morning." She reached over and tousled Tony's dark hair and gave him a smile. "You look pretty."

"I don't look pretty! Girls look pretty."

"Well, you look handsome then," Dani said. She turned and left the apartment, and somehow she felt as she got back into the car and started it up that something would come of this visit. Her heart had gone out to the family, though she herself had never had the problems that Allison St. John had to face. She was puzzled over the fear that Allison obviously felt, but she knew she could not force the woman to talk.

Threading her way through traffic, she got to the office thirty minutes later. When she entered, she found Overmile flirting with Angie, and distaste came over her. "Don't you have anything to do, Al?"

"Sure. Just leaving."

As soon as the big man was out of the building, Dani hesitated, then went over to stand beside Angie. "I don't want to sound like a broken record, but going along with Al's flirtations isn't such a good idea, Angie."

Angie didn't pretend to misunderstand. "Well, he's somebody to talk to and to go out with once in a while."

"He's not much good as a man, and you know that."

"Oh yeah, I know that. I've had enough practice." Bitterness came into Angie's voice, and she dropped her eyes for a moment. Finally she looked up and asked directly, "Don't you ever get lonely, Dani?"

For one moment Dani tried to arrange her thoughts, but that moment was too long for Angie. "I guess you don't. But I do, and Al is better than nobody."

"Of course I get lonely sometimes," Dani said quickly. "But I've learned to live with it."

"Well, I haven't. So I guess I'll take Al until something better comes along."

"Watch yourself. You know what he's like." Dani almost came out with a more stern warning, but at that moment the door opened and Ben Savage walked in. When Dani turned, she greeted him, then fell silent, seeing that he was not alone.

"Boss, this is our new agent, Miss Jamie Cordova. Jamie, this is Miss Ross. I've told you all about her."

"How do you do, Miss Ross."

Jamie Cordova was not tall but had an athletic build. She was obviously strong and quick, but Dani noticed most of all that the woman was a beauty. Apparently of Spanish blood, she had coal black hair, brown eyes, and a stunning figure. She was wearing a pair of navy batik pants, a black silk sweater, and a reversible, soft suede coat. Her eyes were almond-shaped and shaded by thick lashes, and her lips were broad and well-shaped.

"How are you, Miss Cordova?" Dani said, "Come into my office. We'll talk."

The three of them moved into the office, and as soon as they were inside and seated, Ben said, "Jamie and I go back a long time, Dani."

"That's right," the woman replied. She had a low voice, rather throaty, and there was something sultry about her, although she made no attempt to emphasize this. "I still have that scar on my back where some clown tried to take me out." She looked over at Dani and said, "Ben saved my bacon that day."

"Just paying her back," Savage grinned. "We took turns saving each other's lives."

Dani listened, but she couldn't shake off some feeling that had come over her. Finally she said, "What do you have in mind for Jamie to do, Ben?"

"It's already taken care of, boss. Jamie's got a job down at Denver's shipyard."

"How did you manage that so quickly?"

Jamie Cordova smiled. "It wasn't hard. They're hiring. A lot of turnover there."

"What will you be doing?"

"Hopefully a gopher," Jamie said. "I'll be working for Mr. Franz—mostly carrying messages and taking notes."

Dani observed, "I'm still surprised you were able to get in so soon."

"She has a way of doing things like that, boss."

"It could be dangerous. Remember, somebody tried to kill J.T. Denver."

"It goes with the territory, Miss Ross. You know that." Jamie smiled.

Dani went over the usual talk about salary and hours and what few rules existed, and finally Jamie said, "I'd better get to work."

"You don't work in that outfit, do you?"

Jamie laughed. She had a most attractive laugh. Her teeth were white, and her skin, which was pale olive, showed them off well. "No. A little less fancy than this."

Ben said, "I'll come by your place to get your report."

"Fine. I'll make you some enchiladas and that cheese dip that you'd die for." She smiled at Dani, then left the room.

"What do you think, boss? She's really something, isn't she?"

"She's not exactly what I was expecting."

Catching some nuance in Dani's voice, Ben studied his employer carefully. He had learned to read her very well in the short time he'd known her, and he turned his head to one side. "Something bothering you? I thought you'd be pleased."

"It's just that she doesn't look like—" Dani couldn't bring herself to finish the sentence, but the implication was clear.

"Well, she's too good-looking to be an agent, but I couldn't find an ugly one."

Dani was upset but could find no way to fault Ben's choice. And after all the woman had worked herself almost miraculously into a place where she could be all over that ship. "She'll be all right, I'm sure. You'd better get back to the hospital."

"No more hospital for J.T. Denver."

"What do you mean?"

"I mean he checked himself out. He's out on his yacht."

"His yacht?"

"Yes. It's called *The Nancy*. You won't believe that ship, boss! You have to come down and see it."

Dani suddenly made up her mind. "I'd like to. I need to talk to him anyway."

"Okay. I thought we'd get Dugan Stokes to take the night shift watching our prize client."

"Dugan's a good man. I'm surprised he's available."

"I turned the charm on. He couldn't resist. Come on."

Dani got into her Cougar and started down toward the bay. As she drove, she asked in what she hoped was a casual voice, "Is Jamie married?"

"Not now."

There was something in Ben's voice that closed the door on that subject, and silence filled the car in a rather thick fashion.

Suddenly Ben turned and leaned forward so he could see Dani's face. "We were never lovers, Dani."

Dani felt her face flush. "I didn't ask."

"Sure, you did."

Dani compressed her lips and ignored him for the rest of the drive. Following Ben's instructions, she came to the docks and saw out in the harbor a beautiful vessel. "Is that it?" she breathed.

"That's it. Beats the little johnboat I go shrimping in, doesn't it?"

The Nancy was, indeed, a beautiful ship. It was long and sleek and so white that it almost hurt the eyes to look at it. Everything about it suggested speed—and money.

"How much did that thing cost?"

"About two million, I think, more or less. But of course that includes the flag flying on the fantail. It has a crew of fifteen, including a chef."

Dani got out of the car and locked it, and the two walked down to the bay. "We go out in that little boat there," Ben said, indicating a small white speedboat with *The Nancy* painted on the side in gold lettering. A man in a blue and white uniform, blue slacks, and a white turtleneck shirt with *The Nancy* across the chest watched them carefully as they approached.

"Why is it called *The Nancy*? That's not one of his ex-wives' names."

"Haven't found out about that yet," Ben said.

"Going aboard, Mr. Savage?"

"Yes. This is Miss Ross, my employer, Tom. Be sure you let her on but nobody else who's not cleared."

"Yes, sir."

Savage helped Dani down into the boat, and the two sat down. Going to the front, the man started the engine. The propellers made a bubbling sound, and after casting off the rope he eased out. The bay was quiet that day, and Dani looked over Mobile Bay carefully. There were a few fishing boats out, and over to her left, she knew, were the shipyards, including a huge derrick. That was rather ugly, but the bay itself was lovely. Turning to the east she saw the Eastern Shore, prime property, expensive and hard to come by. Further out was a narrow corridor, Fort Morgan on the left and Fort Gaines on the right. It was through here that Fairgood had led his fleet to fight the Battle of Mobile Bay. But Dani's thoughts were on other things besides ancient history now, and she said little to Ben.

When they pulled up to *The Nancy* and were helped on board by a steward wearing a spotless white uniform, she glanced around curiously. She had been on more than one cruise ship, rather ornate ones at that, but there was something about this one that spelled "no expense spared" in large letters. Gleaming brass shone everywhere, and the deck itself was dark wood—mahogany, she suspected, or teak. Everything was clean, and the crew she passed were all dressed as if for a high-level inspection.

"Down this way, boss," Ben said. He led her to the lower deck and down a corridor to a door where Dugan Stokes sat in a chair reading a paper. "Anything going, Dugan?"

"Not a thing, Ben. Hello, Miss Ross."

"Hello, Dugan. Glad to have you with us again."

"Have there been any visitors?" Ben inquired

"Just family. Sometimes he sees them, sometimes he doesn't." A wry expression touched Stokes's lean face. He was a tall man of thirty-five with a pair of sharp, gray eyes. "I can hear him cussin' 'em out sometimes clear through these walls."

"Well, I guess we'll go take our cussin' now." Ben winked.

Knocking on the door, he waited until a voice answered and then opened it. He stepped back and allowed Dani to go through. "You first."

Stepping inside, Dani saw Denver sitting in a chair. The entire back wall was glass with a clear view of the harbor. It was the most luxurious room Dani had ever been in, and she said, "Nice place you have here."

Denver was wearing a pair of gray trousers and a white shirt. He still moved stiffly. His right arm was in a sling, but he looked much better. "Sit down. I'll send for something to drink, or maybe we'll have lunch pretty soon."

Dani noticed that Ben said nothing but took his place against the wall. She knew that as usual he was taking everything in. Whenever they compared notes afterward, they were amazed at what they could learn together.

"What have you found out?"

Dani gave her brief report, and then, as expected, Denver was sharp with her. "You're going to have to make better progress than that, Miss Ross!"

"We're doing the best we can."

For the next few minutes Dani talked with Denver about the case. She saw that he was depressed, and finally he shook his shoulders and said, "So you like the ship?"

"It's beautiful! I've never seen anything like it." She wanted to ask about the name *Nancy* but felt she hadn't known him long enough to ask such a personal question. She smiled and said, "What's it feel like to be able to buy anything you want?"

"I don't know."

The answer took Dani off guard. "Well, according to *Newsweek* you can do just that, and *Time* says the same thing."

"Well, the great oracles are wrong." Getting up rather painfully, Denver walked to the large window and stared out at the bay. A group of pelicans flew by in formation and then disappeared. Turning, Denver said, "I've always wanted a son more than anything else. That's one thing money can't buy."

"That's true," Dani said quickly. "'The fruit of the womb is the reward of the Lord.'"

"Who said that?"

"It's in the Bible."

"Where in the Bible?"

"I don't know. I'll look it up for you. Do you have a concordance?"

"No."

"I'll bring you one."

Denver sat down again and took a sip of 7-Up. "I don't know what I'm working for," he said almost to himself. "My family can't stand me." He looked up and said, "None of my families can stand me."

Dani didn't know what to say. He had honor and wealth and yet he was unhappy. It was in his eyes, his expression. "Now that you've found the Lord, things will be better."

That answer hit J.T. Denver hard. He didn't answer for a long moment, then nodded. "I hope so. Will you stay for lunch?"

"Yes. Will your family be here?"

"Most of them. I'll skip it, but you'd better get to know them." A bitter twist came to his lips, and he said, "After all, one of them might have tried to kill me—or maybe all of them formed a committee!"

Six

"THOMAS WOLFE WAS RIGHT"

After Dani made her report to Denver, she was given a tour of the ship by the captain himself. This was not an accident, for Denver had called and said rather shortly, "Captain, I want you to give Miss Danielle Ross a tour of the ship. Show her everything."

Dani enjoyed meeting Captain Iverson, a tall Swede of thirty-nine with frosty blue eyes and a face weathered by years at sea. He had greeted her politely enough and had given her a thorough tour of the ship from the galley to the head used by the crew.

As the tour ended, Iverson lifted one eyebrow and said, "I've never known a private detective before."

"That makes us even," Dani smiled. "I've never known a ship's captain."

"Is your life anything like I read in the mystery novels?"

"Not very much, I'm afraid. Actually it's very boring work. A lot of looking, asking questions, reading over information that proves to be useless, looking for a needle in a haystack that will solve some sort of problem."

Iverson was walking slowly, adjusting his long legs to match Danielle's stride. "It's about the same with captains, I guess."

"I would think your job would be very romantic—a beautiful

ship like this and all. Don't you sometimes go to Hawaii, Australia, and other far-off romantic places?"

Iverson laughed. "Once you get off the tourist track you run into poisonous snakes and bugs that eat you alive. Besides, keeping a ship running is like maintaining any other piece of machinery. It takes a lot of care. Especially one this complicated."

"What do you think of your employer?"

Iverson grinned. He was an attractive man and obviously knew it. Dani wondered how many women on tours had found his charm irresistible.

Iverson thought over her question, then nodded. "I know what you mean. He has a bad reputation in the business world, and he sometimes peels the hide off me and the crew. But I've always had the idea that he's not Mr. Hyde and Mr. Hyde. Somewhere a Dr. Jekyll is lurking under that gruff exterior."

Leading Danielle up on deck, the two strolled around, and she found herself liking him very much. "It's time for lunch. The rest of the family has gathered in the main dining room."

"How many dining rooms are there?"

"Oh, there's one for the crew. We call it the mess. But this is the *royal* dining room where all the wives and the children assemble."

Dani laughed. "It sounds very polygamous. Or is that the right word?"

"I'm not sure. But in any case, if you're looking for a suspect, I suspect you might find one there."

Dani thought about that for a moment. "What do you mean, captain?"

"I mean that people love money. Haven't you found that out?"

"Generally speaking that's true. But what does that have to do with this situation?"

"When a man has as much money as J.T. Denver, somebody's always after it. In this case he's had three wives. Everybody in the family except the twins is a suspect."

"You don't mean that, I'm sure."

"Don't I? Wait until you meet them. Or have you met them already?"

"I met Mrs. Sanderson and her daughter Loreen and Mrs. Bracken and her son Creighton."

"So you haven't met Maris yet. She's wife number three. 1990 to 1995," Iverson said wryly. "She has two girls—twins—Anne and Gayle." He slowed his pace and shook his head. "You'll find out soon enough that Mr. Denver can't stand any of them except Anne and Gayle, and that's because they're just children."

"I understand Mr. Denver's always wanted a son."

"Creighton comes close, though J.T.'s not his father. Besides, he's a playboy. He's never finished anything in his life. Not school, not a job—nothing. He didn't have to. He's almost always had Mr. Denver's money to hang on to."

"What does he do now?"

"He finds rainbows and tries to talk Mr. Denver into investing in them."

Dani wanted to ask more but didn't because they had reached the steps going down to the first deck. The dining room was in the center of the ship, shielded by large double doors. Captain Iverson opened it, and when Dani stepped in she saw a table covered with a snowy white tablecloth and fine, gleaming china and crystal goblets. She saw Vivian Sanderson and her daughter Loreen, Shelley Bracken, Creighton, and a man and a woman she assumed were Maris Nolan and her fiancé.

"I'll leave you here, Miss Ross," Captain Iverson said. "If there's anything more I can do for you, let me know."

As the captain left, Shelley Bracken said, "I think you've met everyone."

"Not quite." Dani turned to meet Maris Nolan. She bore a striking resemblance to a younger Lauren Bacall. Indeed, she had been a top model and then an actress. According to Dani's notes, she had given up modeling and a budding movie career to marry J.T. Denver. Dani didn't recognize the man beside her.

"This is my fiancé, Trevor Fountaine. Trevor, this is Miss Ross, the private detective J.T.'s hired to keep us from killing him."

A slight shock ran over Dani at the brutality of the words. They sounded even worse coming from such an elegant woman. "I'm sure you don't mean that." Trevor Fountaine was a muscular man of about thirty-two and resembled Richard Burton. He had auburn, curly hair and a rather squarish face, and now as he smiled at her, she saw that he was indeed an attractive man. She would learn later that he was British and had lived most of his life in England.

"I'm happy to meet you, Mr. Fountaine, and you, Ms. Nolan." Dani went over to take her seat across from the couple. "I must confess, you've always been an idol of mine."

Something broke then in Maris Nolan's face. "I can't believe that," she said.

"But it's true. I used to cut your pictures out of *Vogue*. But my dreams were hopeless—I was never elegant enough to be a model."

"You mean skinny enough," Maris laughed. "Don't be so polite."

"I wouldn't call it that," Dani said.

"These are my daughters, Anne and Gayle. Say hello, girls."

The twins, apparently about seven years old, were identical as far as Dani could tell. They both had light blonde hair and greenish-blue eyes and were slim. "Which is Anne and which is Gayle?"

"I'm Anne," the girl on the left said.

"How can I tell you from Gayle?"

Anne suddenly grinned. "Because she has a purple birthmark on her bottom."

A laugh went around the table, and Dani joined in. "I need something a little less embarrassing than that."

Gayle said, "I'm the smart one. She's the dumb one who sings."

Anne picked up a piece of celery and smacked her sister in the temple with it, upon which Trevor Fountaine reached out and took it from her hands. "You girls can fight in private. That's the way polite people always do it."

"Well, Miss Ross," Creighton said, "have you discovered who tried to knock the old man off?"

Dani studied Creighton's face. He was handsome, with soulfully dark eyes and carefully styled hair. He was wearing a pair of blue linen slacks, a crisp white shirt, and a blue and red striped sweater tied loosely around his neck. "Not yet, Mr. Bracken."

"Call me Creighton."

"All right then, Creighton. Not much progress yet."

Vivian Sanderson was at the end of the table. She lifted her head at this and glared at him. "You'd better keep your mouth shut, Creighton. You're the prime suspect as far as I'm concerned."

"Why, thank you, Vivian. It's nice to be treated to your usual good manners." Creighton's face didn't change, but there was a grating sound in his words.

It was easy for Dani to see there was no love lost between these two. The meal went on for some time, and the only pleasure Dani got out of it was talking with Anne and Gayle. They seemed to be lively girls, and she could understand why the two were their father's favorites. *But I wonder if it'll be the same as they get older.*

Suddenly the double doors opened, and a beautiful woman wearing a bright orange bikini, accenting her golden tan, made a grand entrance, towing Ben Savage by one hand. She looked around the room, then directly at Dani. "Looks as if all the suspects have been rounded up, just like in the movies."

"Go put some clothes on!" Vivian snapped. "Miss Ross, this is my granddaughter Tara, the outrageous one!"

"I have clothes on, Mother. Ben likes my new suit. Don't you, Ben?"

Savage looked terribly out of place. Dani saw that he was embarrassed, and that delighted her. "Right on the job, are you, Mr. Savage?" she teased.

Tara winked at Dani. "I'm getting real tight with your man here, Ross."

"He's not my man."

"Good!" Tara said and grinned broadly. "Then I won't have to fight you for him. Come on, Ben, sit down and eat."

The meal was finished soon, and afterwards Dani got Ben off

to one side. "I have to go back to the office." He followed her up to the top deck and to the boat that was waiting to take her ashore. "Watch out for that woman, Ben."

"Not my type."

"Oh?" Dani said coldly. "What is your type?"

"I like intellectuals, boss. Like you."

Giving him a frosty look, Dani shook her head as she moved toward the ladder that led down to the waiting boat. "Keep away from her."

"She's one of the suspects, Dani."

"You don't believe that."

"Do your homework. I've been snooping around a little bit." Ben took her by the arm and turned her around. The sun was going down, and the waters of the bay looked very blue indeed. They reflected in Dani's eyes, and for a moment he didn't speak. "You're much better looking than she is. Now if you'd just get a new swimming suit like Tara's . . . Your old one's got a hole in the knee."

"Never mind that, Ben Savage!"

"Okay, okay, here's the deal. I've been reading up on the family of J.T. Denver. Not only is every one of them broke, they're all in debt over their heads. As a matter of fact, Creighton's in for thirty big ones to Trumps Lamont."

Dani stared at him. "That's a bad move."

"Right. Lamont will take Creighton's right eye for security if he doesn't pay up. He's done it before. So they're all starving, and they all want money."

"But all three wives got a huge settlement."

"They thought it would last forever, but it didn't." He squeezed her arm and said, "Very few things last forever, boss."

◆ ◆ ◆

Dani worked hard at the office for the next few days. She got daily reports from Ben, but for some reason it irritated her when he forwarded the report given by Jamie Cordova. She never asked Ben about his personal affairs, but she knew he was seeing her every night or at least getting her input over the telephone. She suspected the former. On a Thursday afternoon she went back to *The Nancy* to visit Denver. She dreaded it a little, since she had so little to tell him. He was looking much better, and she told him so as she entered. "You must heal quickly."

"Yes, I do. We rich people do that, you know."

Dani had learned that Denver liked to mock his wealth. She sat down and took the Diet Coke he offered her. "What's it really like to be rich?" she asked.

"I've been poor, and I've been rich. Everybody says that rich is better. Let me see your watch."

Startled by the abrupt question, Dani held her arm up, and he peered at it. "How much did it cost?"

"A little over a hundred dollars."

"What time do you have?"

Dani looked at her watch. "It's eleven minutes after 3."

Denver looked down at his own watch and said, "That's right. That's what my watch says too. Eleven minutes after 3." He looked at her with an odd expression in his eyes. He had a rugged look about him. The premature gray at his temples showed clearly in the sunlight streaming through the large windows in the stern. He held out his watch to her. "Look at it."

Dani leaned forward and peered at the watch. The band was made out of stainless steel and gold. The face was circled by a band of gold, and the hours were in Roman numerals with what she assumed were rubies. "It's beautiful." She read the inscription. "Breguet 4107." Looking up at him, she said, "Nice watch."

"Guess what it cost."

"Umm, 2,000 dollars."

"Wrong. Closer to fifty."

"Fifty thousand dollars?"

Denver seemed to find her response amusing. "That's right. I had it especially made. Breguets are expensive anyhow, but I wanted one that nobody else had. But you'll notice it can still only do one thing, and it doesn't do that any better than yours, I don't suppose. So what?"

"Well, I could take that 50,000 dollars and feed a starving African village for a year, I expect."

"I have another 50,000 dollars to do that with."

Dani hesitated, unsure what to say. "So feed two villages."

"But I couldn't feed *all* the villages. At some point I'd have to give up."

Dani wasn't sure how to answer him, so she finally said, "Since you've become a Christian, have you changed your financial habits any?"

"I support missionaries and Bible schools and several other good Christian causes."

"But you still won't go to church."

"No. I told you why." He sat silently, and Dani wondered what was really on his mind. He was not a man to just sit and waste time, but clearly something was troubling him. Finally he leaned forward and said, "I consider you sort of like a priest, Miss Ross. If I make a confession to you, it stops there, right?"

"Of course."

"All right. I want you to find a woman for me."

"A woman! What woman?"

"Someone I knew a long time ago." Leaning back in his chair, he stroked his chin and then began speaking slowly. "Her name when I knew her was Nancy Bayless. She's probably married by now."

"Who was she, Mr. Denver? And why do you want me to find her?"

Denver hesitated, then said, "She was the only woman I ever loved, Dani."

It was the first time he'd used her first name. Always before it had been Miss Ross or sometimes just Ross. But there was a plea in his tone now. "When was this?"

"Nearly twenty-five years ago. I was just a young guy trying to make my way when I met Nancy. I'd like to see her again."

Dani leaned forward and studied his face. She asked, "Did you ever hear of Thomas Wolfe?"

"Sure. I've read his stuff."

"You know his book *You Can't Go Home Again*?"

"I've read it."

"I think he's probably right. When people try to go back to something they once loved, it usually isn't there. One time I went back to a town we lived in when we were children. I was so anxious to get back to the house, but it wasn't the same."

"Houses aren't people, Danielle."

"No. People change more than houses. But tell me about her."

For the next fifteen minutes J.T. spoke in a restrained voice about the woman called Nancy. It was a simple enough story. Two young people meet not having anything, then love each other greatly, but are finally driven apart. Dani wondered what had accomplished that in this case. "Why didn't you marry her?"

"Because I was a fool, like all young men." His tone was bleak, and J.T. Denver said, "Just go find her. You don't have to say anything to her. Just give me a report of what she's doing, who she's married to, her family. Is she happy? That's all I can say right now."

Realizing he would say no more about that subject, Dani decided to try once again to help J.T. spiritually. "I still think you're wrong about church. Go with me on Sunday. You need the Body of Christ, other believers who can encourage and teach you."

"That won't work for me. Money isolates a man. I'm in the castle, surrounded by a moat, and the drawbridge is up."

Dani turned at the door, and a thought came to her. "Except for Nancy?"

J.T. blinked and nodded, his lips growing pale. "Yes. Except for Nancy."

Seven

THINGS ARE NOT WHAT THEY SEEM

"I need a good man to help me find someone, Luke," Dani said earnestly. She was sitting across the desk from the burly homicide detective, and a note of urgency was in her voice. "I thought maybe you could help me. You always have before."

Sixkiller listened carefully as Dani explained her mission. As he looked across the desk, he seemed to see a vulnerability in the woman. It had always been there, but now for some reason he sensed it more intensely than ever. He picked up a rubber band, wound it around his fingers, then pulled it back and sent it across the room where it struck a calendar with a picture of horses looking longingly over a wire fence. "I always hated that picture," he remarked.

Glancing at it, Dani smiled at the policeman's inconsistency. "Why do you keep it on the wall then?"

"Because I'm going to be mad at something. It's easier to be mad at a calendar than it is at a police commissioner or some stupid patrolman on the take." He straightened up and touched the burgundy tie that formed a brilliant color against the snow-white shirt. "I don't see the problem. You want to find somebody? You're a detective agency. Go find them."

"It's not that easy, Luke. I have to find this woman in a hurry."

"Well, with J.T. Denver behind you, I guess you can afford to hire Sherlock Holmes. Why don't you go to the Missing Persons Bureau?"

"Oh, Luke, you know how slow those agencies are!"

"Yeah, I guess so." Sixkiller sat back in his chair, and his obsidian eyes glinted as thoughts ran through his head. Finally he said, "Francis Pink."

"What?"

"Francis Pink. That's your man."

"He sounds like a—" Dani hesitated for a moment. "He sounds like an interior decorator."

"He may do that too, for all I know, Dani." Sixkiller's white teeth flashed against his bronze skin. "But believe me, he'll find the woman if you have the money." Reaching into his desk drawer, he rummaged around, found a stub of a pencil, and wrote a name down, then located the right card in his Rolodex and copied the phone number. "How about dinner tonight?"

"Not tonight, Luke. I'm snowed under with work."

Sixkiller never got tired of Dani's refusals, and now he grinned at her as she rose to leave. "Maybe I ought to arrest you on suspicion. That's the only way I'm going to get to spend time with you."

Dani turned and gave Sixkiller a warm smile. "Suspicion of what?"

"Suspicion of being the most beautiful PI in the business. You'd be found guilty as charged."

"Thanks, Luke. I really needed that."

After Dani left the office Sixkiller took his seat again and, locking his fingers behind his head, tilted his chair back. Thoughts ran through his mind, and finally he shook his head. "That's some babe!" he said with admiration. "I'm liable to break a rule and marry her myself one of these days."

◆ ◆ ◆

As soon as Dani got back to her car, she plucked her cell phone out of her purse and dialed the number Luke had written down for her. The phone rang twice, and then a mild voice said, "Francis Pink."

"Mr. Pink, my name's Dani Ross. I need to talk with you about some work."

"Yes, Miss Ross. Now, all I do is find people."

"That's exactly what I need, Mr. Pink."

"I'm on a job right now. It'll probably be very late before I can get back to you."

"I'll be at my office working late tonight. You can come by there any time." She gave him the address in the French Quarter and her phone number and hung up. As she started the car engine, she thought, *He sounds like a sissy to me. But Luke says he's the best, so . . .*

◆ ◆ ◆

Glancing at the clock on the wall, two lines appeared between Dani's eyebrows, a sure sign she was frustrated. The office was quiet; Angie had already left, and Dani had been alone for the past hour. For the tenth time she glanced over at the phone, willing it to ring, anxious to get Pink started on his assignment.

"He's probably like everybody else in this business," she said aloud. "Not to be trusted."

Her voice sounded loud in the silence of the room, and involuntarily she turned and looked up at the picture of her great-great grandfather. His stern old eyes looked down at her, and Dani managed a rueful grin. "I bet you didn't have to put up with people like this when you were in charge, did you, Colonel?"

The silence was overpowering, and Dani sighed wearily. She locked her hands together and bowed her head. She felt the beginnings of a major headache, and as she sat there, despite her best intentions, the concerns that had been piling up on her rolled across her mind like a thunderstorm. She thought about her father. She and Daniel Ross were much closer than most fathers and daughters. She couldn't remember a time when she hadn't been able to go to him with whatever problem was bothering her at the moment. She thought of how he had always been there for her when she was growing up, even as a small child. For some strange reason she had found it easier to take her problems to him than to her mother.

These days she thought almost constantly about her father's brush with death. True, he was doing better, and the doctor said the heart attack had not damaged his heart significantly. Nevertheless, the ghostly fingers of death had left an imprint on Dani.

Rob, her younger brother, was just at the right age to get into trouble. He was a good kid, but impulsive and highly impressionable. The seventeen-year-old had a bad habit of making a role model out of those not worthy of it, and as Dani thought about him, she murmured, "I have to spend more time with Rob."

Then thoughts of her younger sister, Allison, fifteen, leaped into her mind. She caught a glimpse of Allison's face, sweet but vulnerable, and she knew the young girl was going through a bad time. Dani Ross had little use for the modern psychobabble going around—"Everybody just needs more self-esteem." *Hitler had plenty of self-esteem. A person needs more than just thinking he or she is wonderful. We all need God in our lives.*

Still, she could understand what Allison was going through, for she herself at that age had been miserable and unhappy. She had never been able to convince Allison, not even with photos, that during adolescence Dani had called herself a walking skeleton. She had complexion problems and was totally convinced she would live and die an old maid. She had often wished during that time that she was Roman Catholic, so she could become a nun and hide from all her problems. She turned away from the desk now, walked over to the window, and stared out at the Quarter. The pale light of a streetlight formed a halo. *That's about the only halo there is in this part of the world.* She disliked the French Quarter intensely and more than once had talked about moving the office downtown or outside the city; but somehow she had not quite been able to make that decision.

Another worry came to her. Right now the agency was in the black due to J.T. Denver's money, but that would come to an end someday. Dani was aware she herself had a self-esteem problem. She kept it covered up well, and with her statuesque good looks and firm, aggressive manner very few people knew that she would sometimes wake up at night terrified at what the future held.

Glancing at the clock again, she walked around the room nervously and finally walked over to the desk and sat down. Opening the drawer, she pulled out a worn, black Bible and opened it. She ran her eyes down the page and finally put her finger on a pair of verses, Philippians chapter 4, verses 6 and 7. "I've just about worn these two out." She smiled as she looked at the underlined verses. She had put a star to one side, and several dates were printed there, some going back four or five years. She thought about all the times she'd come to this passage for comfort, and now, although she had it memorized firmly, she traced the words with her finger, speaking them aloud: "Do not be anxious about anything, but in everything, by prayer and petition, with thanksgiving, present your requests to God. And the peace of God, which transcends all understanding, will guard your hearts and your minds in Christ Jesus."

Once again as her words broke the silence, she felt somewhat self-conscious. She closed the Bible, put her hands on it, bowed her head, and began to pray aloud. "Lord, I wish I had great faith. But You and I both know that I don't. All I've got, Lord, is a little tiny grain of mustard-seed faith. I know, Lord, that You said even that much faith is enough to move a mountain. But it doesn't seem like enough, Lord, and I'm asking You again to give me more faith. I know all these problems that trouble me are under Your control. You're able to furnish a table in the wilderness where there is nothing at all. So You're able to help Rob and Allison, and You are able to help me run this agency." She hesitated for a moment and shrugged her shoulders. "I don't have great faith, and I can't bring You what I don't have, Lord. But I give You all I've got. I ask You to help me with all of these problems, and I ask You to give me the peace that passes all understanding."

For a few moments she sat at the desk, not opening her eyes. Finally, taking a deep breath, she smiled and said, "Well, Lord, there it is. It's *Your* problem now." Glancing over at the clock, she gave up on Pink and prepared to go home. Leaving the office, she stepped outside and moved downstairs, then exited the building. The car was parked on a narrow side street almost a block away, and Dani suddenly remembered that she had left her Detective Special pistol in the office. For a moment she hesitated and was ready to go back, but then she changed her mind. "Lord, take care of me," she said and started walking quickly.

The heels of her shoes made a staccato sound on the cobblestone as she crossed the street, and even before she had gotten fifteen yards she was aware that she was not alone. She whirled quickly just in time to see a bulky figure approaching. He was walking swiftly, and fear swept over her. He was a black man wearing some sort of dark trousers and a pullover shirt. A black cap obscured part of his face, but she could see the intensity of his eyes. She knew it was too late to run, for he was almost upon her. She faced him and knew that her only recourse was to scream, though in the French Quarter that was not likely to be very effective against a mugger as large and determined as this one. She stiffened her back and held her shoulders together as the man came toward her. His features were blunt with large lips and a flattened nose, and at that moment Dani would have given practically anything to see Luke Sixkiller or Ben Savage step out of the darkness.

"Miss Ross?"

Dani sighed loudly with relief. She felt as if her body had been wrung dry. It was the same feeling she'd had after narrowly avoiding a bad automobile accident.

"Yes, I'm Dani Ross."

"My name is Pink, Miss Ross. I'm sorry I'm late. I saw you leaving the office. If it's too late, I can come back tomorrow."

"No," Dani said nervously.

"I didn't mean to frighten you."

Taking a deep breath and letting it out slowly, Dani said, "I ought to know better than to be out on these streets late at night. Let's go back to the office."

Five minutes later Dani was seated at her desk, and Pink sat across from her. He was a huge man, and Dani almost smiled as she thought of the remark she'd made about his name sounding like an interior decorator's. "This is the job, Mr. Pink," she said. She handed over a slip with a name on it. "Nancy Bayless was her name at one time. She lived in a little town in Texas called Decatur."

"I've been there. It's just outside of Dallas." Pink studied the paper that Dani had typed out giving all the information Denver had given her, and finally he said, "This pretty urgent, Miss Ross?"

"Very urgent. Use anybody you need, and don't spare the expense."

An amused smile turned the man's huge mouth up at the corners. "That's a dangerous thing to say. How do you know I won't run up the tab on you?"

"Luke Sixkiller wouldn't have recommended anybody who would do that."

"The lieutenant's quite a fellow. Are you and him close?"

Dani felt her face burning. "We're just good friends."

"Good man to have for a friend."

"Do you think you can find her quickly?"

"Yes."

The single word encouraged Dani, and she said, "Isn't it hard to find people sometimes?"

"Not usually. If you have a name and a location, it's generally pretty simple. I have an inside track with some government agencies that keep track of people. All I have to do is find out, for example, where she worked, and they'll have her Social Security number. Once we have that, it'll be easy enough."

"I'd appreciate it if you would finish the job as quickly as possible."

"No problem." Pink got up and said, "I'd better walk you to your car."

"That might be best." Dani reached into the drawer, got the Lady

Detective Special, and clipped it under her jacket in the center of her back. Pink watched and smiled. "It doesn't go with the outfit."

"No. It goes with Bourbon Street though. Good luck, Mr. Pink."

◆ ◆ ◆

Daniel Ross looked up, surprised at the sharpness of his daughter's voice. She had snapped at her mother, and although he said nothing, his displeasure did not escape Dani. She mumbled, "I'm sorry. I'm just irritable today. I'll be back for dinner tonight."

After the door had slammed and Daniel heard the car roar off, he looked over at his wife and took her hand. "She's letting this get the best of her." His voice was heavy, and he said nothing more.

Catherine Ross came over and put her arms around Daniel. "She's doing fine," she said. "And don't get any ideas about rushing to the rescue like Custer."

"He didn't wind up very well, did he? I feel so—so *useless*, Catherine."

"You're going to follow the doctor's orders if I have to tie you in your chair."

"I surrender, dear," he said. Both of them were concerned about Dani, and they had lived together so long that many things did not have to be said aloud.

◆ ◆ ◆

As Dani sped across the causeway and made her way to the shipyard, she was uncomfortable. She had slept poorly, and by the time she got to the shipyard she was thoroughly dissatisfied with herself. She didn't seem to be making any progress with the case, and she knew J.T. Denver would not put up with that for very long. As she turned to walk the length of the huge vessel, she saw Jamie Cordova. The young woman was wearing a tight-fitting, white T-shirt that showed off her figure to the max and a pair of dark green slacks. The two exchanged glances, but not a flicker of recognition showed in either woman's eyes. Dani knew the last thing the agent needed was for the wrong person to see them talking together.

She made her way to the offices, where she found Loreen Franz alone. Looking up as Dani came in, Loreen said, "Well, do you have anything?"

Dani had already decided that if J.T. wanted anybody to know about her search for Nancy Bayless, he would tell them himself. "We're narrowing it down a little bit," she said, giving the standard answer.

"That means you haven't got anything." Loreen was wearing a gray business suit, and there were lines of fatigue on her face. She pulled a cigarette out of a platinum case and offered it to Dani. When it was refused, she lit up and puffed nervously. "I'm going to quit these things one of these days," she said irritably.

"That's not a bad idea."

"Everybody knows it's not a bad idea. I've tried everything including those little pieces of paper they stick on your skin. Did you ever smoke?"

"No. I never started."

"You're lucky." Loreen crushed the cigarette out and turned to face Dani. "I know you detective people keep things to yourselves, but I'm gonna tell you something, and you forget where you heard it."

"Of course, Miss Franz."

"I think Creighton is responsible for that accident."

Dani narrowed her eyes. There was something almost frightening about the woman's intensity. She was an attractive woman, but there was a hardness about her that Dani knew was not only on the surface. "Why would you think that, Mrs. Franz?"

"Because I've heard him threaten to kill my father."

A chill suddenly touched Dani, but she kept her voice calm. "When was this, Mrs. Franz?"

"More than once. We aren't very close now, but there was a time when we tried to get along. Creighton's always been a heavy drinker, and when he drinks he talks. I never paid much attention to it. He's a spoiled brat! He reminds me of the John Kennedy type—the handsome playboy. But he never finished anything. Went to law school, didn't finish. All he wants to do is to get his hands on Dad's money."

Dani almost replied that he would have to get in line for that, but she carefully said, "Did anybody else hear this threat?"

"I don't know. He talked to me a lot when he was drunk. The last time he told me this was about a month ago. Ever heard of a man named Trumps Lamont?"

"I know of him. He's a big-time gambler, and a pretty dangerous one too."

"Well, Creighton owes him a lot of money. He came to my place one day trying to borrow some money to pay that gambler off. I didn't give it to him, of course. He was drunk, and he was scared. That's when he said, 'Why doesn't J.T. have the decency to die?'"

"That's not a death threat, Mrs. Franz."

"No, but that's not all he said. He mumbled it, but as he was leaving, he turned around and said, 'If he doesn't come through, I'll kill him. He's got to help me. He's got to!'"

"Do you think he's capable of violence? A lot of people talk, but not many people can actually go through with it."

"You ask around about Creighton Bracken's violent ways. He beat one poor man who stole one of his girlfriends so badly that the family had to pay over 100,000 dollars in damages."

Dani listened as Mrs. Franz went on, and finally she knew she would have to take it seriously enough to look into it. "I wouldn't tell this to anyone else if I were you, Mrs. Franz."

"I'll tell anybody I want to. And by the way, tell that agent of yours to stay away from my daughter."

Dani blinked with surprise. "Ben Savage always stays away from the women involved in a case we're working on."

Loreen Franz hesitated. "Tara's hard to discourage. She's got a crush on him. Do something—get another agent, whatever. I don't want her mixed up with a seedy private detective."

"Maybe you'd better talk to her."

That suggestion did not sit well with Loreen, and Dani left the office at once. She spent an hour talking to Bobby Franz, whom she found elsewhere in the plant. Dani brought up the question of Creighton. "Your wife thinks he has ill will toward your father-in-law."

"Sure, he does," Bobby said. He had a round, innocent-looking face, and the glasses he wore added to his innocent appearance. "But he wouldn't try to kill him."

"You sure about that?"

"Of course!"

Dani saw that the man was in earnest. She wanted to tell him that far more people were killed by relatives than by total strangers, but she said only, "I'll be checking back with you, Mr. Franz."

◆ ◆ ◆

By the time Dani got back to the office it was nearly noon. She entered and started to speak to Angie when suddenly she saw Francis Pink sitting in one of the leather-covered chairs. "You're here!" she said inanely.

Pink got to his feet. "Yes, ma'am. Have you got a few minutes?"

"Of course. Angie, hold my calls."

"Yes, Miss Ross."

Dani went into her office and at once turned to meet Pink, who reached into his shirt pocket and gave her a paper. "Here's what you need."

Dani could not believe what was happening. "But—but you don't mean you've already found her?"

"Wasn't too hard. Unless somebody's trying to hide, it's pretty easy to trace them. Especially a lady like this. She's Nancy Livingston now. Her husband died three years ago. She has a house just outside of Colorado Springs. The address is 1123 Payton Road."

Dani took the paper and stared at it as if it were a strange specimen under a microscope. She looked up, admiration evident in her voice. "I appreciate this, Mr. Pink. Luke was right. You know your business."

"Well, I'd like to take credit, but this one was like shootin' fish in a barrel."

"How did you find her?"

"I called Decatur and found out that the vet she worked for in that place was still in practice. He was fond of the woman. Told me she married a man named Livingston and had moved to Colorado Springs."

"How'd you get the address?"

"You want me to give away my trade secrets?"

"I wish you would. I may need them."

"Well, the vet still gets Christmas cards from her. How easy can it get?"

Dani could not praise Pink enough. They went back out to the reception area, and Dani insisted on giving him a bonus.

"You don't have to do this," Pink said.

"I'm not, but J.T. Denver is."

"Well, in that case I expect I'd better take it."

After Pink had left, Dani called Angie into her office. "Get me a ticket to Colorado Springs. Round-trip."

"When?"

"The first thing out. And, Angie, make it first-class."

♦ ♦ ♦

"And so, Mr. Denver, finding the woman was apparently fairly simple. A plane leaves in three hours, and I'll be on it and will go talk to this woman. Are you sure that's what you want?"

J.T. Denver was looking better. His color had come back, and although he moved carefully there was a light in his eyes Dani had not seen before. "Of course I want you to go," he said quickly.

"And what should I tell her?"

"Just tell her the truth—that you're working for me, and I wanted to know how she was. That I've worried about her." He hesitated, then said, "I thought about writing a letter, but what could I say? Just tell her I'd like to see her again if—" He broke off and gnawed on his lip nervously. "Do you think she might after all these years?"

"Anything's possible," Dani said. She took a deep breath and added, "You want me to ask her to come back with me?"

Eagerly J.T. Denver said, "Yes! See if she'll come. You're a woman. You could talk to her. Tell her I—" He hesitated, then said, "No, don't tell her anything. If she won't come, she won't."

"I'll tell her how anxious you are."

"Thank you, Dani."

Two hours later Dani parked her car in the long-term parking lot at the airport. As she went through the procedures of getting her ticket cleared, she was thinking about the job that one of the richest men in America had given her. *I've never seen a thing like this work out, but maybe this will be the first.*

There had been a time, Dani remembered, when she'd found commercial flights an exciting adventure. That, however, had been a long time ago, and now she had reached the point where only through necessity did she ever get on a commercial liner. She had had a bad night, sleeping poorly again, and something about going to Colorado Springs to interview a woman out of J.T. Denver's dim past troubled her.

After arriving at the airport an hour earlier and going through the rather humiliating exercise of obeying the terse commands of airline employees, she had waited impatiently, glad that at least the flight was on time. That, however, proved to be false hope.

She had walked onto the airplane, settled down, and waited for the takeoff, but nothing happened. Time passed, and like the other passengers Dani grew restless. The air conditioner was off while the plane was on the ground, and sweat began running down her face, and her clothes began sticking to her body.

"This is the captain speaking. We apologize for the delay, but we have had a slight malfunction in one of the elevators. There's no problem really, but we want to be absolutely sure things are checked out. So, if you'll just be patient, we'll get aloft as soon as we get clearance."

"Fine!" Dani muttered under her breath. "Just what I needed."

The seat next to her was filled to overflowing by a young man no more than twenty-five. He was a large, rawboned man with flaming red hair and a homely face scarred from encounters with fists or whatever. Dani noticed that his hands were enormous, and they bore various scars of past injuries. He wore a pair of high-heeled ostrich boots, jeans, and a belt buckle so big that a plumber could use it for a wrench. His shirt was so yellow that it almost hurt her eyes.

"Looks like we're stuck on this thing, don't it?"

"Yes, it does," Dani answered briefly. She had figured that sooner or later the young cowboy would try to get acquainted. Men often approached her on airplanes, and she had learned to turn off their advances without being nasty about it.

"My name's Red Bassinger."

Dani nodded briefly but made no reply.

"What's yours?"

Dani could not avoid the direct question. "My name is Ross," she said.

"Your first name?"

"No. That's my last name."

"What's your first name?"

"Dani—Dani Ross."

"Well, that's right unusual." The tall young man removed a box of snuff from his hip pocket with some difficulty, and held it out to her, but a quick look from Dani caused him to change his mind. "Reckon you don't dip, do you?"

Dani could not help being amused at his mannerisms.

"No, I don't dip, Mr. Bassinger."

"Oh, shucks, just call me Red. Everybody does."

Dani tried to concentrate on the in-flight magazine, which was boring, as usual, and finally put it back and decided she might as well listen to Red, who obviously was not going to hush.

"You ever go to rodeos?"

"I rode the barrels in high school rodeos."

"You don't tell me! You still got your hoss?"

"Yes, I do."

"What kind is he?"

"A quarter horse. His name is Biscuit."

Bassinger began firing questions at her, and Dani didn't mind talking about Biscuit. He was still one of the pleasures of her life that she treasured the most, and finally she opened up enough to say, "I think I get too fond of that horse sometimes."

"Well, that ain't all bad," Red grinned. "I get that way about all my hosses. I'm in the rodeo, you know."

"I guessed as much."

"You ever see me ride?"

"I don't think so. I don't go to the rodeos much. I'm too busy."

The cowboy leaned forward and extracted a billfold from his hip pocket. Plumbing the depths of it, he came up with a ticket and said, "Here. Be proud to have you come and watch me. You going to Colorado Springs, ain't ya?"

"Yes."

"Rodeo's there tonight. If you'd like, I'll come by and take you there."

"No, I don't think so. But thanks anyway."

Red didn't seem put off by her rather cool manner. He began to talk about the coming rodeo, and Dani grew interested. "I've often wondered why anybody would take up riding wild horses for a living, Red. It's not a very steady occupation, is it?"

"You got that right." Red sighed heavily. He was wearing a battered, white Stetson that he had not bothered to put in the overhead, and now he took it off and ran his hand through his bright red hair. "I've always said that the best qualification for ridin' in a rodeo is gettin' kicked in the head a few times."

Dani laughed. The young man was likable enough. "Well, what's it really like?"

"Well, ma'am, I'll tell you, it's get up every day and get in a pickup and pull a hoss trailer to a town 500 miles away. You get there just in time to pay your entrance fees and unload the horses, and then the rodeo starts. I ride bareback and saddle broncs too, and Brahma bulls. So, by the time you get all that done it's ten o'clock, so you go get somethin' to eat, maybe have a few drinks, go to bed.

And if the rodeo lasts two or three days, you just keep doin' the same thing. Then you get in the trailer, and go another 500 miles or a thousand or whatever, and do it all over again."

"Does it pay well?"

"It does for about a dozen fellows, but they have to work at it."

"Why do you do it? You just like to ride?"

"Oh, I don't know. I guess it was just a dream I had when I was younger. I seen pictures of folks like Jim Shoulders and Casey Tibbs, and they was makin' hundreds of thousands of dollars, and all the pretty gals was hangin' onto 'em, and it looked like a pretty good life. But it ain't. Just one accident, and you're out for the year if it's bad enough. If it's real bad, you may be out for life."

Dani was fascinated by the rather tragic cycle, and she tried to plumb further into what would make a man do it. "Couldn't you do something else, Red?"

"I reckon I could, but it'd be powerful dull. You know, you only got to stay on a buckin' bronc for ten seconds, but durin' that ten seconds a man's blood gets to poundin' and his head gets to poundin' too. And it's just you against the hoss. Well, I just like it, I guess."

"Do you have a family?"

"No. It ain't a good life for a family man. Someday, I guess, maybe I'll have to quit."

"What about your parents? Are they still living?"

"My mom is. She just about raised me."

Something in the man's tone troubled Dani. "Where does your mother live?"

"Tucson, Arizona. That's where I growed up. Ma don't like me rodeoin'. She always hoped I'd be a preacher."

Dani smiled briefly. "Do you think you might be someday?"

"Me? No, ma'am. Not much hope for that."

"Your mother must be a wonderful woman."

Red Bassinger fell silent, and Dani saw that for some reason her words had troubled him. She heard the thumping as the mechanic worked on the plane for what seemed like a long time.

Finally Red said, "I'll tell you what, Miss Dani. I can remember bein' out in the front yard, and my mama was up in the second floor in her bedroom. And even outside playin' like I was, I could hear her prayin' for me. She didn't mind liftin' up her voice."

"That's a wonderful memory, Red. And I think God's going to answer her prayers."

"You do? Well, he'd have quite a chore with a maverick like me."

"We're all mavericks, Red."

Bassinger looked at the elegantly dressed young woman with the smooth complexion and knew that she came from a different world. "I reckon you're a Christian yourself, ain't you, Dani?"

"Yes, I am." Dani began giving the young man her testimony. It was very simple and not dramatic, but just as she was finishing it up, the pilot spoke. "All right, folks, we'll be taking off in five minutes. Please fasten your seat belts."

Red fastened his seat belt, put his feet out in front of him, and studied his boots. He didn't comment on Dani's words about God, and when the plane took off he pulled his hat down over his face and apparently went to sleep.

Dani watched the earth fall away, and as the plane turned northwest toward Colorado, she prayed that God would touch the young man's heart.

The flight was uneventful. It seemed rather long to Dani, and since she had slept little the past few nights, she found herself dozing off. Once she awoke and found that Red was awake and was watching her curiously. He said nothing, however, and she went back to sleep.

The plane landed at the Colorado Springs Airport, and Dani waited until all the other passengers had departed. She saw little sense in fighting to get off, and Red nodded. "That's smart, Miss Dani. You don't save no time hurryin', and I always bump my head on the ceiling of these blasted airplanes."

Dani struggled with her carry-on, but Red reached up and

pulled it down for her easily. "You got somebody meetin' ya?" he said.

"No. I'm going to rent a car. I'm here on business." She reached into her purse, pulled out a card, and said, "I wish you'd call me when you find the Lord. It would do me good to know you're on your way, Red."

Red looked at the card and said, "What's this PI?"

"Private investigator."

"You're a detective?"

"Yes, I am."

"Never met one of them before. Of course I met the police under not very good circumstances." He tucked the card into his shirt pocket and studied her carefully. "Maybe I *will* give you a call."

"And maybe I'll come out and watch you ride tonight. Can't promise because I don't know what direction my business will take me. But good luck to you, and I'll be praying that your mother's prayers get answered."

It was time to file off the airplane then, and as soon as they got into the cavernous interior of the terminal, Red took his hat off and commented, "Like I said, I'm kind of a maverick, but I reckon I need your prayers about as much as anybody, Miss Dani. Good-bye."

"Good-bye, Red." Dani watched the man go, towering over the other passengers. She followed the white hat until he was lost to sight. With a sigh she turned and made her way to the car rental agency.

It took her only a few minutes to check the car out. It was a one-year-old Taurus. Dani looked around as the young woman finished the paperwork. "Beautiful airport," she said.

"Most people would rather come here than to Denver. It's a lot easier to get to, even if you have to drive a little farther. That Denver airport's a mess."

"I thought it was new."

"It is. They put in a new baggage system that was going to save the world. All electronic. You never saw such chaos in all your life! Everybody's baggage gets lost. Welcome to Colorado, Miss Ross."

"Thank you."

Dani took the keys and wheeled her suitcase across the terminal, following the signs. When she stepped outside, she saw that the skies were bluer and bigger than in New Orleans. Far over to the west a line of snowcapped peaks bordered Colorado Springs. The snow was so white, it almost hurt her eyes. She made her way to the lot where the cars were parked. Putting her bag in the trunk, she got inside and started the engine, then pulled out of the airport. As always, getting out of a large airport was confusing, but Colorado Springs was simpler than most. There was a frontier look about Colorado Springs, and she drove until she cleared the airport, then pulled into a gas station. She purchased a city map and, once back in the car, unfolded it. She could not find Payton Road on the map and sat there wondering what to do.

I guess I'll get a room, she thought, *and then maybe I can get directions.*

The Radisson was crowded, but the clerk found a room for her with one king-sized bed on the seventh floor. Dani signed for the room, carried her bag upstairs, and then put the little card in the door. For once it worked, but she thought, *I liked it better when you had keys. I guess I'm just old-fashioned.*

Stepping inside, she saw that it was an attractive room with a window looking onto the Rockies' snow-white peaks to the west. Quickly she unpacked. After a plane trip for some reason she always felt grimy. She showered and put on a pair of tan dress slacks and a lightweight yellow sweater, then moved downstairs. Going to the desk, she asked the clerk if she knew where Payton Road was. The clerk said, "No. Why don't you go outside and ask one of the cab drivers? They'll know."

"Thank you."

Dani moved outside, where several cabs were lined up. She walked up to a driver leaning against his cab reading a magazine Dani wished would go out of business.

"Excuse me."

"Take you somewhere, lady?"

"I'm sorry to bother you, but I'm looking for Payton Street. I can't find it on the map."

"You mean Payton Road?"

"That's it! It's not on the map anywhere."

"You've probably got an old map. Payton Road is in a new subdivision. Not much out that way. Be glad to take you."

"No thanks. I have a car if you could just give me directions."

The cab driver spat with disdain and rattled off directions so rapidly that Dani had trouble keeping up. She asked him to repeat them, and she jotted them down as best she could. "Sorry I did you out of a fare, but here's a tip anyway." She handed him a five dollar bill, and the driver's face brightened.

"Thank you, ma'am."

"You're sure about Payton Road?"

"There's not much out there. It's kind of wild. As a matter of fact, I think it's a county road."

Dani thanked him again and went to the garage. It was still early, so she thought she might as well make her initial contact with Nancy Livingston, perhaps her only contact. That thought troubled her as she pulled out of the Radisson parking area.

She saw signs advertising Pike's Peak and thought maybe she'd have time to take it in if she couldn't see Mrs. Livingston right away. She wasn't much for tourist sights, but for some reason she'd always been fascinated by that particular peak.

She soon cleared Colorado Springs and was headed toward Denver, but she kept seeing more of the signs and landmarks the driver had told her about. Finally she turned off the main highway and followed a county road. The trees began to get thicker, all tall evergreens, and she lost sight of the Rockies. She brought the car to a stop when a beautiful eight-point buck stepped out onto the road. She'd never seen such a beautiful animal so close up. He didn't seem to be afraid of her, and he stared at her for a time, then sniffed and ambled off at his own easy pace.

She followed the directions carefully and finally found a sign that said Payton Road. There were no buildings, no houses, no gas stations or anything else, but she turned and made her way down a pristine, winding road that finally emerged on a level plain at the very base of the foothills. She could see the Rockies clearly as they rose beautifully to the west. She drove for five minutes and then saw the house. It was made of stone and cedar and was nestled against a rise of gray granite, almost seeming to meld into the land itself. Dani liked it instantly. She got out of the car and started toward the house. She had gone only halfway to the steps when suddenly from around the corner a huge pit bull came toward her at a fast gallop.

The animal moved so fast that Dani had no chance to react. She had heard of pit bulls' reputation for fierceness, and the dog had a broad head, wicked-looking teeth, and a pair of beady-looking eyes that he kept fixed on her.

"Nice doggie," Dani said though it sounded rather foolish to her.

The dog didn't advance any farther, but he didn't back off or lose interest either. Dani had always heard you should not turn your back on a dangerous dog, but neither did she feel inclined to advance. She stood there uncertainly, and then with some relief she saw a woman mounted on a beautiful, black horse ride around the edge of the house. The woman took in the situation at one glance and dismounted. She patted the horse and led him forward. "The dog's harmless," she said in a pleasant, low-pitched voice.

"That's good to hear."

The woman came over and patted the dog's broad forehead. "He's just a big baby," she said. "I know pit bulls have a bad rep, but he's gentle enough."

The dog suddenly left the woman's side and came over, and Dani wondered what the dog intended to do. But when he got to her, he sat down—right on her feet.

The woman laughed. "He loves to sit on people's feet. Just shove him out of the way. Get off of her feet, Trouble."

The dog was heavy, and Dani moved back a little, but he leaned suddenly over against her leg and looked up, his huge red tongue lolling. He seemed to be grinning at her, and as she backed away, he advanced, still leaning against her and nearly knocking her over.

"Trouble, come here!"

Reluctantly the huge, white dog swaggered back to his mistress, where he sat on her feet.

"Get off my feet! I don't know what's the matter with this dog. That's what he likes to do better than anything—sit on somebody's feet. Can I help you?"

"I'm looking for Mrs. Nancy Livingston."

"I'm Nancy."

Dani had assumed this was the woman she was looking for, and now she had a chance to look at her. What she saw was a woman apparently in her early forties with a mass of auburn hair or somewhat redder. She had green eyes set in a square face, a pleasant wide mouth, and a trim body trained by hard work or sports. She was wearing a pair of chinos. A man's shirt open at the throat revealed a tan, and there was a directness about her gaze that Dani rather liked. "My name is Dani Ross, Mrs. Livingston. I'd like to have a few minutes of your time if I may." Quickly Dani saw something leap into the woman's eyes, and a no began to form. "I'm not selling anything," she assured her. "I've come all the way from New Orleans just to talk with you."

"New Orleans!" Surprise washed across the woman's face. "Well, if you've come all the way from New Orleans . . . But a lot of people say they're not selling when they really are."

"I'm not a salesman for anything. I just need to talk with you."

"Come inside. Let me tie this horse up first." The woman tied the horse to a hitching post, a statue of a jockey with a ring held in his immobile hand.

Dani followed the woman inside the house, and the huge dog forced his way in before the woman could close the door. "That dog thinks he has to be in on everything."

The room Dani stepped into was enormous. It had a huge, cathedral ceiling with exposed beams and windows that went all the way to the top, allowing the brilliant sunlight to filter through. The floor was hardwood, but brightly colored Indian rugs, probably Navajo, were scattered about, and the furniture was all leather. Everything looked worn and comfortable.

"We might as well have some coffee."

"Don't make it for me."

"Oh, I keep it made. Sit down, Miss Ross."

Dani did so, and the woman soon brought a pewter tray back with two cups of coffee and two pieces of cake. "That's store-bought cake. I hate it, but I'm not much of a cook."

Dani smiled. "This is fine."

The two women sipped their coffee, and Dani saw that the woman had opened the door but would offer no more information on her own. "Did you work for a veterinarian named Wilson in Decatur, Texas, some years ago?"

"Why, yes, I did!" Something changed in Mrs. Livingston's face. "There's nothing wrong with him, is there?"

"Not that I know of. I just traced you through him."

"That sounds rather ominous. I haven't inherited a million dollars or something like that, have I? I've always heard about things like that, but I never expected to wind up being an heiress."

"It's not exactly that either, Mrs. Livingston." Dani shifted uncomfortably and tried to think of some way to approach the subject. Deciding that Nancy Livingston was a woman who could be best approached directly, she said, "I'm employed by a man named J.T. Denver." Something did change in Nancy's face then. It was only a flicker in her eyes, but Dani didn't miss it. She noticed that the woman grasped her hands together to conceal a slight trembling. Dani knew she had hit a nerve. "Mr. Denver hired me to find you, Mrs. Livingston."

Dani expected the woman to protest and to ask her to leave, but she did no such thing. The silence in the room was broken only by the ticking of a grandfather clock on the wall behind Dani. The big white dog lifted his head in the sudden silence, got up, moved even closer, and sat down beside Nancy Livingston.

"Why would he do that?"

"I'm not sure. You know he's a very wealthy man."

"Yes, I know. He can afford to do anything he wants to."

Dani hesitated, then said, "From what little he told me, I gathered he was a little worried about you. He wanted to be sure your life was all right. He didn't tell me that exactly, but . . ."

"What *did* he tell you?"

Dani could not meet the woman's gaze. She glanced down for a moment, then lifted her eyes. "He said he knew you very well at one time."

Nancy Livingston seemed to consider some hidden meaning in those words and finally said, "Yes, we did know each other very well, but that was a long time ago."

Again silence prevailed, and finally Dani broke it by saying, "He would like very much for you to come back with me. He'd like to see you."

"I don't think that would be proper at all." She hesitated, then put her full gaze on Dani. "We were in love once. We were both young and poor, and it was the first time either of us had ever been in love." Gazing out the window, she continued to speak in a low tone. "I loved him as I never knew a woman could love a man, and I thought he loved me the same way. I'd been brought up in strict circumstances and had never expected to give myself to a man before marriage. But—I loved him too much, or at least in the wrong way."

Dani didn't move; she hardly even breathed. She was beginning to see something about J.T. Denver she'd never seen before. His other wives were hard, foolish women, all of them, but this woman had a quality that was real and deep and true.

"I told him I couldn't live with him anymore. I asked him to marry me, but he wouldn't do it. I couldn't live like that, Miss Ross. So I ran away from him."

"I see," Dani said. "And you haven't talked to him in all these years?"

"No. Not once. Of course I've kept up with him in the newspapers and the magazines. He hasn't had a very happy life."

"No, he hasn't. "

"I suppose he—" Whatever Nancy had intended to say she didn't finish because just then a door slammed, and a young man came in from the back. He was no more than twenty-five or twenty-six, Dani estimated, but it was not his age that brought a gasp to her lips. She blinked with shock—the young man was the exact image of J.T. Denver!

"This is my son Travis, Miss Ross."

"Glad to know you, Miss Ross."

Travis bore a startling resemblance to a younger J.T. except for the thick auburn hair, which came from his mother. He looked fit, and there was a brightness about his eyes that indicated high intelligence. "I didn't mean to bust in," he said. "I just wanted to tell you, Mom, that next week I'm going over to Idaho to see Frank."

"All right."

"Good to meet you, Miss Ross." The young man hurried up the stairs with the exuberance of youth.

When his footsteps faded, Dani faced the woman across from her and waited.

Nancy Livingston said quietly, "I know you can see the truth."

"No one could miss it who has seen the two of them. Some children look exactly like their parents, and your son looks exactly like a young J.T. Denver."

Nancy rose and walked over to the window. She looked out for a long time, then turned and said, "J.T. never knew I was pregnant. I didn't know it myself until a month after I left."

"You've never told your son who his father was?"

"I married Pete Livingston a year later. I never told Travis who his real father was. Pete was a good husband and a good father to Travis. It broke Travis's heart when Pete died in a wreck three years ago."

Dani knew she was on dangerous ground now, but she had to say something. "Mr. Denver longs for a son, Mrs. Livingston. He has daughters, but he wants a son—a son he can be proud of."

"I can't bring the truth into the open," Nancy said quickly. "I don't know what it would do to Travis."

Dani felt it was time to leave. If she put too much pressure on Nancy Livingston, getting her to talk any further would be impossible. "I can't tell you what to do. I've done what Mr. Denver asked me to do, and I know what he's asked is a hard thing for you." She hesitated, feeling she should say more, but wanting to find the right words. "I'm a Christian, Mrs. Livingston, and I believe that God has a hand in everything that happens to us. Sometimes He even takes the wrong things we do and makes something good come out of them."

Surprised at Dani's words, Nancy Livingston didn't answer for a moment, then said quietly, "I'll have to think about it. Where are you staying?"

"At the Radisson."

"I'll call you, but don't expect anything."

"Thank you for talking to me, Mrs. Livingston."

Dani left the house but did not go back to the hotel. For over three hours she drove around the Colorado Springs area. She saw with her eyes the beauty of the place, but her mind was occupied with Nancy Livingston and her pain. *What would I do in her place?*

Nancy Livingston was a proud woman, and she had made a life for herself and for her son after she'd been rejected by J.T. Denver. And now the man wanted her back in his life. Dani knew instinctively that Denver's riches would have no appeal for this woman. Her only concern would be, "What's best for my son?"

◆ ◆ ◆

For two days Dani stayed at the Radisson. She didn't call back to the Livingston house, though she could have. Finally, at the end of the second day, she ate supper and went up to her room. She knew she was beaten, and she felt the defeat keenly, though also understanding and sympathizing with Mrs. Livingston's feelings in the matter. She turned on the television, watched the news, then turned it off. Just as she did a knock came at her door.

When she opened the door, her heart leaped within her, for there was Nancy Livingston. "Come in, Mrs. Livingston."

"Call me Nancy."

"All right, Nancy. And I'm Dani."

When Nancy stepped inside, Dani knew that her mind was made up. "I've told Travis the truth—all of it."

"How did he take it?"

"I don't know. Travis is a quiet young man. He thinks things over for a long time, but we both talked about it and prayed together about it. And we think he needs to at least go meet J.T. one time."

"I'll purchase the tickets. I think you're doing the right thing, Mrs. Livingston."

"I'm not sure. It's so easy to go wrong. Travis is such a fine young man. He took over the trucking business Pete built up. He owns five trucks now and could own more if he wanted. He flies a plane. He loves stock car racing and is thinking of going into NASCAR. But for right now all that's on hold. I guess it's natural enough for a man to want to know his father—his biological father, I mean."

"Well, he'll get the chance. I must also tell you that there's considerable trouble in J.T.'s life right now." Dani asked Nancy to sit down, and she went over the situation J.T. Denver was facing.

"So you see, Mr. Denver has some serious problems that have to be solved."

"I can't be involved with any of that. All I want is for Travis to meet his father."

"We'll leave as soon as I can get the tickets. And again let me say, I think you're doing the right thing."

After Nancy left, Dani picked up the phone and made the reservations. When she hung up the receiver, she had an eerie feeling. "Am *I* doing the right thing?" she whispered. "J.T. Denver's life is a mess. It would be awful if this woman and her son were ruined by meeting him." But she couldn't turn back now, and she resolutely began to make plans for what would happen when they got back to New Orleans.

Nine

"CAN YOU FORGIVE ME?"

Looking out the jet window, Dani marveled at how white and fleecy the clouds looked. Yet, there was a hardness and an apparent solidity about them. One of the things she liked about flying was watching the clouds beneath her instead of looking up to admire them.

A slight movement to her left drew her attention, and she shot a quick glance at Travis Livingston. He had a flight magazine in his hands, but she noted that he was staring at the back of the seat directly in front of him. That gave Dani a chance to study his features, and once again she marveled at how greatly he resembled his father. The same tapered face and identical brown eyes. His crisp hair had some of his mother's auburn in it, but the wide mouth and the deep dimple on the chin spelled J.T. Denver. Even now as she watched there was a nervous flicker in his eyes, and he suddenly turned to face her, catching her off guard.

"This is all pretty hard for me, Miss Ross."

"I can imagine. It's a very strange situation. I've never heard of anything exactly like it."

"Did you ever think you had come to the bottom of some steps in the dark but there was one more and you nearly doubled up when you hit it?"

"Yes," Dani smiled. "Or it's like walking along on firm ground, and you step in a hole. It jars you clean up to your skull."

The flight attendant came by, a short, well-built woman in her mid-thirties. She had merry blue eyes, and there was a chirp in her voice as she said, "Can I bring you cocktails or anything?"

"Nothing for me," Travis said. Dani shook her head. After the attendant had left, Travis commented, "You paid a fortune so we could fly first-class, and all we get is a free cocktail, which I don't want, and the chance to get on and off the airplane first."

Dani knew the young man was simply making conversation. "Yes, it is kind of a waste. I don't like to fly anyway. I understand you're a pilot."

"Yes. I have my license. My dad paid for it for my twentieth birthday. Paid for the lessons, I mean."

"You and your dad were very close, weren't you?"

Travis dropped his head for a moment, and when he turned to meet her gaze, there was evidence of loss in his eyes. "As close as two men can be, I guess. That's why this thing has hit me so hard."

Dani said very carefully, "I don't think you ought to make any quick decisions, Mr. Livingston."

"Oh, call me Travis."

"Fine. And I'm Dani. What I mean is, when we hit an emotional bump it's easy to make a wrong decision. When we get angry or upset or something goes wrong, that's the worst possible time to make a choice."

Travis grinned and studied her more carefully. "What do you mean? I can make a bad decision *any* time. It reminds me of what Harry Caray said once. Somebody asked him if the Chicago Cubs usually lost at Colorado because of the altitude, and Harry said, 'No. The Cubs can lose at any altitude.'"

Dani laughed.

The two sat quietly talking, and Dani was encouraged. She wanted to help the young man deal with the shock he'd experienced. Right across the aisle she saw Nancy with her head back, apparently asleep. However, Dani suspected she was not. *These two have had a rough bump*, she thought, *and I don't know how they're going to handle it.*

The plane droned on, and Dani wondered if Travis wanted to

talk about it anymore. She was looking down at the clouds again when suddenly he said, "I can't decide how I feel about J.T. Denver."

"What do you mean, Travis?"

"Well, he did run out on my mother by not marrying her. Out on me, too, in a way."

"He didn't know about you," Dani said quickly. "Your mother told you that, didn't she?"

"Oh yes, she told me, but that doesn't make much difference. He ran out on her. And the more I think about it, the more angry I get about the whole thing. I've never known a woman like my mother, Dani. She's generous, gracious. I've never known her to say an unkind thing about a human being in my whole life."

"I can see that. I already admire her greatly."

"What kind of man must he be to have walked out on her?" Bitterness etched Travis's face. He seemed to be struggling to hold his words back, but he couldn't. "When somebody hurts the one you love, it's worse than hurting you, isn't it?"

"I think so. We can handle personal trials pretty well, but when somebody touches our family . . ."

"What should I call him anyway? Dad? He's not my dad. Pete was my dad, and he always will be."

"I understand why you feel that way. From what you tell me, you and Pete were father and son in every way except blood, and that's not always the most important factor."

Something in Dani's words encouraged Travis, and he put the flight magazine away and turned to face her. His eyes were troubled, and he shook his head with a gesture of resignation. "I've been a Christian since I was fifteen years old, Dani, and I've always tried to be obedient to what the Bible teaches. I know that as a Christian I'm supposed to forgive those who sin against me. And so far it hasn't been hard because, really, I've had an easy life in that way. I never had any real enemies. But now it's different."

"I know," Dani said sympathetically. "So much of the Bible turns out to be hard when we have to put it into practice. As long as it's just words in a book, it's easy. But something like this brings you back to who you really are as a believer." She thought for a moment, trying to find words to comfort this young man. His whole world had been shaken, and now everything he had trusted was suddenly falling apart. His voice was unsteady, and she saw that he was clasping his hands tightly together.

"You know, Travis, I've read through the Bible several times, and there are some hard things in it. But a long time ago I decided the hardest thing that I ever heard of was when Jesus was on the cross. He said, 'Father, forgive them.' Can you imagine that?" Dani's eyes closed for a moment. "It always gives me a terrible feeling when I think of the Lord Jesus being nailed to a cross by men whom He Himself had made. He made us all, didn't He?"

"Yes, He did."

"So there was the Son of God being executed like a thief and a criminal by those profane, sinful Roman soldiers. And there were the Pharisees, the Sadducees, the scribes, the Roman soldiers—all of his enemies jeering at Him, calling Him names, challenging Him to come down from the cross. And yet when Jesus looked out on that group, He said, 'Father, forgive them.'" Dani was silent for a moment, and when she lifted her head, Travis saw that tears had come to her eyes. This shocked him a bit, and he reached out and put his hand on her arm in an impulsive gesture.

"Sorry. I don't mean to be a weepy female, but every time I think of how much Jesus loves us—even the worst of us—I see that I have no reason to have bitterness or anger or hatred toward anyone." She put her hand into her purse for a Kleenex and wiped her eyes.

Travis said, "I know that's true. It's just a little hard to learn all at once."

◆ ◆ ◆

The New Orleans Airport was as hectic as usual. But it was not as traumatic to navigate as Atlanta or Chicago's O'Hare, and Dani had become familiar enough with the routine. She led Travis and

Nancy down to the baggage pickup, and they waited until the luggage appeared on the rotating stand. Then Dani led them to the parking lot, where they loaded their luggage into the trunk of the Cougar. When they got inside, she drove out of the parking garage and headed for downtown New Orleans. Neither of her passengers seemed talkative, and Dani understood that they both felt somewhat overcome by the circumstances.

Suddenly Nancy asked, "What's that?"

Glancing over to one side, Dani said, "That's a cemetery, Nancy."

"But it looks like they are all on top of the ground."

"They are. The ground's very soft and mushy around here. They had some sad experiences of coffins floating up during floods, so now they put the crypts on top of the ground. Even single ones."

This interested Travis. "How do they build buildings if the ground's that bad?"

"Well, they don't build very high ones. They have to drive piers down hundreds of feet to make anything like a stable platform, so you won't see any skyscrapers like in New York or Chicago."

"Good," Travis said. "If you've seen one skyscraper, you've seen them all."

Dani laughed. "I said that once when I was visiting in England. I was with a friend, and when we went through a tower, down below were the crown jewels. The pride of the whole collection was the Star of Africa. It's one of the biggest diamonds in the world. Well, we were moving along in the line, and I looked at it. By that time I was pretty well touristed out. I'd seen so many things, I was tired of it all. My friend said, 'How do you like it, Dani?' and I'm afraid I said, 'When you see one Star of Africa, you've seen them all.'" Dani laughed suddenly. "The guard didn't like that at all because I wasn't showing proper respect for British tradition."

Dani threaded her way through the traffic and arrived at the Radisson. She got out of the car and said, "I'll walk up with you." To the doorman she said, "If you'll please park this, I'll be back in a few minutes."

Going inside, Dani went to the desk where she obtained the keys and signed the necessary papers.

"You're on the fourth floor," she said, then led them to the elevators.

The rooms were very nice. Dani had spared no expense. After all, it was J.T. Denver's money. She knew he would want the best for these two; so each of them had a suite. They went inside the first one, which was Nancy's. "Why, this is as big as a house!" Nancy exclaimed. "What could anybody do with this much room?" Walking to the bathroom, she stopped abruptly. "Look at this!"

Dani and Travis walked over to see what had caught her attention. "Look at that," she said. "It's big enough to take swimming lessons in."

The bathtub was indeed enormous. It was fitted with a Jacuzzi and was extra-deep. There was also a large, triangular shower in the corner, and as Travis flipped on the light, he grinned. "This would light up Yankee Stadium."

"I'm not sure I want to see myself quite that clearly," Nancy said. She turned and walked out of the bathroom and stopped beside a huge basket of flowers, fruit, nuts, and other goodies. "I thought you might want to snack a little bit," Dani said. "I think your suite is just like this one, Travis." She hesitated for a moment, then said, "I know you'll want to get rested up. When you're ready to go see Mr. Denver, just let me know."

Nancy lifted her head suddenly, and her chin had a determined look about it. "I'd like to see him right now."

"Now?" Dani said with surprise. "Aren't you tired?"

"No."

Dani was somewhat taken aback. She had expected that the two would want to rest up and had planned to take them both to see J.T. the next day. But the determination in Nancy was unmistakable. "All right, if that's what you want."

"You want me to go with you, Mother?"

"No, Travis. Let me see him alone first." She hesitated and then said, "You may not want to see him at all."

This enigmatic statement struck Travis, and he studied his mother. "Why do you say that?"

"It may not be a good thing for you two to get together. I will leave it up to you, of course. After all, he is your father, but—"

"No. Pete was my father."

Nancy went over and put her arm around her son. "I know you feel that way, but let's give him a chance. He can never be what Pete was to you, but maybe you two could get to know each other on some other level."

"I'll go with you now if you'd like."

"No. You just wait here."

The three left Nancy's suite, and Travis went to his own next-door. When the two women were back in the car, Nancy was silent. Feeling compassion for her, Dani said, "It'll be all right, Nancy."

"I don't know whether it will be or not. It was a long time ago. We have our own lives now, and I just can't imagine getting close to J.T. Denver. I've seen his pictures in the magazines and the newspapers so often, but they don't seem like the young man I knew so many years ago."

"He's not the same man, but God will give you wisdom." Dani pulled the Cougar out and headed toward the dock. She was actually nervous herself because even on short acquaintance she had formed a good opinion of these two. *Maybe I've done the wrong thing. I've known money to ruin people before. These two seem solid enough, but a billion dollars is a big temptation.* Dani began to pray for the three as she headed for the dock, and when they arrived, she got out of the car. She saw that Nancy was staring at the yacht. "Is that where he is? On that boat?"

"That's it. Enormous, isn't it?"

"It looks like a cruise ship. I don't know—" Nancy suddenly broke off and leaned forward. "Why, it's called *The Nancy*."

"Yes, it is," Dani said. She watched something change in the woman's face, then said gently, "Come along. I'll take you to his cabin."

♦ ♦ ♦

J.T. stared across the room at Creighton, who was standing as stiffly as if he were a soldier at attention. The young man's handsome face was tense, and there was an urgency in his voice as he continued to speak. Denver listened but only halfheartedly. He had other things on his mind. Besides, he had heard Creighton's spiels before. They were all just about the same: "If you'll help me, I can make us both rich. It can't miss."

The trouble was, Creighton's schemes often did miss. Tiring of the scene, J.T. glanced over at his ex-wife Shelley, who sat in a chair twisting her handkerchief nervously. She had been drinking heavily, Denver knew. He should know because he'd seen her in this state many times. Once again he wondered why he had ever married this woman. He knew deep within that his loneliness made him want to have somebody near, but he had tried to meet that need in three marriages, and in all three he had found no companionship, just new problems.

Creighton wound up his plea. "It would only take 300,000 dollars, and it's a surefire thing."

Wearily J.T. lifted his eyes and studied Creighton. He had always wanted a son, and he had fully intended to adopt Creighton. But it soon became apparent that Creighton would never finish anything. He had furnished the young man with plenty of money, and Creighton had thrown it all away. Because Creighton was lazy and dishonest, J.T. would never finance any project he brought to him. But he didn't dare say so outright, or Shelley would go ballistic. So he had to pretend to be interested.

"Write it up as a proposal, Creighton. I'll look it over."

"A proposal!" Creighton said, anger flickering in his eyes. "I thought I was family!"

"Creighton, even in a family you need to put things in an orderly fashion. Besides, this is business."

Creighton cursed and stormed out of the room. As expected, Shelley began to cry. A brief spark of compassion for this woman who had brought nothing but trouble into his life came over J.T. Denver. He rose, walked over to her, and put his left hand on her shoulder. His right arm was still in a sling, but he had regained most of the use of the left one. Not wanting to explain why he didn't just give Creighton the money, he decided to discuss another issue. "Shelley, that drinking is going to kill you."

"You always say that," she wept.

"Because it's true. Have you thought about going to Betty Ford or someplace like that?"

"If I felt more secure financially, I wouldn't have to drink."

J.T. turned away from her and went to stare out the porthole. He watched some pelicans as they flew by, admiring their airborne grace, then turned around and said, "How much do you need?"

"I need 5,000 dollars, J.T."

Without a word Denver moved over to the rosewood desk, pulled out a checkbook, and wrote a check. He handed it to her, and she quickly stood up and started to put her arms around him.

He didn't push her away, but something in his expression made her pull back. "I wish you'd take my advice and go do something about that drinking," he urged.

But Shelley had what she wanted, and she was already on her way to the door. "I hope you'll help Creighton," she said. "He's a good boy. He just needs somebody to stand behind him."

The door closed, and Denver walked around the stateroom restlessly. He turned on the stereo, and the sounds of a classical symphony filled the room. He picked up a book, but he had to force himself to take in what he was reading. A knock on the door caught his attention and, happy for any relief, he opened it. "Well, come in, Dani," he said.

"You're looking better, Mr. Denver. How's that left arm?"

"It's okay. This right wing's going to need a few more weeks though." He closed the door behind her and searched her face. "Did you find her?" he asked anxiously.

"Yes, I did."

"Where was she? How did you do it?" He began to pepper her with questions, which Dani answered as thoroughly as she could.

"What did you think of her, Dani? You're a woman, and you've been around. Was she married?" he said suddenly.

"She's a widow. Her husband died three years ago."

Denver digested this information, then said, "What does she look like?"

"You can find out for yourself. She's outside now waiting to see you."

Dani had never seen J.T. Denver seriously disturbed, but she did now. His face seemed to grow pale, and a tremulous look appeared around his usually firm and strong mouth. He looked like a man standing on the edge of a very high cliff. "You brought her back with you?" he whispered.

"Yes."

J.T. Denver turned and walked away. He stood in front of the desk with his head down, and when he turned back he had better control of himself. "Did you check her for weapons?" he asked wryly. "She might want to shoot me."

Dani saw through his frail attempt at humor. "I don't think so. Shall I send her in?"

"All right. Yes, please do."

Denver watched as Dani left the room. In the old days he would have immediately poured himself a drink, but he had given that up when he gave his heart to God. He had thought for years about this woman, and now he was prepared for disappointment and rejection. He well knew that few people could go back again, but this woman had been in his memory for years. One of the few pleasant memories he had. *Perhaps I've blown it all out of proportion*, he thought as he stood waiting nervously.

The moments seemed like an eternity, and many conflicting thoughts flashed through his mind as he waited. Then the door opened, and she came in.

Nancy! His lips formed the words, but there was no sound. He stared at her, unable to speak.

Coming over to him, Nancy put out her hand, then smiled. "It's good to see you, Travis."

Hearing his first name, Denver blinked. Nobody ever called him that except Nancy. He looked at her now and found it hard to believe that she was forty-three. She looked ten years younger. She was still slim, and her hair was as he remembered it—the most beautiful auburn he had ever seen. Without meaning to, he blurted out, "Do you dye your hair?"

Nancy laughed, and he remembered how he had always loved her laughter. "No," she said. "Do you?"

"No. You could ask if I wear a toupee, but I don't." He could not think of a thing to say. Finally he took a deep breath and noticed that she seemed as nervous as he was. "I've never felt so—so helpless in all my life."

"It's a little awkward, isn't it, Travis?"

"Come. Sit down." He waved her to one of the mauve-colored, overstuffed chairs, then sat down across from her. Clearing his throat, he said rather formally, "Would you like something to drink?"

"No. Not really."

"Are you hungry?"

"No. Nothing for me."

The silence that fell on the room was almost palpable, and finally Nancy asked directly, "Miss Ross tells me you had an accident."

"Oh yes. I'm better now. This arm is pretty well banged up, but I don't want to talk about that." His eyes went over her face eagerly. He could still see the young girl he'd known in this mature, attractive woman. "Tell me about yourself, Nancy." He sat there listening as she reviewed her life since their parting. She told him how she had found a man who had been good to her. They'd had a happy life together, and he had died three years earlier.

"It sounds like you've had a good life."

"Yes, thank the Lord. Very good."

"Well, if you read the newspapers, you know mine hasn't been that nice."

Nancy gave him an odd look. "You have what you always wanted, Travis."

Her words felt like a knife in his heart. "I guess I do." He dropped his head and for a time did not speak. When he lifted his face to her, she saw the lines that had not been there as a young man. "You know, Nancy, out there somewhere there's a poor, ambitious, young kid saying, 'If I had what J.T. Denver's got, I'd be on top of the world!' But he's wrong."

Again the silence seemed to come between them, and finally J.T. said, "I guess you're wondering why I sent Miss Ross to find you."

"You could have found me years ago if you'd wanted to, Travis."

"I know. But what would I have said?"

"Why did you decide to do this now?"

"Well, I treated you—" He had trouble getting the words out. "I've never forgotten how I treated you. I've tried to put it aside, to forget it, but something's happened lately that brought it up again."

"What was that?" Nancy asked curiously. Leaning forward, she studied him carefully.

"Well, it always sounds funny to me when I hear myself saying things like this, but . . . Well, to put it bluntly, I found God, and I've been trying to set some things right." He hesitated and looked for mockery in her face, but he saw none. "Some of it was easy, Nancy. It just took money. But I haven't been able to forget how I walked out on you. Can you forgive me?"

Nancy Livingston had thought about this man for years. During her married life she had put him aside with other memories because of her loyalty to Pete. But she knew now that she had never really forgotten J.T. Denver.

"I did that years ago, Travis."

The simple words brought tears into J.T.'s eyes, and as soon as Nancy saw them, she thought, *He has changed! I never saw him cry. Not once.*

"I made such a mess of my life, Nancy. And I can't ever make up for the things I've done."

"Don't let the devil torment you, Travis. Jesus paid for your sins. If you have taken Him as your Savior, you'll never have to pay for them again."

Travis passed a hand in front of his face, a hand not entirely steady as he said, "That sounds too good to be true, though I know it is."

"You've started over, Travis, and I'm glad."

Dani had waited outside the door, not knowing whether the interview would be five minutes or five hours. It turned out to be nearly an hour, and she somehow took satisfaction from that. Finally the door opened, and J.T. Denver said, "Dani, take Nancy back to the hotel please." He turned suddenly and said, "Nancy, you're having dinner with me, I hope?"

"I'd like that."

"I'll have Dani pick you up. Will 7 be all right?"

"That's fine."

The two women left, and when they were in the car headed back toward the Radisson, Dani could not hold in the question any longer. "What did he say about Travis?"

"I didn't tell him." Nancy turned to look at Dani. "I'll let Travis decide if he wants to meet him or not."

Ten

DENVER GETS A SHOCK

Looking from the balcony of his suite, Travis studied the landscape below him. Far off to his left he could see the Mississippi River as it wound around New Orleans. To the right planes were taking off from the New Orleans Airport. He had sat there for a long time, looking up occasionally at the gulls flying overhead. Suddenly hearing a sound behind him, he turned and watched as his mother took a seat beside him on the cushioned chairs.

"Did you see him?"

"Oh yes, I saw him." Nancy said no more for a time, then turned and said, "He's living on a yacht. A huge one." She hesitated for a moment and said, "He calls it *The Nancy*."

This bit of information startled Travis. "I guess that means he hasn't forgotten you after all these years."

"I'm not the only woman named Nancy, you know, though you're probably right."

"What did he say? What did he want? Why did he decide to look for you after all these years, Mom?"

Quietly Nancy told Travis the essence of her visit. Finally she said, "I asked him the same question you just asked me. After all these years, why would he suddenly want to see me?"

"What did he say?"

"He said he'd come to know the Lord, and he wanted to ask my forgiveness." She briefly related the story of Denver's conversion as he had given it to her and then sat there quietly. She had done what she could, and now she waited for her son's reaction.

"Mom," he said hesitantly, his brow furrowed, "when you knew him, I mean, all those years ago, were you in love with him?"

"Very much."

"Why didn't you stay with him?"

"He didn't want to get married, and I knew what we were doing was wrong. So I left him." From nowhere a gray pigeon appeared and fluttered down onto the railing of the balcony. Making its distinctive soft cooing sound, he walked back and forth. Then, seeing there were no morsels for him, with a noisy flutter of wings he rose into the air and went elsewhere to seek better fare.

"You loved him, Mom?"

"It was the hardest thing I ever did in my life to give him up, but I had to do it. There was something in him that disturbed me. He wanted money and power, and nothing else mattered very much."

"So he didn't love you."

"Not as much as he loved some other things."

Suddenly Nancy turned and said, "I know what you're thinking, Travis—you're wondering if I loved your father. I want to tell you now, and you must never forget it, yes, I loved him. He was the most gentle, loving man I've ever known. I never saw a better husband or a better father, and I miss him more than I can say every day."

Travis's eyes brightened, and he smiled. "You should have been a gypsy, Mom—reading minds like that."

"Pete is your father, Travis. Blood may be important, I'm sure it is, but it's not everything. Pete loved you and invested himself in you. He never missed a Little League game, did he?"

"No, he didn't. Remember the time he drove all the way from Maine to Colorado without a stop when our team played for the championship?"

"I remember. I remember everything about him. He was my life for all those years, and yours too." She turned toward him. "Whatever happens with Travis . . ." She saw his startled look. "Yes, that's his name too. Jonathan Travis Denver. I always called him

Travis. I named you after him, although Pete, of course, never knew. Two Travises. I'm going out to dinner with him tonight unless you think I shouldn't."

"Well, we've come this far, so I don't see why not."

"Travis, we can leave anytime." She hesitated, then said, "He doesn't know you exist. He doesn't have to know."

"I think he does, Mom," Travis said slowly. "Bring him by the hotel after your dinner. I want to meet him."

♦ ♦ ♦

Ben was unusually serious as he drove the Jaguar down the busy streets. He had never driven a Jaguar before and decided that he didn't like it. Basically it was a rich man's car, and Ben Savage's early life had ground economy into him. *Nothing you can do in this car you can't do in a '66 Studebaker Hawk,* he thought with disdain. He took great pride in the vintage automobile he'd restored and had just recently had shipped from Denver, where he formerly lived and worked, to New Orleans.

He finally pulled up in front of Raoul's and parked the car. He opened the door, and Nancy Livingston stepped out. She was wearing a calf-length, black linen dress with a V-shaped neckline and short sleeves. Over the dress she wore a long black duster jacket that was edged in dark purple, a pair of satin high-heeled shoes, and a small evening bag decorated with pearls. He waited until Denver came up to them and said, "I'll stay nearby, Mr. Denver."

"I don't have to be watched like a child," Denver said petulantly.

"Yes, sir, you do."

Nancy gave Ben Savage a quick look. He did not look particularly dangerous, but there was something in his mannerisms and in his steady, dark eyes that told her he was more than just a chauffeur. Dani had told her about some of J.T.'s trouble, so she assumed Ben had something to do with that. She smiled and said, "Come in and eat with us, Ben."

"No, thanks. I'll just float around, Mrs. Livingston."

The two entered the restaurant, and the host, a tall, thin man with a beard and a pair of sharp gray eyes, led them to a table and gave them menus. "We're glad to see you, Mr. Denver. You haven't been in lately."

"No I haven't, Tony. But I've missed you." After the host left, he asked his guest, "Have you eaten much Cajun food, Nancy?"

"No, not much. Why don't you order for me? I'd like to try it."

The meal was different from anything Nancy had ever had. It began with boudin, a spicy mixture of pork, onions, cooked rice, and herbs stuffed in sausage casings. Next came court bouillon, a rich soup made from fish fillets and dirty rice. This was followed by a dish of cooked rice sautéed with green peppers and onions. The main dish was a crawfish étoufée, a succulent, tangy tomato-based stew.

Nancy listened as Travis talked rather rapidly, mostly about the food. When the waiter brought a platter of crawfish, he said, "These are known as mud bugs." Nancy saw that they came whole, with head and legs still attached. She watched as J.T. expertly shelled the little crustaceans, grasping the head between the thumb and the forefinger of one hand, and the tail between the thumb and fore-finger of the other, then twisting and pulling until head and tail were separated. She blinked when he sucked the contents of the head, then squeezed the tails to crack the shells, popping out the meat and gently pulling the vein free, then putting the meat into his mouth.

"We call these things fish bait further south," Denver said.

As the meal progressed, Nancy became more and more aware of J.T.'s nervousness. "Do you remember Mom's Place?" she said.

Denver stopped abruptly and then laughed. "How could I for-get? How many times did we eat at that place, Nancy? It was the cheapest place, but it was good. I always remember what Hemingway, or so I'm told, said about a cafe called Mom's."

"What was that?"

"He said, 'Never eat at a cafe called Mom's, never play cards with a guy named Doc, and never have anything to do with a woman who has more troubles than you have.'"

Nancy laughed. "I doubt if he said that."

"So do I. But I do remember Mom's." He chewed thoughtfully on a piece of crawdad, then said, "You know, those were the best days of my life, Nancy. I didn't have anything and didn't think I would ever have much."

"Yes, you did. You always knew you'd gain success, Travis."

"Well, I have it, and what does it amount to? I guess you know what my life's been like."

"I'm worried about you. Miss Ross told me somebody tried to kill you."

"Probably not. It was probably just an accident." He wished he really believed that.

Nancy, however, would not be put off. "So many people depend on you, Travis."

"Depend on me! A room full of ex-wives?" His tone was bitter, and she quickly changed the subject. There was an obvious unhappiness about him, a deep dissatisfaction. They stayed for a while after the meal was over, steering away from anything serious. Then she said, "I think we'd better go now." All during the meal she'd been wondering if she should really ask him to go back to the hotel with her, but now she knew that it must be done.

Back at the hotel, standing outside the door of Nancy's suite, J.T. asked, "What are your plans, Nancy? You're going to stay for a while, aren't you?"

Savage had brought the two back and was lounging at the end of the hall, seemingly paying them no attention and just staring out the window.

"I'm not sure, but come in, Travis. I want you to meet someone."

J.T. Denver stiffened. "I bet I can guess."

"I would think not."

"A prospective husband's in there, right?"

Shaking her head, Nancy said quickly, "No. Nothing like that." She hesitated for a moment and then said, "I hope I'm doing the right thing." Going inside the room, she walked to the phone and dialed three numbers. She waited for a moment, then said, "Please come to my room."

She put the phone down. Turning to Denver, she said, "I may be doing the wrong thing, but . . ."

Puzzled by all this, J.T. said nothing. A knock on the door sounded, and he watched as she went and opened it. His eyes fastened on the young man who entered, and he heard Nancy's voice saying, "This is my son Travis."

Travis stepped forward and put his hand out. "I'm glad to meet you, sir."

J.T. Denver tried to speak, but he couldn't. He was staring at the young man, his eyes fixed on his face.

"He's always looked exactly like you, Travis."

There was no mistake. Denver's mind whirled, seeing that the young man was a mirror image of what he himself had looked like when he was a young man. *This is my son!* He turned to Nancy and said hoarsely, "You—you never told me about this."

"When we separated, Travis, I didn't know. Later when I found out I wanted to write you, and I almost did. Maybe I should have. But by the time I made up my mind you were married, and it was too late."

The older man turned and said, "Your name is Travis?"

"Yes, sir."

"How long have you known—about this?"

"I just found out," Travis said quietly. He said no more. He was studying the man whose picture he'd seen often in newspapers and on television. He could not verbalize it, but just seeing the man had somehow changed him. He wondered why he'd never noticed the resemblance, but it probably just didn't seem possible he could be related to someone so famous.

"There was one Travis, and then there were two. I should have told both of you," Nancy said quietly. "I was wrong, but I didn't think it would be fair, Travis."

"I need to sit down," J.T. said shakily. He slumped down in the chair and stared at his son. "What do you do, Travis?" he said, trying desperately to collect his thoughts.

"I took over my dad's trucking business."

"Do you like it?"

"Sure. I went with Dad a lot as the business was building up. Being a trucker isn't bad. The business has five trucks now."

"Are you going to stay with it long-term?"

"I don't know. I'd rather race cars."

"NASCAR?"

Travis suddenly laughed. "There's a rich man talking. You know what one of those cars costs?"

Denver listened as the young man spoke of his dream of someday racing with the greats. Finally the conversation ground to a halt, and Denver said quietly, "I abandoned your mother. I suppose you hate me for that, and I can't blame you."

"I don't hate you. I don't even know you. And I've had a good life. No man could have been better to me than my dad."

Nancy suddenly said, "You look tired, Travis." Both of them looked at her, and she laughed nervously. "I guess I'll have to call you J.T. to avoid confusion. You look tired. Go home and get some sleep."

J.T. Denver got to his feet. "I do feel pretty shaky, but I don't think I'll sleep much." He waited for a moment, then said, "Travis, I've asked your mother to forgive me, and she has. It's too soon to ask, but I'd like you to think about the same thing." He turned without another word and left the room. When the door closed, Travis was silent for a while. Then he turned to his mother and said, "He's not what I expected."

"He wanted to ask you to forgive him right now, but he was afraid to, I guess."

"I can do that, Mom—I really can."

Meanwhile, as J.T. stepped outside, he found Savage suddenly beside him. "Ready to go home, Mr. Denver?"

J.T. couldn't speak. He just nodded and followed the younger man down to the car. As the Jaguar moved through traffic, he asked, "Do you have a family, Savage?"

"No such luck." Ben saw that Denver was hurting, and he thought, *I guess having a billion dollars doesn't solve everything.*

Eleven

A *VERY* UNHAPPY FAMILY

Nancy crossed the room, picked up the phone, said "Hello," then listened for a moment. "All right," she said. "We'll be right down. Thank you." Putting the phone back in the cradle, she turned to Travis. "That was Ben Savage. He's come to take us out to the yacht."

Travis had been standing beside the large patio-type door, looking down on the traffic below. He had been quiet for most of the morning, and now he turned, an odd expression on his face. He studied his mother for a moment, then said, "All right. I guess we'd better go."

"Travis," Nancy said, coming over to stand beside him, "how do you feel about—" She hesitated, then laughed nervously. "I don't know what to call him. I always called him Travis, but everybody else calls him J.T. I don't want to call him your father because that's what Pete was."

"It doesn't matter much, does it?"

"I think somehow it does."

Quickly Travis searched his mother's face and saw the trouble that clouded her eyes. "We can leave here anytime we want to, Mom. We can go back, be what we were before, and just erase this from our minds."

"I don't think it works that way."

"What do you mean?"

"Well, some things come into your life and exist for a moment, then they're gone, and you never need to think of them again. But somehow I don't think meeting with J.T. Denver is going to come under that heading." Studying the face of her son, Nancy put her hand on his cheek. "You know, you're very much like him."

Startled, Travis demanded quickly, "How could that be?"

"I've always seen little parts of him in you. Things you do, ways you act that remind me of him."

"I don't know if that's a compliment or not."

Nancy shook her head and patted his cheek, then stood for a moment irresolutely. She had slept little, and now the problem of what to do about this man who had entered her life so abruptly after many years would not leave her mind. "What do you think about him, Travis?"

"I don't know anything about him. I know what I've read in the papers and the tabloids, but that probably isn't a true picture."

"I know. I don't think of him like that. I think J.T. Denver's two people. One was the young man I knew—full of energy, generous, really kind. But even then I saw the signs of selfish ambition in him. And that, I think, is what ruined him."

"It's ruined a lot of people, including Macbeth and his wife."

"Do you think we should leave?"

Travis paused and chewed on his lower lip. J.T. had always done the same. "I don't think so, Mom. I think maybe we're here for a reason. Remember the Scripture you drilled into my head? 'All things work together for good to them that love God.'"

"I've just about worn that one out." Nancy smiled briefly.

"How do you feel about the situation?"

"Oh, Travis, I don't know. I was very young when we met, and I loved him, and I think he loved me. But that all ended. At least it should have. I've tried to put it out of my mind . . . And I had such a good marriage with Pete."

The two stood there, not knowing how to bring the subject to a conclusion. Finally Travis said, "Let's go see him, Mom. I'm going to do the best I can to get to know him while we're here."

The two left the suite, went downstairs, and found Savage waiting for them. He was leaning against the Jaguar, his arms folded, but quickly opened the rear door for them. Going around the car, he got behind the wheel. "Hang on," he said cheerfully. "The worst drivers in the world inhabit New Orleans—and the stuffiest cops. They'll give you a ticket for spitting on the wrong side of the street."

As Savage threaded the traffic and made his way to the dock, his two passengers said little. From time to time Ben would glance in the rearview mirror, and he noted that both of them were sober, even troubled. *I can't blame them*, he thought. *They have a hard nut to crack here. That boy sure looks like his dad. I wonder what he's like on the inside?*

When they reached the dock, he led them up the gangplank and on to J.T. Denver's suite. Knocking on the door, he heard a voice, then opened the door. Stepping back, he nodded to the pair who went inside and then stepped inside himself. He saw Dani sitting across the room from J.T., who got up at once and came over to Nancy. Savage saw the light in his eyes as he greeted her, and he was sure Dani had observed it as well.

"I'm glad you could come," Denver said. "Did you have a restful night?"

"Fine," Nancy said. "We walked down to St. Charles Street, a most pleasant evening stroll."

"Better let me go with you next time," Ben said.

"Why?" Nancy asked in surprise.

"New Orleans isn't a good place to go walking after dark."

"That's right." J.T. nodded quickly, then turned to Dani and said, "But I'm not sure I need all this security around *me*. Nothing more has happened, Dani."

"That's not quite the case, but you're the boss," Dani said. "You're paying the bills."

J.T. moved his battered right arm and grimaced at the discomfort he felt. "I wish this thing was stronger."

"Better be glad you're able to walk. If that semi had hit you," Ben said, "all your problems would be gone."

J.T. laughed suddenly. "That's a funny way to put it."

"I think you'd better listen to Miss Ross," Nancy said. "If there's any danger, there's no point in taking chances."

"Are you making any progress?" Denver asked the detective.

"Not a whole lot," Dani admitted reluctantly. "But I am convinced something's wrong. There was another 'accident' at the shipyard last night."

"What sort of accident?" Denver demanded, his face alive with interest. "Was anybody hurt?"

"No. It was a mechanical matter. The support that holds one of the engines collapsed. No damage done really, except it'll take time to fix it."

J.T. said, "That'll give Mad Jack a better shot at winning this race."

"Who's this Byron? Is he a threat?" Travis asked.

"He and I are competing for a contract to build a new ferry. And he's a shark, a killer. I've bumped up against him before. Sometimes I've won, sometimes I've lost, sometimes we just beat each other half to death. But this is the biggest thing we've ever knocked heads on. I wish I was at my best."

The younger Travis studied the face that was so much like his own and said, "I'd like to know more about this. Maybe I can be of some help. I don't know how though. I don't know anything about ships."

Instantly J.T. straightened up. "I don't know anything about ships either. We don't have to, Travis. We have people who can build the ship. What we need to find is some way to get it built before Mad Jack gets his into the water. I believe I'll take you up on your offer."

"I have things to do," Ben said. "If you'll all stay on the yacht for about an hour, I'll be back then."

"All right, Ben," Dani said. As soon as Ben left the room, she nodded. "It's a good thing we're on this ship. It's easier to keep a watch on you here."

Impatiently J.T. Denver shook his head. "I suppose so," he said. He hesitated, then turned to look at Nancy and Travis. "I asked you to come here for a reason. I want you to meet some people."

Nancy blinked and then asked cautiously, "People? What kind of people?"

"Well, I want my family to meet you. Or actually, to put it bluntly, my *families*. It sounds awful when I say it, but I've asked all of my exes to come."

"Why would you do that?" Nancy asked, repelled by the idea.

"I want them to know you, and I want them to know Travis. You may never meet them again, and I don't want them to hear gossip about you. I want them to get it straight from me."

Travis shifted his feet, then grinned. "I don't imagine they'll be too pleased to see us, but lead on."

Denver flashed a quick grin at the young man, then said, "They're waiting down in the dining room. Come along."

The party, including Dani, made their way to the dining room. Dani kept looking around in every direction. It wouldn't be impossible for a good marksman with a scope and a high-powered rifle to take a shot at J.T. Denver from the shore. Without saying anything, she kept on the outside as they walked down the deck. When they came to the dining room, Dani stepped aside and let the party enter. But as she stepped inside and took a place along the wall as unobtrusively as possible, she saw the shock that leaped into almost every face. Vivian Sanderson was nervously puffing on a cigarette as usual. Dani saw her eyes fly open as the visitors entered the room, and she almost gasped audibly.

Loreen, her daughter, standing next to her mother alongside her own daughter Tara, showed a similar reaction. Dani saw that Shelly Bracken and her son Creighton had pulled themselves apart as if to keep their own space. They had their eyes locked on the face of Travis Livingston. Across the room Maris Nolan and her fiancé Trevor had turned to meet the party. The Englishman's eyes narrowed as he studied the young man, and Maris turned pale. The twins, Anne and Gayle, were playing a game of checkers. They looked up and smiled but said nothing.

J.T. then announced, "I have someone I'd like you all to meet. This is Nancy Livingston and her son Travis."

For a moment he hesitated, then he said, "I knew Nancy years ago before I met any of you, and I'll be seeing quite a bit of her, so I wanted to tell you face to face about the situation."

Tara was absolutely still, but her eyes were searching Travis Livingston's face. Finally she laughed sharply. "Well," she said loudly, "you gave her something to remember you by, didn't you?"

Travis flushed, and Nancy said nothing. Tara walked right up to Travis, studying his face feature by feature. "Here's the younger J.T. Denver. I'm glad to know you, Travis. You're as good-looking as your dad."

"Tara!" Loreen snapped. "Don't be ridiculous!"

Maris spoke up quickly, saying, "Yes, Tara, you're always talking when you should be listening."

Tara was wearing scarlet lipstick that emphasized her sensuous mouth. "I know a Denver when I see one. Call yourself Livingston if you want to, but you can't deny that face, can you?"

Travis Livingston was startled. He stared at the young woman and tried to think of a reply but felt it was not his place to do so.

Quickly J.T. called out the names of his ex-wives and children. He went over to stand beside the twins, and both of them at once got up and gave him a hug. "This is Anne and Gayle. They are seven years old and my pride and joy."

Nancy immediately went over and smiled down at the girls. "I'm glad to meet you, young ladies. Which one is Gayle, and which one is Anne?"

"I'm Gayle. I have a mole on my fanny."

Nancy laughed. "Well, if I want to know who's Anne, I'll have to do some inspecting."

"No," Gayle said. "I'm the smart one. Just ask me a question, and I can answer it. She can't."

"Who cares about your dumb old questions?" Anne frowned.

"That's enough, girls." J.T. turned away from them and stood beside Nancy. "I don't think I'll have to say anything else. I just wanted you to hear this from me and not from someone else."

"What does this mean, J.T.?" Loreen said, her face tense. She glared at Nancy Livingston. "Obviously you had an affair with this woman, or did you marry her?"

"We were never married, Mrs. Franz." Nancy turned to face the woman who was glaring at her and took a deep breath. "And the answer is yes, we had an affair, but I broke it off. I had a son later, but J.T. never knew about him. He didn't know, as a matter of fact, until Miss Ross found us."

"But why are you here?"

"I asked her to come," J.T. said. He glanced over at Travis and said, "Nancy married a good man, and he was a good father to Travis. I'm not sure if Travis will ever want to acknowledge me, but I'm acknowledging him."

"Acknowledging him *how*?" Creighton demanded, and a harsh light in his eyes flickered briefly.

"That will be up to him. I'll do anything I can for him. We haven't talked about such things yet." J.T. glanced at Nancy and saw that she was unhappy. "That's enough for now. Come along, Nancy, Travis."

As soon as they left followed closely by Dani, a babble of talk broke out. Everyone tried to talk over the others, and finally Maris said, "I think we all know what this means. J.T.'s always wanted a son, and now he's got one. A son of his own blood."

"That's right!" Loreen said bitterly. "Now we can kiss anything we hoped for good-bye forever!"

Tara glanced around the room with a cynical smile on her face. "It looks like the golden egg is going to go somewhere else. But—"

"Be quiet, Tara!" Loreen said. Shaking her head, she said, "I'll have to tell Bobby about this."

They continued to talk louder than usual, though they all knew there was really nothing to say. Finally Shelley began to cry. "I need a drink," she said.

"You'd better cut down on your drinking, Mother," Creighton said. "It looks like there's a new son and heir, and you know what that means for us."

◆ ◆ ◆

As Dani shadowed J.T., she caught a glimpse of Nancy's face. The woman was pale and troubled, understandably so. When they reached the gangplank, J.T. turned suddenly. "I'm sorry about all that, but I hate gossip. I like everything out in the open."

Nancy said quietly, "It's all right, J.T."

Travis said suddenly, "I'd like to see the ferry you're building, the one you and Mad Jack Byron are racing to finish. Would you show it to me?"

At once J.T. said, "Yes. Of course."

Dani inquired, "Would you go too, Mrs. Livingston?"

"No, I think not."

"If you'll wait here, I'll take you home after we return. Or you can wait, Mr. Denver, until Ben gets back before you go to the ferry."

"We'll be all right," J.T. said.

"I'm sorry, but I can't be in two places at the same time."

"Maybe she's right," Travis said. "We can wait. Are you sure you feel up to going there at all?"

"Yes. I need to spread my wings. Well, my *wing* I guess I should say."

The four of them went into J.T.'s suite, where he paced the floor nervously. Dani sat beside Travis and started a conversation about racing cars. The young man brightened up and soon was entertaining all of them with stories of his adventures on local tracks.

Ten minutes later Savage appeared, and Denver said, "This young fellow would like to see the ferry, and I'm going too."

"Fine," Ben said. He turned and asked, "Any instructions, boss?"

"No. I have some things to do myself."

They all left the ship, Nancy getting into Dani's car.

In J.T.'s car Travis said, "I've never driven a Jaguar. Do you mind if I try it?"

"Have at it. You're the race driver." Ben grinned.

They made their way to the dock with Ben telling Travis about the '66 Studebaker Hawk he had restored.

"I'd like to see it. That was a great car. I've been told it could beat anything on the road in its day."

"Anytime. Maybe you could help me tinker with the engine."

When they reached the dock, they went at once to Bobby Franz's office.

Franz nodded as they entered, speaking pleasantly to J.T. and to Ben. But when he saw the young man with them, his expression was identical to that which had been on the face of his wife and mother-in-law.

"I've already given this speech once, Bobby," J.T. said, "but here goes—this is Travis Livingston, and as you can see he's my son."

Bobby Franz looked stunned, but he quickly recovered. "I'm glad to know you, Mr. Denver—uh, Livingston."

"I've asked Travis to give us a hand on this blasted boat. It's about as big as Noah's Ark. How long did Noah work on that thing?"

Instantly Travis grinned. "I think several hundred years."

"Well, Mad Jack Byron would like it if we could equal Noah. Come along, Travis. I'll show you around."

Savage trailed along, his eyes constantly vigilant. When they reached the top of the huge boat, he looked over and shook his head. "This is a mighty big ship," he said. He noted the workers who were scurrying around like ants, and he heard Travis ask, "This is almost like a building. Don't those fellows ever worry about falling?"

"The union's got some pretty strict rules. Nobody's fallen yet, though there's been every other kind of accident."

Savage listened as J.T. explained what he knew about building ships, and he saw that Travis was deeply impressed by what he was hearing. He was distracted for a moment when Jamie suddenly walked by. She whispered just loud enough for only him to hear, "I have something. Come to my place tonight about ten o'clock." Savage didn't move, but he felt encouraged. *I knew Jamie would come up with something*, he thought. *She always does.*

Twelve

IF ONLY . . .

Nancy was sitting beside J.T. on the bow of *The Nancy*. The two had talked together quietly there for some time because Nancy enjoyed watching the gulls. She'd brought a loaf of bread out with her, and as usual greed quickly spread among the gull population. At first only a single creature swooped down when she tossed morsels into the air, but soon the area was full of fluttering birds, the bright sunlight reflecting off their white wings. Finally J.T. grinned at her. "Why don't you let them take it right out of your hand?"

"Will they really do that, Travis?"

"I think they'd take it out of your pocket." Standing up, he broke off a piece of bread. "Don't throw them any more for a minute." He held the piece of bread in his hand, and a bird swooped down but veered away when it drew within three feet. Another followed, coming still closer, and finally one of them swooped down and snatched the morsel right out of his hand.

Nancy laughed and stood up to join him, and soon the creatures were coming one after another.

"Don't let them bite your finger. Their teeth are pretty sharp."

"I never liked gulls much," Nancy said. "They remind me of greedy, noisy people—like people waiting in line to buy tickets for a concert that's sure to be sold out—yapping and pushing and shoving."

"I think the gulls have better manners than that." J.T. grinned. He watched her as she continued to feed the gulls, marveling how the years had failed to touch her as it did so many. As she reached high, holding bites of bread for the hungry gulls, he remembered something from the past. He and Nancy had been on a picnic beside a river, and after they'd eaten, the two of them had strolled along beside the water. They stopped to peer down into the river, and she pointed out the silvery minnows darting back and forth in the shallow water. "Look at them. They all know exactly what to do!" she had exclaimed.

J.T. remembered the scene clearly. As they watched the myriads of tiny minnows, he said, "What do you mean they know what to do?"

"Well, look at them. They don't just each go their own way. Somehow when they change direction every one of them knows exactly what to do."

"Birds do that in the sky sometimes too. Blackbirds especially."

"I wonder how they do that. It's like each of them has a built-in radio and they keep in touch so they can all dart away at the same time."

He remembered answering, "I'm glad people aren't like that. It's better to do your own thing instead of just going along with the crowd."

He remembered taking her in his arms and kissing her, and she leaned against him and whispered how much she loved him.

"Do you remember the time we went on that picnic down by the river over near Gainesville?" he asked now.

Turning quickly, holding a morsel of bread in her hand, Nancy smiled. "You still remember that?"

"I think I remember everything we ever did."

"I doubt that."

"Try me."

"Well, what did we talk about that day?"

"We talked about how minnows all go the same way without a leader, how they dart around by the hundreds, all of them turning exactly at the same time."

Nancy was struck by his memory. "That's right," she whispered. "I've thought about that often. That was a good day, wasn't it?"

"Yes, it was. We had a lot of good days. Remember the time we went to the John Denver concert? We didn't have the money, but I borrowed it and we went anyway."

"I remember." Nancy came over and sat down beside him. Reaching over, he took her hand, and the two sat silently for a long while. A flight of pelicans flew over, and then two jet-skiers went by, weaving and shouting at each other and sending up silvery drops of water in a cascade in their wake. They looked young, not over seventeen or eighteen, and had been turned golden by the sun.

"Do you wish you could go back and be like those two?" J.T. asked.

"We can't do that. And I wouldn't really want to."

J.T. turned and studied her. "You've had a good life, Nancy."

"Yes. I had a good husband, and Travis is a fine son. "

From far away they heard the throbbing of a tugboat, and they watched it move slowly across Mobile Bay. J.T. sighed. "I wish I'd lived my life as well as you have. I spend a lot of time wallowing in regrets."

"Don't, J. T.," she said quickly. "You don't have to do that."

"You don't know what a mess I've made of things. Then again, I guess you do." His lips twisted to the side, and he shook his head almost violently. "It's been in the papers and the magazines enough."

Sensing his discontent, Nancy wanted to help him find a way out. "Let's do something different today."

"Different? You want to find some railroad tracks and throw rocks?"

"No," she laughed. "Don't be silly!"

"How about we go down to the barber college and watch a couple of haircuts?" He grinned as he made several more ridiculous suggestions. Finally he grew serious. "There's one thing I'd like to do, if you would go with me."

"What's that?"

"I'd like to go pick up the twins and take them somewhere. I've tried to do something with them every week if I can. If you and Travis would go with me this time, I'd appreciate it."

"Why, of course we will! When do you want to go?"

"Whenever you're ready."

◆ ◆ ◆

Anne and Gayle came to the door as Ben Savage brought the Suburban to a stop in front of the house. As he stepped out of the vehicle, he glanced up and down the street just as he always did. He didn't expect any trouble, but the habit was deeply ingrained. As a UPS truck turned the corner, he moved over toward J.T. and stood there, his attention firmly fixed on the driver. He waited until the truck passed, then turned to see J.T. kneeling down and laughing with the girls, their voices sounding like bells in the morning air. Ben glanced over at Travis and winked at him, and Travis smiled back. The two of them were obviously thinking the same thing— this was a side of J.T. Denver that the media never cared to report. Writing about a messy divorce or a bloody fight against his competitors sold more papers or attracted more viewers than a man enjoying the company of his two daughters.

"Well, what do you want to do today?" J.T. asked. "Mr. Savage will take us anywhere you want to go. Nancy and Travis are coming too."

"Let's go to Alligator Annie's," Anne said. She was the loudest of the two and the most outgoing. Gayle was quieter and more thoughtful. That was one of the few ways one could tell the difference between the two. Anne was always jumping and running and crying at the top of her lungs, while Gayle was generally quiet and smiling to herself as if she had a secret joke.

"We've already been to Alligator Annie's five times. What do you say we hit the zoo?"

"We've been there too," Gayle said.

"I know, but there's so much to do and see there."

"All right, Daddy," Gayle said, and Anne immediately began asking if she could ride the elephant.

"Sure, you can. Now go get ready."

"We are ready."

"I need to talk with your mother. You go get in the car." Turning, he said, "Can you watch these two hooligans, Nancy, until I get back?"

"Of course. Come along, girls."

"I want to sit with Daddy," Anne demanded loudly.

"All right. You can sit with Daddy going, and Gayle can sit with him coming back."

Maris looked up as J.T. entered the house. "Where are you taking them today?" she asked.

"To the zoo to begin with."

Trevor Fountaine was sitting there enjoying a cup of tea. As he stood up he said, "Have you given any more thought to the film, J.T.?"

"Yes, I thought about it, but I don't know enough about it to make a decision yet."

Trevor quickly responded, "I realize that, but it's not difficult to obtain any information you need. Have you talked to anyone about it?"

"Not really. I haven't had the time." He studied Fountaine carefully, noting again the man's close resemblance to a young Richard Burton. There was an aura about Fountaine, just as there is about any good actor or actress. In a way he wanted to help the man, and yet . . . "The trouble is," he said slowly, "I've read about some big bombs that almost destroyed whole studios. *Cleopatra* and *Heaven's Gate*, just to name two examples from the past, cost millions—and lost millions. I'm sure you're even more aware of such busts than I am, including some very recent ones."

"But those are exceptions to the rule," Fountaine said smoothly. An urgency came into his voice as he said, "You need to make up your mind. I have commitments to other projects too, but I want to put my whole heart into this one." He looked at Maris. "We both do, don't we?"

"J.T., please think about it," she added.

For a moment J.T. was almost ready to commit himself, but something stopped him. He couldn't define it—it was an instinct that came to him often in the business world. It didn't come from study or learning or any sort of logical and reasonable source. It was deeper than that, and he'd learned to trust it more than balance sheets or the advice of experts. "Give me a little more time," he said. Anxious to be on his way, he added, "I don't know when we'll be back. We'll probably take the girls out to eat, perhaps even let them stay with us overnight if that's all right with you."

"We? Who's *we*?" Maris said.

"I have Nancy and Travis with me."

An expression of displeasure flickered in Maris's face, but being an actress she quickly concealed it. "I see. Just so you get them back home tomorrow.

"I'll have them here."

As soon as the door closed, Maris went over and put her arms around her fiancé. "Trevor," she said, "I'll persuade him to give us the money."

"You'd better! It looks like he's our only hope, Maris. If he doesn't come through, everything goes down the drain."

The two stood there for a moment, and then Trevor said softly, "With all his money he can't spare a little bit for one project? Yeah, right."

"He will. Don't worry. I might even know a way to hurry him up."

Trevor stared at her. He knew her very well and finally said, "What are you thinking?"

"He's crazy about the girls. He loves them more than he ever cared for me. I was thinking . . . I could tell him he can't see them unless he backs the movie. Of course I wouldn't put it exactly like that."

"How would you get him to buy that?"

"You know his reputation. Everybody does. If I were to take this into court and get a woman judge, a grandmother type, I'm sure I could convince her he's not a fit parent, and J.T. knows it. I threatened that very tactic one other time, and he almost panicked."

"It's worth a try. Go ahead with your plans."

"Oh, I will, believe me I will."

◆ ◆ ◆

Most people found the zoo a delightful place, but Nancy didn't particularly like it there. She loved animals, but she hated to see them caged up. She mentioned that to J.T. while the girls were taking a ride on the elephant. She smiled and waved at them as Anne shouted, "Look at me! Look at me!"

"I hate to see animals so confined, don't you, J.T.?"

"Well, they say they're better off here—better protected. That sounds right to me." He turned to glance at her, admiring the outfit she was wearing. She had on khaki-colored linen pants and a white T-shirt, with a khaki and white scarf tied around her neck. She carried a straw bag that was now filled with the sweaters the girls had discarded. On her head was a wide-brimmed straw hat. "You look beautiful today, Nancy."

"Thanks. You look beautiful too." Her eyes sparkled as she laughed at his expression. "Well, you are a beautiful man."

"I don't know whether to take that as a compliment or not."

The two laughed at their silly repartee. From time to time J.T. glanced around looking for Ben. He didn't see him, but he knew he was close. "That fellow's like a chameleon," he murmured.

"You need him for a while longer though, until this thing is settled," Nancy said firmly. "Come on, that's the end of the elephant ride."

The afternoon passed quickly, and after a while J.T. groaned, "I'd hoped to tire the girls out. But it's the other way around."

Nancy suggested, "Let's go home."

"Home? Yours or mine?"

"Yours. We'll take the girls out to the boat. I bought them a Monopoly Junior game, and I'm sure they'd love to play it."

◆ ◆ ◆

The Monopoly Junior game did indeed turn out to be a lifesaver. Nancy set it up on a card table when her son went with Ben to fish off the bow of *The Nancy*. The girls, Nancy, and J.T. ate Oreos and drank Cokes during the game. The twins manifested the traits Nancy had observed in them earlier—Anne loud and exuberant, shouting when she won and sulking when she lost; Gayle steady and smiling, win or lose. Gayle was more dependent on her father, Nancy saw, than her sister, going to stand beside him more than once. She needed the security of his arm around her, and she would look up at him with admiration in her eyes.

Finally they ate the supper brought in by the steward, and Nancy said firmly, "All right, it's time for you girls to go to bed."

"It's too early!" Anne protested.

"Not really, dear."

"Will you come in and say good night to us, Daddy?" Gayle asked.

"Sure, I will."

"Come along, girls. It's time for a good shower, then bed. "

J.T. took a stroll out on the deck. When Travis saw him coming, he grinned and teased, "Did you get the gold dust twins to bed?"

"Nancy's showering them and putting their jammies on. Are you catching anything?"

"Nope," Travis said. "Don't want to really."

"I know what you mean. Sometimes I just like to sit here and watch the sun go down. All quiet on the western front, Ben?"

"Everything's as fine as frog hair," Savage said. "It's almost a shame to take your money."

"Maybe I don't need you anymore."

"Talk to the boss."

"Maybe I will—tomorrow."

The three men talked until Nancy called saying, "Travis, the girls are waiting for you."

"Okay. I'll be right there." He quickly accompanied Nancy to the stateroom where the two girls were already in bed.

"Tell us a story," Gayle said quickly.

"All right, I will." He sat down and smiled. "Do you want me to tell you the story of the monster that caught the young girl and chopped her head off?"

"No!" Gayle said quickly. "Don't tell one like that. Tell us a *good* story."

"I want to hear about the girl with her head chopped off," Anne protested.

"I think your father can tell a more pleasant story than that," Nancy encouraged. She came over to stand beside J.T. and rested her hand lightly on his shoulder. He smiled up at her.

"Why don't you tell the story? They've heard all of mine."

"I'd like to hear you," she responded.

"All right, here goes." J.T. began a rambling story that he made up as he went along. He had always done this for his children, and Nancy saw that the girls loved it. It was a wild, fanciful story with beautiful young girls and ships and forests and good fairies and all sorts of things that would give young girls pleasant dreams. He often wished that the rest of his life had been like this part of it, that his story times with the twins hadn't been the exception rather than the rule.

Finally J.T. said, "And that's the end of the story."

"Tell us another one," Anne demanded.

"Nothing doing," Nancy said. "We have a busy day tomorrow." She turned to J.T. and suggested, "Why don't you say a prayer for the girls, Travis."

Travis blinked with surprise, then said awkwardly, "Well, I haven't quite got the handle on that. Why don't you show us how?"

"All right." Nancy knelt down and took both girls by the hand. "You take their other hand, Travis," she said. When he had done so, she said, "Lord God, we thank You for this day we've enjoyed, and we thank You for the great time we've had together. Be with Anne and with Gayle, and help them grow up to be servants of Yours. Be with Travis in his work, and give him complete healing for all his injuries." She went on to pray for others as well, including the twins' mother. Finally she said, "We ask this in the name of Jesus."

As Nancy stood up, Gayle held on to her hand for a moment. "That was nice," she whispered, then her eyes went to her father. "Will you do that when Nancy's not here, Daddy?"

"Well, I'll try, but I hope she'll be here."

As the two went outside, he said, "This has been a good day. Let's go sit on the stern and watch the moon's reflection on the water."

"All right."

As the two made their way, Nancy looked around. "I haven't see Ben for a while."

"Good. I'm tired of having a chaperone. I feel like a sixteen-year-old boy going on his first date, with the girl's daddy aiming his shotgun at me to make sure I behave myself with his daughter."

Nancy laughed.

The two stood there and watched the moon as it rose. Nancy whispered, "I can't get over how it looks so much larger sometimes than at other times."

"That's because of the atmosphere."

"Don't you have any romance in you? I don't want to hear a scientific explanation. Let's just look at the moon and appreciate it."

They could hear sounds of traffic, but it seemed far away. The serenity of the moment was healing. J.T. said, "I wish it could always be like this."

"So do I," Nancy said.

He pulled her to him and kissed her. She put her arms around him and held onto him for a moment. He said, "I love the way you love those girls."

"I'm glad to hear you say that," Nancy said.

♦ ♦ ♦

Savage stopped the Jaguar, turned the engine off, and got out. He paused for a moment, looking at the vehicle, then shook his head. "A fellow could get spoiled driving one of these things," he murmured aloud, then turned and walked into the apartment building. As always, he automatically checked his surroundings for possible trouble. When he realized what he was doing, he laughed softly, thinking, *They're after J.T., not me.* He knocked at Jamie's door, and she opened it a few seconds later. "Hey, Jamie."

"Ben! Come on in."

Savage entered and said, "Is it too late for you?"

"Nope. I'm not sleeping much these days. I'm glad you came by. Have you eaten?"

"As a matter of fact, I am hungry. I'll go get us some Chinese food."

"No need. I'll fix something. Come into the kitchen."

"Sounds good to me."

The two went into the kitchen, and Ben leaned back with two chair legs braced against the wall. He crossed his arms and studied Jamie as she pulled out a frying pan. She was, he'd often thought, one of the most vibrant people he'd ever known. She was still a beautiful, desirable woman, but she'd lost her enthusiasm somewhere along the way, and he was saddened at the change.

"Will an omelette be all right?"

"Sure. I love 'em."

"What do you want in it?"

"Everything you've got."

Jamie laughed weakly and turned to face him. "You haven't changed. You've always had a cast-iron stomach. I believe you could eat a dead armadillo."

"Better than eatin' a live one."

Shaking her head, Jamie began to prepare the meal. As she did, the two talked about the days they'd worked together. When the omelettes were ready, Jamie asked, "Do you still like Tabasco sauce on it?"

"Oh yeah."

"I'd believe you'd put Tabasco sauce on toast."

"It's not bad that way." Ben grinned at her.

Ben ate hungrily, but he noticed that Jamie only picked at her food.

"What's the matter? Not hungry?"

"What? Oh, I guess not."

"Is the job bothering you?"

"No, it's not that."

The detective chewed thoughtfully for a moment, then took a swallow of the strong, black coffee. "You still missing that husband of yours?"

"Ex-husband."

Ben shook his head. "You know, Jamie, it hit me hard when you two broke up. You seemed so right for each other. What went wrong?"

"*I* went wrong," Jamie said.

"I can't believe that."

"That's the way it was. I wanted to rise through the ranks in the department, and I put in as many extra hours as I possibly could trying to make a name for myself."

"And you did it too. That's what Kimbrough said." Kimbrough was the police chief who had trained both of them. "And when Kimbrough endorses a woman, you can bet she's really something. You know what a chauvinist he is."

Jamie toyed with her coffee cup and shook her head. "I suppose so. I got what I wanted, but I lost a husband in the process."

Ben said, "I would have thought you and Dave could have weathered just about anything."

Jamie just looked down at her hands. Ben had noticed long ago that whenever she was having a tough time with something, she'd lock her hands and stare at them, saying nothing. She finally looked up and said, "Dave wanted a family, and I wouldn't give it to him."

Savage had no idea what to say to that but finally said quietly, "It's not too late, Jamie."

Jamie looked at him, tears suddenly filling her eyes. "Yes, it is." She wiped the tears away, then said, "Enough of my woes. I can only stand to talk about it so long. What's new on the case?"

Ben felt depressed by what he'd heard. He'd seen so few successful marriages, and he'd bet on this one. Now it had gone to pieces, and he couldn't help feeling somewhat angry, though he didn't know whom to direct his anger at. Jamie? Dave? Marriage's being out of fashion and living together being in?

When he left a short while later, he turned to Jamie who had accompanied him to the door. He leaned forward and kissed her on the cheek saying, "You know what they say. It ain't over 'til the fat lady sings."

"Thanks, Ben." Jamie tried to smile. "I'll remember that."

Thirteen

"THEY CAN ONLY KILL YOU ONCE"

"I don't know why you like to eat at this place," Dani complained. "It's awful!"

"It's only the decor that's awful. The food is great."

Ben Savage had brought Dani to his favorite restaurant in the Quarter. It was called Della's Delight, and it was in a neighborhood that was once high-rent and silk stockings. The houses were enormous and had once been beautiful and ornate. Now, however, they were deteriorating like derelicts parked in a ship's graveyard.

Della's Delight, on the first floor of one of those ancient mansions, was run by a tall, black woman with a regal face. She came over and greeted the two with a smile and brought tea for Dani and coffee for Savage. "What'll you have today?"

The menus were encased in clear plastic, and the checkered tablecloths were red and white. "The pig lips look good, boss," Savage said with a grin.

Della nodded. "Neck bones and gravy is our special today."

"Maybe I'll have the chitlins," Ben said. "On second thought, I think I'll have some pigs' feet, yams, and dirty rice."

Dani suppressed her shudder at the thought of eating rice mixed with an animal's internal organs and picked what she con-

sidered the most civilized item on the menu. "I'll have some boiled
river shrimp and a salad."

"Be right up. You folks be comfortable now."

"A real fine lady, Della is." Savage nodded.

"How'd you meet her?"

"Her son was gettin' involved with some bad guys over in the
Quarter. I had a talk with them and persuaded them to leave the boy
alone. I take him down to the Y every once in a while, about once
a week, and give him boxing lessons. He's getting good too. Nearly
tore my head off last Tuesday."

When the meal came, it was delicious. Halfway through the
meal Dani said, "What do you make of the Denver case?"

"It's like a real bad soap opera."

"It is, isn't it?" Dani agreed. She peeled the shrimp and took a
tiny bite of a fragment of a lettuce leaf from her salad. "Have you
noticed how close J.T. and Travis are getting?"

"Yeah. It's hard to miss. The boy had a good father from what I
hear, but J.T.'s always longed for a son. It's almost pathetic how
eager he is to get close to the boy."

Taking a sip of the sweet tea, Dani suddenly said, "You probably haven't noticed Nancy's reaction to all this."

"Sure, I have. She's head over heels in love with the guy."

Dani suddenly laughed. "Why do you say that? What makes
you an expert on love?"

"Oh, I read *True Love Magazine* every month. Tells you all about
stuff like that. And I bought a book written for women—*How to
Make Your Man Happy*—I think that's the name of it. I'll give you
my copy. I have all the good parts underlined—the parts that would
help you out, boss."

"Keep your dumb old book!" Dani snapped, then softened. She
could never stay irritated with Savage for very long. "The situation's really sad, Ben."

"What's sad about it?"

"Why, it's plain as you can see, at least to a woman. Nancy was
in love with J.T. Denver once, and she still is."

"Love is eternal. Is that what you're saying?"

"Well, I don't know if I'd put it like that."

"Sounds to me like that's what you're saying. She was in love with him once; therefore she's still in love with him. What about the marriage she had with her husband Pete?"

"He must have been a fine man, and I'm sure Nancy was a wonderful wife. But I think she's never gotten away from those echoes of her affair with J.T. Denver when they were young."

"You're just a romantic, boss. You need to be a hardheaded realist like me."

"I'm not sure you're that much of one. You still haven't gotten over that aerialist, Florrie, you were in love with when you were with the circus."

Instantly Savage's face turned stony, and he took a bite of pigs' feet and said nothing.

"I'm sorry, Ben, I shouldn't have said that. It's obvious that you still think about her a lot."

"Sure, I do. So what? Don't you think about that guy you were in love with? The one who was killed in the car wreck?"

Now it was Dani's turn to be silent. She sat there so long that Ben finally said, "Look, let's just leave those matters alone."

"Getting back to Nancy, I can't help noticing the way J.T. looks at her."

"Yeah. I've noticed that too. After three wives and three horrible marriages, I guess he's thinking about the good old days when things were simple."

The two went on with their meal, but a gloominess had come over Ben. Finally he said, "I don't think we're getting anywhere with this case. Maybe it really was an accident."

"Could be," Dani agreed wearily. "We've tried everything and have found nothing."

"What about Allison St. John?"

"She won't talk. I can't tell whether she's afraid or just doesn't know anything. In any case, we're spending a lot of Denver's money and not coming up with much."

"But we can't be sure. We may have scared off whoever tried to do him in."

The two finished their meal. When they got to the car, Ben said, "I'll take you home now."

"Where are you going after that?"

"Jamie slipped a word to me today. She says she's learned something, so I'm going to her place."

A little too quickly Dani said, "I'll go with you."

Savage suddenly grinned. "Jealous, are we?"

Dani was used to Savage's mild teasing, and on the way they talked mostly about the case. When they got to the apartment house on Rose Street, a rather nice section of town, they both got out. There were four apartments on the first floor, and Jamie's was number 2. Ben rang the bell. When no one answered, he shifted his feet restlessly. He rang the bell twice more, and when still no answer came, Dani suggested, "Maybe she's gone out."

"Not Jamie. She said 10, and she's always precise when it comes to time."

Savage tried the door. It was locked. Pulling a small leather case from his hip pocket, he opened it and removed a pick.

"Breaking and entering?" Dani asked only half seriously.

"Yep," Savage said calmly, then opened the door as easily with a pick as most people could with a key. When the door swung open and he stepped inside, Dani followed him. He turned on the lights and quickly went through the living room. Coming out of the bedroom, he said, "She's not here." He stood there for a moment, and Dani waited silently. "We'd better go to the ferry," he said.

As Ben led the way back to the car, Dani said nothing. She saw an intent look on Savage's face that she'd seen before, and she noted that his knuckles were white as he held onto the steering wheel.

When they pulled up to the dock, Dani got out and followed Savage up to the gate, where they found Juan Martinez who seemed surprised to see them. "Hello, Miss Ross, Ben. What's up?"

"Have you seen Jamie Cordova?"

"Sure. I saw her about six o'clock. She was coming out of Mr. Franz's office."

"I mean, have you seen her later tonight?"

"No." Martinez stared at them. "Something wrong, Ben?"

"I think there might be. I want to take a look around the ship."

"I have some flashlights. I'll help you."

The three quickly started a search, and Dani was again impressed at how enormous the vessel was. She covered the second deck, while Ben went down into the engine room and Martinez searched the first deck, which was essentially the lounge. They met a few minutes later on the first deck.

"Didn't see anything, Ben. What makes you think she's here?" Juan asked.

"She was supposed to meet me, and she didn't show up."

Dani walked to the rail and glanced down. Suddenly she stiffened. "Ben!" she said urgently. "Come here!"

When Ben came to her side, she pointed down. "What do you see?"

Savage took one look, then whirled and broke into a run. Dani and Martinez followed him. When they emerged from the ship, they came upon the still form half hidden in the shadows. Dani leaned over Ben's shoulders and saw that the young woman's face was pale, and blood was running from her ear and nose.

"I'll call 911," Martinez said quickly.

Dani knelt down beside Ben. She put her finger on the woman's throat and said, "She's still alive, Ben."

Savage glanced up and said, "I don't think this was an accident."

Martinez returned and said, "The ambulance is on the way." He glanced up and chewed his lip. "It looks like she might have fallen from up there."

"Jamie doesn't fall. She's a free climber. She climbs mountains steeper than you'd believe, with no gear—just her bare hands and tennis shoes."

Dani had seen Ben Savage in all kinds of tense situations, but she noticed that his hands were shaking as he caressed the woman's hair. She heard him whisper, "Hang on, Jamie. Hang on."

◆ ◆ ◆

The ambulance came no more than five minutes later, and Martinez led the medics to the spot. Carefully they put the woman onto a stretcher, strapped her down, and said, "We'll take her to the emergency room at Baptist."

"I'll ride with you," Savage said.

"We don't allow it."

"I said I'll ride with you." Something in Savage's expression changed the EMT's attitude.

"Well, I guess just this once."

Dani drove to the Baptist Hospital and after parking the car went at once to the ER.

She found Ben sitting in the waiting room.

"How is she?" Dani asked.

"I don't know. They're checking her now."

As the two sat there, the situation was unbearable, as such experiences always are. The hands on the clock moved slowly, and neither Dani nor Ben said a word. After a while Dani went to get them some coffee. They both drank silently. Finally an attendant in surgical greens came out and said, "Cordova?"

Ben stood urgently. "How is she?"

"I'm Dr. Simms. I'm afraid she has serious internal injuries . . ."

"Can I see her?"

"She's in intensive care. Follow me."

Simms was a young man, no more than twenty-five from his appearance. He was tall and lanky and had a Texas drawl. When he took them inside, Dani stood off to one side. Jamie Cordova was lying motionless with tubes running into her nose and arms. She was hooked up to the usual battery of monitors. The lanky doctor said, "We don't know exactly how bad her injuries are, but the worst is probably her concussion. What happened to her? Did she fall?"

"Nobody knows—yet," Ben Savage said. "Doc, is she going to be all right?"

"I don't know, Mr.—"

"Savage. This is Miss Ross."

"Are you family?"

"No. She works for Miss Ross, and I'm an old friend of hers."

"Well, I wish I could be more optimistic, but she's hurt very badly. You say you don't know how it happened?"

"She may have fallen."

"That would answer some of the questions we had about the internal injuries. But she struck her head, and that's what worries me the most. When she wakes up, we'll hopefully find out more."

"Can I stay with her around the clock?"

"No. Only family can come in at all, and only for ten minutes or so every four hours."

"I'll be here."

Ben reached over and touched the woman's shoulder lightly while the doctor and Dani watched. Then he turned and shook his head as he left the room.

As soon as they were in the waiting room, Ben said, "You'll have to hire some more help. I'm going to have to be here a lot."

"I can stay with her some too, Ben."

"I'd better do it," Savage said briefly, and by the tone of his voice there was no arguing the point. "I think this was deliberate," he went on. "I want you to get a friend of mine to work on the case."

"What's his name?"

"Lonnie Beaudreaux. They call him Beau. Hire him, and tell him to stick with Denver like a tick on a dog."

"Who is he, Ben?"

"A friend. He was a Navy Seal—and other things not quite so admirable."

"Where will I find him?"

"There's a poolroom on St. Charles Street in the 700 block called Charlie's Place. They'll tell you where he is."

"I'll go right now."

As Dani drove to St. Charles Street, she couldn't get Ben's look when he saw Jamie out of her mind. She'd always been curious about the relationship between the two, although Ben insisted there was nothing personal in it. Still, she couldn't forget the expression in his eyes as he looked down at the fallen woman.

Charlie's Place was easy enough to find. Dani parked the car, locked it, and got out. She went into the smoky interior and at once was approached by several young men. Two of them were black, one of them a huge man wearing a vest that couldn't cover all his tattoos. "Hello, darlin'," he said. "How about you and me havin' a good time?"

Dani felt surrounded but not afraid. "I'm looking for Lonnie Beaudreaux."

"Hey, Beau," the big man grinned. "It looks like you're steppin' up some."

Dani watched as a rather slender man came from the back table. He was no more, she guessed, than thirty years old with a dark olive complexion and liquid black eyes almost hidden by heavy lids. "I'm Beau," he said simply.

"Could I talk with you—outside?"

"Why not?"

The two left amidst whistles and advice from the pool players.

As soon as they were outside, Dani said, "Ben Savage sent me." Quickly she explained the situation and said, "Ben said you might be willing to help."

"I owe Savage one. I'll be working for you?"

"Yes."

"And somebody's tried to clip J.T. Denver?"

"We think so."

"Why would anybody want to toast him? But then I guess most rich guys have enemies."

Dani said quickly, "I want to be completely honest with you, Beau—this job could be dangerous. One of our agents there had some sort of—accident."

Beau shrugged his shoulders. "Living is dangerous, Miss Ross. But," he said, smiling lazily, "they can only kill you once."

Fourteen

RIPPLES FROM THE PAST

Dani stood in the back of the room watching Ben as he sat beside the still form of Jamie Cordova. It had been four days now since she had been brought into the intensive care ward, and Dani could see no change at all in her condition. She'd been present the previous day when Dr. Simms talked with Ben, and the physician had not been optimistic.

"I would've thought she might have come out of it by now."

"What do you mean, doc?" Ben had asked.

"Mr. Savage, we doctors can't really do much in cases like this. We like to pretend we can, but there are so many things we don't know. The human body is a complex piece of machinery. Sometimes just one microscopic part of it keeps the rest of the body from functioning. I can't tell you when Miss Cordova will recover. She might never come out of it. That's the worst-case scenario. Or she might wake up this morning and be as bright as ever. At this point we've done all we can medically."

Dani studied Ben's face and saw there were hollows in his cheeks that hadn't been there before. He never had a surplus ounce of fat, working it off constantly in the weight room and by doing acrobatics. But now the stress was telling on him, and she noted the tiny marks of strain at the corners of his eyes and how thin and pale his lips were.

The humming of the monitors never varied, and Dani could hear various hospital sounds filtering vaguely through the walls.

Nurses in white uniforms moved busily back and forth through the unit. Dani thought, *I could never be a nurse or a doctor. I could never get used to being a witness to suffering like this every day.*

One of the nurses came in and said, "Technically your time's up, but you can stay a little longer if you'd like, Mr. Savage."

"Thanks. I appreciate that."

As soon as the nurse turned and left, Dani stepped forward and put her hand on Ben's arm. "I know she's going to be all right." When Savage made no remark, she said, "Why don't you go home and get some sleep, Ben."

"Maybe later."

Dani had tried this before. As far as she knew, Ben stayed at the hospital twenty-four hours a day. Sometimes he went out for a walk on the grounds while waiting for the next visit. She had forced him to go eat in the cafeteria several times, but he merely picked at his food. Now she said quietly, "I'll stop in later."

"All right, boss." Savage turned to look at her. "Thanks for coming by."

"The Lord's a great healer, Ben. You have to believe that." She saw something change in his eyes. He was not a believer, though there were times she was certain he was becoming a bit more open. She smiled encouragingly and said, "Jesus is the Great Physician. He can heal us in body, spirit, and soul. I know He can heal your friend."

Turning quickly, she left the hospital. All the way to the dock she thought about Ben's still figure. She was amazed that anyone could be so patient and long-suffering. But if anyone could, it would be Ben Savage. She knew he had deep feelings, although he refused to let them show. There had been times in the past when he'd drawn the curtain back, and she had seen that beneath the sometimes cynical exterior Ben Savage was as tenderhearted as anyone.

Reaching the ferry, she passed by Juan Martinez, who nodded and said, "How's the lady doing, Miss Ross?"

"Still hasn't recovered consciousness."

"I've been over everything, and I can't figure it out. She had to fall from up there, but from what Ben says, she wasn't a woman given to such things. But we all slip, I guess, from time to time."

"What would she be doing up there at that time of the night, Juan?"

"I don't know. Nobody does. She was supposed to have left two or three hours earlier."

"Have you seen Mr. Franz?"

"Yeah. He's in his office. His wife is there with him. They're both worried about this job."

Dani turned and made her way to the office, where she found Bobby Franz and his wife Loreen sitting at the desk together, apparently going over the books.

As soon as she entered, Bobby stood up. "Hello, Miss Ross."

"Hello, Mr. Franz."

"You can just call me Bobby. Everybody does. How's Miss Cordova?"

"Still not conscious."

"We'll probably get a lawsuit out of this," Loreen said. She was wearing a light-gray suit, and her hair was done up in a new style. She looked thin and lit a cigarette nervously.

"I wish you wouldn't do that, hon. It's a little late in life to take up smoking."

"What difference does it make?" Loreen snapped.

Franz blinked at her sharp words, but Dani had already observed that the two were not exactly soul mates. Franz was a nervous young man, always soft-spoken and eager to please. Loreen was harder and much more demanding. She puffed defiantly on the cigarette, then turned abruptly to ask, "What have you found out about all this anyway, Miss Ross?"

"Not a great deal, I'm afraid."

"Nothing on that truck that tried to run Dad down either?"

"Nobody saw the accident, so it's hard to determine exactly what happened." Dani still had not given up hope that Allison St. John remembered more than she had admitted, but she knew better than to admit this to a client.

A peculiar light flashed in Loreen Franz's eyes. "What do you know about Nancy Livingston and this son of hers?"

"There's not a great deal to know, I don't think," Dani said evasively.

"They lived up in Colorado," Bobby said. "What did her husband do?"

"He ran a small trucking business."

"They didn't have a lot of money then?" Loreen asked sharply.

"Not really. It was a very small business."

Loreen stared at Dani almost accusingly. "I always thought Dad had good sense, but this dredging up an old lover from twenty-five years ago or whatever—well, there's something not right about it. She's out to get his money."

"I don't think so," Dani said confidently. "She could've done that years ago."

"What about this boy?" Loreen demanded. "He and Dad have been thicker than thieves. He doesn't have any ideas of adopting him, does he?"

"I couldn't say, Mrs. Franz."

"It would be natural enough, I suppose," Bobby said quickly. "J.T.'s always wanted a son, and the young man seems nice enough. He's been in several times with J.T., and he's pretty sharp. He could learn the business quickly if he set his mind to it."

"That's just what we need!" Loreen snapped. "Another handout for Dad to waste money on."

Although she had her own opinions, Dani knew better than to express them right then. It was family business. She turned to Bobby and said, "How's the schedule going?"

"Terrible," Bobby groaned. "One little slowdown after another."

"Will you finish on time, do you think?"

"Maybe. I've talked to J.T. about putting on a second shift, and he agreed. We have to get that contract."

Dani said, "Perhaps we should increase security."

"That wouldn't be a bad idea. I'll tell Juan to hire a couple more people."

"No. Let me find the men."

Loreen suddenly narrowed her eyes. "You don't trust Juan?"

"I don't really trust anybody in a situation like this, Mrs. Franz. And I know some very good people who could keep their eyes on things around here."

"Well, get them here quick. We'll need 'em," Franz said. "I hate to let J.T. down. And I'm afraid I always have."

Loreen turned to her husband. "Don't talk foolishly, Bobby! You've always done a good job for Dad."

"Not good enough, I'm afraid."

"I'm sure it'll come out all right, Mr. Franz." Dani turned and left the room, thinking of how mismatched the couple were. But she had seen mismatched couples before who made it to their golden anniversary.

◆ ◆ ◆

Dani spent the rest of the day going through the finances of the ex-wives of J.T. Denver. It was not difficult for a trained investigator and a CPA, and she did the work herself. There was something, she decided, terribly wrong with the situation. To her, marriage was a sacred thing, and the abyss that J.T. Denver had plunged into—marrying women and getting rid of them, spawning children that he could not or would not father—was a terrible tragedy.

Finally she decided to go talk to J.T. Denver directly about the situation. Arriving at the dock, she greeted Beau, who nodded and gave her a brief smile. "Hi, Miss Ross."

"Hello, Beau. Any kind of trouble?"

"Nope. Everything's fine as frog hair."

"I'd tell you to keep your eyes open, but I know you will." Dani smiled.

"How's Ben's lady doing?"

Something about the way Beau phrased that did not sit well with Dani. She was tired and had been sleeping poorly. "She's not his lady."

"Oh, I thought she was." Beau's eyes were innocent enough, but she saw a flicker of what could have been amusement in them.

"She hasn't recovered consciousness yet."

Dani left Beau, feeling his stare as she went along the deck and turned into the passageway. She knocked on the door of J.T.'s suite, and when he said, "Come in," she entered at once. Sitting at a desk covered with papers, he stood up and said, "I'm glad you came, Dani. I need a break from all this paperwork."

"You look much better," Dani said as she took the seat he offered. She also let him fix her a Diet Coke and a glass of ice. As he fussed over her, she thought, *If he'd shown the good manners toward his wives he shows toward me, he might have been able to hang onto one of them.* She didn't say what she was thinking, however. J.T. sat down and said quickly, "Nancy and I are going out this afternoon and will have dinner together tonight."

"Where are you going?"

Denver laughed. "She saw something on television about Alligator Annie's. She wants to go out and watch the woman feed the alligators."

Dani smiled. "It's quite a sight all right. She treats those monsters like they're kittens."

"I've never been there."

"It'll do you good to get out some, and I'm sure Nancy will enjoy it."

"Look, Dani, I feel like a fool with Beau trailing behind me. Couldn't I leave him home just this once?"

"I don't think so." Dani saw an argument coming, but before he could say anything, she went on, "How much money did each of your ex-wives get when they divorced you?"

"What?"

"I'd like to know how much the settlement was on all three of your ex-wives."

J.T. Denver's eyes narrowed, and he forgot all about disliking bodyguards. He was a very intelligent man, and his mind ran quickly to a logical deduction. "You don't think one of them could be behind this, do you? That's impossible!"

"It probably is," Dani agreed. "But just in case, tell me."

J.T. did not need to look anything up. Each one of his divorces had been rather bitter, and when he reeled off the amounts each had been awarded, Dani's eyes widened. "None of them have any worries at all. Not with that kind of money!"

"They wouldn't if they had kept it."

"Kept it? What did they do with it?"

"They threw it away. Shelley has no sense at all about finances. Creighton doesn't either apparently. He wasted most of the money his mother received—he's a gambler. So they're both broke."

"What about Vivian?"

"Vivian's a compulsive gambler too," J.T. said. "She always was, even before I married her, though I didn't know that. I don't even know how many of her gambling debts I've paid off. I knew it would be a mistake to give her any money, but the law said I had to. And she's spent it all. Loreen makes a living with Bobby's help."

"What about Maris?"

"She loves the theater crowd, so she put everything I gave her into producing plays. But they all bombed, and she lost it all."

"So they're all broke."

"Pretty much. I have to jump in from time to time to help them out. Especially for the twins' sake. I know Maris doesn't mean to, but she neglects them. She doesn't really care for those girls, not like I do. What she wants is a career, and that's why she and Trevor are after me. They want me to finance a film. They had me read a screenplay, and it sounded idiotic. Of course, idiotic films make lots of money sometimes."

"Will you give it to them?"

"I don't know. I do want to make sure Anne and Gayle are provided for."

"So what's the current arrangement with your money? What provision have you made for everyone, in case, you know . . . ?"

Again a cryptic, rather cynical look came over J.T. "I've left

each of my ex-wives enough to have another spree. About three million each, I think."

"Three million dollars?"

"Probably more than that. I haven't thought much about it
lately, but I bought a lot of insurance back a ways. Now that I think
about it, with my investments and the life insurance and all, they'd
probably get closer to five or six."

"That's a lot of money, Mr. Denver."

"Not to them. They'd go through it in a year," Denver said
wearily. "But as far as one of them being a threat to me, my ex-wives
can be pretty stupid, but they're not killers. I'm sure it's Mad Jack
Byron. That's where you ought to be looking."

"We'll do that, Mr. Denver. We began to check into that, but
with all that's happened, we got sidetracked a bit."

"I understand. Now, about this bodyguard . . ."

"You still need one, so you might as well just make the best of it."

J.T. unexpectedly laughed with delight. "And people say I'm
tough. They ought to listen to you boss me around and make me
like it. All right, all right. By the way, Beau's the best I've ever seen.
I never see him when we go someplace. He just seems to disappear.
Maybe he hides in the chandelier or behind the bushes, I don't
know. But I have the feeling he's close enough. If anybody made a
move, he'd be right there."

"He's a good man. I hope you and Nancy have a good time.
You both deserve it."

◆ ◆ ◆

"I don't think I've ever laughed so much in my whole life. This
was really fun, J.T."

Denver had pulled the Jaguar up in front of Nancy's hotel. He
shut the engine off, then turned to face her. "It was fun, wasn't it?"

"The most fun I've had in years."

After Alligator Annie's, the two had taken in a show at Saenger's
Theater, then went out for a late supper. Now it was well after 1:30

in the morning. Nancy smiled, reached over, and put her hand atop his on the steering wheel. "I thought you'd have to wrestle with Beau to make him let you drive your own car."

"So did I. He's a stubborn fellow." Glancing up into the mirror, he saw the dark Chevrolet parked thirty yards behind. He couldn't see Beau's face, but he knew the young man was watching him carefully. "I feel sort of naughty," he said. "Like I'm bringing a date home late to face a mad dad. I'm afraid Beau doesn't approve of all this."

"But he is a nice young man, and I feel better that he's watching out for you. Well, good night, J.T."

Suddenly reaching over with his good hand, he caressed Nancy's shoulder. Her eyes opened with surprise, and he couldn't quite read the emotion there. When he pulled her closer, she didn't resist. He put his arm around her, and when he kissed her, she kissed him back. When he released her, he said, "I've missed you, Nancy."

Nancy didn't answer. This time his kiss troubled her more than she cared to put into words, and she whispered, "I'd better go."

"Nancy, I feel like a fool saying this, like mediocre dialogue in a bad movie, but . . ." J.T. paused for a moment, then shook his head. "I remember the old days. I've never gotten away from those times we had and how much fun they were and how much I loved you." She didn't answer, and he ran his hand through her abundant hair. "I couldn't wait to get home to you in those days. There's been nothing, no one, like you in my life ever. No one."

"I really have to go, J.T."

He released her at once and got out of the car. She waited for him to open the door, and when she stepped out they both saw a man walking rapidly toward them, right past Beau's car. Beau leapt quickly onto the sidewalk and matched the man's pace. The man gave the couple a look, nodded, and passed on by. Beau waited until the man was twenty yards away, then turned around and said, "Better safe than sorry."

"That's right, Beau." Nancy smiled. "Take good care of this man, okay?"

"I will, Mrs. Livingston."

"Good night, J.T. I'll see you tomorrow."

The two men watched the woman leave, and J.T. seemed to have forgotten that he was standing in the middle of the sidewalk in the early-morning hours.

"Something wrong, Mr. Denver?"

J.T. blinked and turned to face the bodyguard. "A lot of things have been wrong in my life, Beau. And that lady was the one right thing."

"It's good to know there is somebody like that," Beau said. He studied Denver's face and said no more. When J.T. finally got back in the Jag and drove off, Beau followed him closely. "I wonder what that was all about," he said to himself. But since he wasn't being paid to wonder about such things, he just kept concentrating on everything that moved in J.T. Denver's direction.

Fifteen

A VISIT FROM MAD JACK

"I've never understood high finance," Travis said. He had been sitting across from J.T. Denver, taking him on in a game of chess. So far Travis had won three games out of five, and each was delighted to face a worthy opponent.

Leaning back in his chair, J.T. Denver said, "I don't understand it either."

Travis grinned broadly. "I don't believe that."

"Well, you don't get the financial picture by going to college. It's a very practical sort of thing—learned on the job."

"That doesn't sound right to me."

"Well, let's see . . . How can I explain it?" Denver mused. Then he said, "Look at this." He went across the room, rummaged through a drawer, and came back with an 8 x 10 glossy photo. "This is a picture of the Mirage Resort down in Biloxi, Mississippi."

Travis stared at the picture. "Beautiful," he said.

"Well, it's beautiful all right. It was supposed to cost 110 ten million dollars. It wound up costing 680 million."

"Wow! Somebody took a shellacking on that!"

"*I* almost did. I would've lost my shirt, but just as I was ready to sign the papers I had a bad feeling about it. So I put it off. I took *The Nancy* down to Biloxi and stayed there a week. I talked to bartenders, waitresses, guys who mixed concrete—everybody I could think of. I had a partner in the deal, and the way he had it figured out, we were going to make millions. Well, I went back and told him what I'd found out. He got mad at me and said he'd do it by him-self—and he did. He's about to declare bankruptcy."

"What was wrong with his ideas?"

"Almost everything. The main thing was, my partner didn't understand the people down there. It's Mississippi, not Florida. He wanted a casino, and he got one. But like I say, he spent 680 mil-lion dollars. The casino was a 150,000-square-foot barge with gam-ing, entertainment—everything he thought folks would like. The trouble is, it wasn't southern."

"What's that mean?"

"It means he invested in fine linens and marble bathrooms when people in the Biloxi market are interested in barbecue and country music. And he threw money away, spent it when he didn't need to. He put in fifteen seventy-five-year-old live oak trees. They cost 67,000 dollars each. And everything had to be first-class. He came up with an insane idea about the riverboat mooring ramps. Thompson Engineering adapted offshore oil platform technol-ogy, and he floated the casino on five barges anchored by nine million pounds of structural steel. He added a ten million-dollar, thirty-one slip floating marina built of Brazilian hardwood. The resort claims it's the world's most expensive marina in the world, and I suppose it is. Then he expanded the motel from 1,200 to 1,780 rooms and from four restaurants to twelve. The cost went up like a rocket."

"But why'd he do that, umm . . . ?" Travis laughed. "You know, I don't know what to call you. I can't call you Mr. Denver, and some-how J.T. doesn't sound right. Would it be all right, do you think, if I call you Dad? You are biologically, you know."

J.T. Denver had been a hard man. He had handled many tough situations in his life. But he couldn't remember a time when he'd been so speechless. He looked at the young man sitting across from him and saw himself as he'd been twenty years earlier, and suddenly his throat was dry, and he had to blink to clear his vision. "I think that would be fine, son. There's nothing I would like better."

Travis was somewhat embarrassed, but he had grown very fond of J.T. Denver. The man had not been what he had expected at all, and he had quickly sensed his father's yearning to bond with him. Now he laughed. "Maybe I could call you 'Pop' when I don't like something you say."

"That'll be all right too, Travis." J.T. cleared his throat. "I always wanted a son, but I never expected to have one."

"So what happened to the Mirage Resort in Biloxi?"

"Well, it's been a mess. They just didn't know what in tarnation they were doing. For one thing they scheduled events on days when Ole Miss played. In Mississippi you don't schedule anything on *those* days. If I had invested in it, I would've lost my shirt. It was just sort of a hunch, I guess." He paused suddenly and said, "I've been thinking about what you said about racing cars. Would you really like to give it a try? In NASCAR?"

Travis shook his head. "Not really, Dad."

"I thought that's what you wanted."

"When I was younger, I wanted to be a forest ranger and jump out of airplanes and fight fires too, but not anymore. Sure, I still dream about racing, but I've been thinking a lot about my life lately, and I'd like to do something more important, something that counts."

"You don't think automobile racing does?"

"I think it's like a football game. It means something while it's going on, I suppose, at least to those interested in it, but after it's over it's over."

"You could say that about a lot of things."

"I suppose that's true, but racing just isn't what I want to do with my life anymore. It would be fun, and maybe in a couple of years I'll decide that's what I should do."

"Maybe so. You know, I've done a lot of things not nearly as honorable as NASCAR." J.T. grinned and shook his head. "I hope you don't find out about some of them. What would you really like to do with your life?"

"I've thought about that a lot, and the thing I enjoy most is something that Mother and I do together."

That caught J.T.'s immediate attention. "What's that?" he said.

"We've traveled a lot down in Central America and South America, and even some in Europe. We've gone with mission groups that go out into the boondocks to try to help people. Of course, I'm not a doctor or a dentist. But we've helped build homes and churches and stuff. Last year I took a crew to Belize. We built four houses for national pastors. All fine men, but so poor you wouldn't believe it. They were just simple, little houses, but you would have thought we'd built a Taj Mahal for them. Dad, you can't imagine how good I felt, and Mother too. She got out and banged nails with the rest of us. We're supporting as many of those national pastors as we can—some in Belize, some over in Romania. We've been there too, even in Russia. Those poor pastors and their families are really laying it all on the line for God. That's what's important to me."

"How about if I go down there with you and your mother?"

Travis suddenly laughed aloud. "You mean in all your glory? When we're there, we live like the people do, Dad. We eat whatever they have. I've even eaten monkey once or twice, but you can't show you're bothered by it. They're wonderful people. A hundred dollars a month to them is almost the difference between life and death."

"You're really serious about this, and your mother is too?"

"Very serious."

"All right, I'll do it. You pick the spot. I'll buy some blue jeans and a denim shirt and a pair of boots and see if I can keep up with you."

Travis stared at his father. "You really mean that, Dad?"

"Try me."

"Mom will be glad to hear that. We're already planning a trip to Haiti. You can't get much more backward than that, but there's a wonderful pastor down there. He's really struggling financially and facility-wise. So we're going to go down and build him a church. Just a little one—concrete blocks. If we could do it together, that would be awesome."

"We will. That's a promise."

◆ ◆ ◆

Two men walked up the gangplank as if they owned *The Nancy*. As they stepped on deck they were confronted by an olive-skinned young man who said, "May I help you?"

"We're here to see J.T. Denver." The speaker was a tall man, wiry, with black hair cut short and hazel eyes. He had authority in his voice, and he gave Beau only a careless glance.

"You can't see him until I shake you down."

"Listen, I'm Jack Byron. I don't get shaken down! And neither does my bodyguard here. Now, sonny, you run along. I know where J.T.'s stateroom is."

Beau smiled pleasantly enough. "Sorry, Mr. Byron, but we've had a little trouble lately. Nobody comes on board carrying any firearms."

"Phil, you talk to our friend here while I go find Denver."

The man called Phil was a thickset man with his eyes almost closed, and yet the eyes were still sharp and piercing. He stepped forward at once, saying, "Look, friend." His tone was soft but unyielding. "Let's not have any trouble. Mr. Byron's not going to hurt anybody. He just wants to talk."

"Sorry. No exceptions. Let me check you over, and I'll be glad to see if Mr. Denver can see you."

"Take care of him, Phil."

The bulky man shuffled forward, and his left shoulder dipped. Obviously a professional, he threw a wicked left that would have demolished Beau had it landed.

However, Beau simply put up his right forearm and blocked it, at the same time striking the large man on the side of the head with the hardened edge of his left hand.

"Phil, I said take care of this guy!" Jack Byron called out.

"I'll take him out, Mr. Byron. No problem."

As Phil spoke, he slipped his hand inside his coat. He came out with a nine millimeter automatic and leveled it, but before he could even turn the safety off, Beau kicked it out of his hands, sending it spinning into the bay, then, shifting to his right foot, gave a kick that caught Phil in the side of the head. Mad Jack's bodyguard dropped to the deck but was still not out. Beau reached down and, grabbing the man by the belt, lifted him, then casually tossed him over the side.

"What do you think you're doing? What if he can't swim?"

"Maybe he should take swimming lessons before he comes here again. You're not going in to see J.T. Denver, Mr. Byron—not unless I check you out first. Make up your mind. You can either let me frisk you or go swimming with your friend."

Mad Jack Byron was not accustomed to being treated like this. He glanced down, saw Phil sputtering and splashing, then shook his head. "Maybe you'd better come to work for me. Go ahead—frisk me."

Beau's hands expertly went over the tall man. He removed a revolver and smiled. "Come along. I'll see if Mr. Denver will see you now."

"Where'd you learn to fight like that?" Byron asked.

"The streets of New Orleans, Golden Gloves, and the Navy Seals."

"I'll pay you twice whatever Denver's paying you."

Byron got no answer, but when they reached the door Beau said, "Wait here. I'll see if Mr. Denver's receiving guests."

Knocking on the door, he waited until he heard Denver's voice. Opening it just a crack, he slipped inside, keeping the door closed. "Mr. Jack Byron to see you, Mr. Denver."

"Has he got his bodyguard with him?"

"Not anymore. I threw him in the bay. You want to see Mr. Byron?"

J.T. laughed. "Sure. Show the *gentleman* in."

Byron stepped inside, noticing that Beau didn't take his eyes off him but just moved over to one corner of the stateroom and stood as still as a statue. Only his eyes showed any life, and he kept his hand under his light gray jacket.

"Quite a bodyguard you got there. He threw my man over the side."

"Those are his orders. How are you doing, Jack?"

"Not bad. Not bad at all. I wanted to talk a little business."

"Sure. This is my son Travis." There was pride in J.T.'s voice.

"I want to talk alone."

"You're not going to, Jack. Sit down. Would you like a Coke? Or perhaps some coffee?"

"How about some scotch?"

"I don't have any hard liquor."

"That's a switch for you."

J.T. laughed suddenly. "I've hit the glory road, Jack. I'm a good boy now."

"You got religion?"

"I think it's got me. You want to hear about it?"

"No. I want to talk business."

"Sure. Sit down."

Byron sat down, and his eyes flickered toward the younger man. "He looks like you," he said. "I didn't know you had a boy."

"Well, I do. How's your ferryboat coming?"

"Fine, but I'm getting tired of all the pressure. I'll get right down to my point, J.T. There's no sense us beating each other's brains out. Why don't we go at this thing together? We'll split the contracts and the profits two ways. Fifty fifty."

"Thanks for the offer, Jack, but no thanks."

Byron's face suddenly reddened. "Wait a minute—you can't turn me down. I know you're behind schedule."

"And I know your boat will never pass the inspection. It'll blow over in the first heavy breeze that comes along."

"That's a lie!"

"I have some reliable information, Jack. You tried to save money on the designer you hired, and if you'd been a little more careful, you would have learned that he designed those two ferry-boats that capsized over in the Philippines. He built this one along the same lines."

Byron's eyes grew very still. "Somebody gave you a bum steer."

"So just go ahead and build your boat, and I'll build mine. When they go out for testing, we'll see who gets the contract."

Byron stood up. He said nothing, but the fury in his face was more intense than Travis had ever seen. He waited for the man to speak, but he didn't. Without another word he left the room, followed by Beau.

As soon as the door closed, J.T. said, "Now that's an evil man, Travis."

"I don't know much about him."

"I've been reading a book called *The Screwtape Letters*."

"Sure. I've read that. I've read everything written by C. S. Lewis."

"You probably remember that in that book Lewis says the really evil men are not those who go around shooting people in the head or burning villages down. They're the men in three-piece business suits in air-conditioned offices. That's where the evil comes from. And that's what Byron is."

"I don't think he's going to leave you alone, Dad."

"You saw that, did you?" J.T. said. "I'm glad you did. I'm more and more convinced that if we dig deep enough, we'll find out he's behind all these accidents that have been happening."

"What are you going to do?"

"Well, I've been trying to read the Bible, and I found a verse that has helped me. I've memorized it, and I put it in my billfold too."

"What verse is that?"

"Proverbs 3, verses 5 and 6. 'Trust in the Lord with all your heart and lean not on your own understanding; in all your ways acknowledge him, and he will make your paths straight.'"

"That's been a favorite of mine for a long time," Travis stated proudly. He got up and said, "I have to get back. I promised to take

Mom shopping. Imagine that. If there's anything I hate, it's shopping."

"You think it'd be okay if I come along?"

"Sure. You can pick up the tab," he said teasingly.

"It would be my pleasure."

"Mom's going to church tomorrow with Miss Ross. I'm going along. How about you?"

The suggestion seemed to trouble J.T. "I don't know, Travis. I don't feel comfortable in church. People are always looking at me."

"Let 'em look. It would make Mom happy, I'm sure."

"You think so?"

"I'd like it too."

"All right, I'll go."

◆ ◆ ◆

"I feel out of place," J.T. muttered as he turned to face Nancy on his left. On her other side Travis leaned forward and grinned. "It's okay, Pop," he said. "Nobody knows you're a filthy rich person."

Nancy stifled a giggle and said, "Just be still and listen, both of you."

Dani, sitting on J.T. Denver's right, added, "I don't think most people come here to look at others' clothes or to see people's bank accounts. It's a fine church, Mr. Denver. We're just here to worship the Lord and learn more of His Word."

"I'm sure that's true. It's just that—well, I've been a lone ranger for a long time. I don't know how to relate to people except in the business world."

Further conversation was cut off when a short young man with a guitar stepped forward and began to play. Other musicians joined him, playing a keyboard, a piano, a bass guitar, and a set of drums. Soon the church sanctuary was filled with joyful sounds as people lifted their voices to God. They sang songs J.T. Denver had never heard before, but he felt the power of them. Beside him Dani was singing beautifully, and Nancy and Travis knew some of the songs and joined in. He still felt out of place, but the worship service was refreshingly different from what he'd been expecting. At times the music was loud and triumphant, and people sang lustily; at other times there was a gentleness as people practically whispered the words. Once the song leader paused and said, "Let's just praise God without instruments, without hymns, in our own spirits. Let's just tell God how much we love Him."

J.T. could think of nothing to say. He heard Nancy beside him whispering, "I love you, Lord. Thank You for saving me from my sins. Thank You for Jesus and His great sacrifice at the cross."

This was a new experience for J.T. He didn't know how long the prayer time lasted, but finally a tall man in his mid-thirties came to stand behind the pulpit. He was not wearing a suit and tie but had on a white T-shirt with an emblem of a fish over the pocket. He looked athletic, and there was a light in his eyes and a lilt in his voice as he said, "We have been worshiping our wonderful Lord. Now I want to encourage us to give something to God. As most of you know, a terrible hurricane has devastated Nicaragua. Thousands of people have no shelter, no food, no medicine. Many are grieving for dead loved ones. I think it would be a fitting way to worship Christ this morning if we would reach out to our brothers and sisters and even those who do not know Him and help minister to their physical needs. We can pray here for their spiritual needs, and we will. But just now I want to ask you to make a sacrifice, above your normal giving. I want us all to give a special sacrifice to God. Every penny of today's offering will go to our distressed friends in Nicaragua. Whatever you give will be blessed."

The appeal was short, but the Spirit of God was moving powerfully. Dani felt it, and she was certain that J.T. Denver did as well. She noticed him pull out a checkbook, and she couldn't keep from glancing at it. Her whole body stiffened as she watched him make out a check for 1,000,000 dollars! She couldn't hold back the gasp of amazement and delight. When J.T. saw her shock, he shrugged, saying, "It's only money. I'm way behind in helping people."

The offering was taken, and the minister, whose name was Ray

Oldham, said, "God will bless your giving. It's impossible to out-give God. Now then, it's time for the message, and it will be very brief this morning. Turn with me, if you will, to the book of First Corinthians, chapter 12."

Dani noticed that J.T. was fumbling through the Bible and had an impulse to help him but decided against it. He found the place just as Oldham said, "Those of you who are familiar with this book know that the thirteenth chapter is probably one of the most well-known in the Bible. It's the Love Chapter. 'If I speak in the tongues of men and of angels, but have not love, I am only a resounding gong or a clanging cymbal.' We all know that passage. That is a very private chapter; it deals with me and you as individuals. But the twelfth chapter does something entirely different. We will begin in verses 13 and 14: 'For we were all baptized by one Spirit into one body—whether Jews or Greeks, slave or free—and we were given the one Spirit to drink. Now the body is not made up of one part but of many.'

"I hope you will go home after we leave this place and read this entire chapter. My remarks this morning will simply reinforce verse 14—'Now the body is not made up of one part but of many.' Many of us spend so much time thinking about our own needs, our own problems, our own griefs that we sometimes forget we are not alone. We are part of a body, as this verse teaches. I want this morning somehow to bring to you a joy that God would have us know and experience. A joy that comes from the fact that we are not alone. Not only do we have Jesus Christ in our hearts, but every living Christian is connected to every other living Christian in what the Bible calls the church or the Body of Christ."

The minister spoke quickly, and the excitement and joy on his face and in his voice moved Denver. He was not accustomed to men like this. He had attended few churches, and as he sat there between Dani and Nancy, he knew he was encountering something different from what he'd known before. He leaned forward to listen.

"The apostle Paul continues by saying in verse 15, 'If the foot should say, "Because I am not a hand, I do not belong to the body," it would not for that reason cease to be part of the body. And if the ear should say, "Because I am not an eye, I do not belong to the body," it would not for that reason cease to be part of the body. If the whole body were an eye, where would the sense of hearing be? If the whole were an ear, where would the sense of smell be?'"

The preacher suddenly smiled broadly. "Can you imagine a body that was composed of nothing but an eye? A huge eyeball walking around. No doubt it could see better than any of us, but could it taste? Of course not. Could it smell anything? No. It could do nothing but see. That's why the apostle is saying the eye, the ear, the legs, the tongue all go together to make up one body. And when any of those members are lost, the body is less. You probably remember John Donne's famous saying, 'No man is an island.' That is what the apostle is saying here. That's why I want to speak to you this morning, especially to those of you who are lone rangers. You think you've made it on your own. You think you can continue to survive on your own. But I am here to tell you that you cannot. The body of Christ is made up of and depends on *all* its members—white, yellow, and red, rich and poor. All who come to the cross and receive Jesus Christ as Savior are part of His body."

Denver had never heard of such a concept, and he listened avidly as the preacher spoke for forty-five minutes. "'If one part suffers, every part suffers with it; if one part is honored, every part rejoices with it. Now you are the body of Christ, and each one of you is a part of it.'"

The preacher looked out over the congregation as he said, "The church has been torn apart by battles and conflicts of many kinds, but I say to you this morning that if you have truly received Jesus Christ into your heart, you and I are one. We are brothers and sisters with the same Father. I should feel your pain, and you should feel mine. The Scripture says, 'A brother is born for adversity.' This morning when we reached out to our believing brothers and sisters in Nicaragua who are facing terrible adversity, we were caring for our own body. This morning I want you to give yourself to the Body of Christ, to serving our Savior by serving others. Let me ask you a question—could you be a Christian on a desert island?"

J.T. blinked with surprise at the question. Then the pastor said, "Some of you think you could because you wouldn't have the irritation and the problems that people bring into your lives. But can you imagine Jesus being content to be on a desert island?" He paused for a long moment and shook his head. "I can't. When I read about Jesus in the Gospels, He's usually in the middle of a crowd. He's healing a leper. He's giving sight to a blind man. He's picking up a child and hugging him and praying for him. Again and again He said, 'I have not come to be served but to serve.' And when He left this earth He said, 'You are to go into all the world. Preach the Gospel. You are to be one.'"

The preacher brought the sermon to a close by saying, "If any of you have put yourself on a desert island and have cut yourself off from others, I challenge you to get off that island. Come to us, for we need you, and Jesus is calling you."

When the preacher issued an invitation, many went forward for prayer or counsel. When the service ended Nancy stood and J.T. with her, and the four made their way quietly out of the church.

J.T. said little afterward, but Travis and his mother discussed the sermon vigorously. "He's a wonderful preacher, Travis," Nancy said. "Not as good as our pastor though, is he?"

"I don't know, Mom. He's pretty good."

Nancy said wistfully, "Your church is wonderful, Dani, but I miss my church back home."

They walked toward the car, shadowed by Beau, who had put on a necktie for the occasion but still looked out of place. Nancy added, "I've been thinking about how things will be in Heaven. When I go into a strange church, I don't really know anybody. I'm a visitor. But I think that when we get to Heaven, we'll know everybody. Not just those we knew on earth, but everybody. There'll be no strangers there."

"I don't know if I'd like that," J.T. said suddenly. "Everybody knowing everything about me, considering all the wrong things I've done."

Nancy reached out and took J.T.'s hand. "But you've been washed in the blood of the Lamb. All your sins are gone, Travis." She used the old name for him, and the younger Travis exchanged glances with Dani. Both of them knew something had happened to J.T. Denver, and that it was definitely good.

Sixteen

THE PERILS OF AMBITION

Late afternoon sunlight filtered through the window of Dani's office. Sitting at her desk weary of reports, paperwork, and thinking about cases, she watched hundreds of dust particles spin and whirl in the golden bars of light. A sudden thought came to her. *The Bible says the hairs of our head are numbered. I wonder if God keeps track of every bit of dust all over the world too?* The thought intrigued her, and she leaned back, allowing her mind to dwell on the significance of God's omniscience. She considered the teeming life in the ocean and the countless birds and mammals spread all over the world from the frozen cold to the tropics. She'd read somewhere that there were a million earthworms in one small section of earth, and she wondered if God gave every earthworm His attention just like He did with the billions of stars flung into the darkness of space.

It thrilled her to think about the vastness of creation and to know that God was keeping track of every atom of it. "You're a great God," she said. "If You can keep track of all those stars, surely You can watch over one worn-out private eye."

The week had been trying for her, not so much physically as mentally as she tried to keep the agency financially balanced. It had grown since her father had been forced to withdraw due to his heart attack. Dani had not regretted for a moment leaving Hayworth Divinity School and coming back to take over. She had hopes, of course, that one day her dad would be strong enough to resume full speed, and she knew that was possible. But right now she was fatigued, and she moved her shoulders in a gesture of semi-rebellion.

"I'm tired of all this," she announced as she stared defiantly at the portrait of her ancestor in his ash-gray Confederate uniform. "I'm going to go home, General Daniel Monroe Ross. You take over." The general's features didn't move, and Dani smiled as she recalled a remark her father had made about the man. "He was one of the most stubborn men who ever lived—so that's probably where you get your stubbornness from." She chuckled.

Gathering her things, she stepped out of the office and nodded at Angie. "See if you can get Ben on his cell phone."

"He just called in."

"Where from?"

"He's at the hospital visiting Jamie." Angie watched as discontent flickered across Dani's smooth features. She had learned to know this boss of hers very well, and a slight streak of mischievousness cropped up within her. "It's understandable for a fellow to care about a good-looking woman like her."

Dani shot an angry glance at Angie and saw she was being teased. "Never mind about that. He just better get his reports in on time. I'm going home."

Angie laughed. "Good-bye, boss. Don't get too jealous now—you might break up a beautiful romance."

Dani made her way to the Cougar, started the engine, and soon was headed out of New Orleans. As always, it was a relief to leave the city behind. She wondered suddenly if she would ever learn to like the city. She'd grown up in Mandeville just outside New Orleans, but that was different. It often seemed to her like there was a fence around the city itself. When she stepped inside it, evil seemed to surround her. She knew that was probably her imagination, but she also knew sin had had plenty of time to soak into the city—especially in the downtown area and most especially in the French Quarter.

Forcing the thoughts away, she sped over the causeway and

turned south toward her home. When she pulled up and got out, she saw that Biscuit, her quarter horse, had come to put his head over the fence and utter his shrill neighing demands.

"You just watch out, Biscuit," she said. "I'm gonna come out and ride some of that meanness right out of you."

Inside the house she found her mother cooking supper and said, "I'm going to take a ride. What's for supper tonight?"

"Crawfish étoufée."

"Sounds good."

Going upstairs, Dani put on a pair of old jeans. She noticed they were just a little tight. "I'm getting fat," she said with discontent. "I'm going to have to work it off." Actually she had the kind of figure other women would kill for, but like most attractive women she was never quite satisfied with her looks. She knew this was a matter of pride, and she fought against it, often telling herself, *It doesn't matter what I look like. It's what I am that counts.*

She pulled on a T-shirt that once had been white, then slipped into a pair of short stockings and half boots. Leaving her room, she made her way to the pasture. Biscuit followed her, pushing her with his nose as she went to the small barn. "Let me get this saddle on you, you ornery creature," she said with a smile. Quickly she saddled the horse, slipped on the bridle, then stepped in one swift motion onto the saddle. She swung the rust-colored quarter horse around, touched her heel, and shouted, "Eeeeya!" at the top of her lungs. Dani leaned over as he shot out of the barn, and the thundering of his hooves and the wind in her hair washed away all thoughts of the pressures of Ross Investigation Agency. She guided the horse with her knees and felt him cut quickly. Quarter horses were made for such short turns. That was what made them the best barrel riding horses in the world.

For half an hour Dani rode hard, driving Biscuit into more sharp turns. She even thought about putting the barrels up and running them, but she decided against it. Finally she rode Biscuit slowly through the gate and back into the woods behind the house. It was quiet as a cathedral in there, and the late afternoon sunbeams breaking through from time to time made a shattered pool of light on the ground and warmed her face. Once a gray squirrel chattered angrily at her for disturbing his peace, but she only laughed. He followed her from tree to tree scolding her. Then, apparently happy that he had succeeded in driving the menace away, he disappeared with a twist of his tail and a long leap from one tree to the next.

Finally she patted the horse on the neck and said, "Good boy. Let's go home now." Biscuit broke into a slow gallop. Back at the barn, Dani took the saddle and bridle off, hung them up, then brushed the horse for twenty minutes and put some grain out. "I wish everybody was as reliable as you, Biscuit."

She headed for the house and a relaxing shower. Afterward she picked up the phone and dialed the office.

"Let me speak to Ben, Angie."

"As far as I know he's still at the hospital."

After a long silence, she added, "If he ever does call in, tell him I'm trying to reach him."

"You could call him there."

Dani put the phone down with more force than usual and continued to dry her hair. For a long time she sat staring out the window at the falling darkness and watching the swallows perform amazing acrobatics. The sky was amethyst, and ordinarily she would have delighted in it, but she was too busy fuming over Ben Savage's devotion to Jamie Cordova. Finally, irritated with herself, she said aloud, "I don't care if he moves in with her— which he probably will as soon as she regains consciousness!" This was so unreasonable, she even recognized it herself. She knew she should feel more compassion for Jamie, but she just didn't want to deal with her own attitude. She angrily brushed her hair, tied it up with a ribbon, and put on a dress and walked downstairs. When she walked into the dining room, she smiled at everyone, hoping to hide her discontent. *What a hypocrite I'm getting to be*, she thought.

◆ ◆ ◆

Dani rose early the next morning but didn't go to the office. She stayed around the house talking to her mother, then ate a leisurely breakfast with both parents. Allison was off visiting a friend, and Rob was spending the day with friends, hopefully better ones than she'd met when she went to a rock concert with him recently. The lines around her father's face bothered Dani. He had always been the handsomest man she'd ever seen with his clean-cut features and distinguished gray at the temples of his dark hair. But now she saw the look that sick people have sometimes, a weakness around the eyes and a tightening of the mouth. She wanted to ask him if he was in pain but knew that would disturb him. She finally left the house. When she reached the office she said, "I don't want to be disturbed, Angie."

"All right. I'll keep the reporters out."

"Very funny." Entering her office, she sat down and began making phone calls. She was determined to find out more about Trevor Fountaine. She finally obtained the name of a man who could give her some information about him.

"Mr. Clements?"

"That's me. Who is this?"

Dani said, "Jack Bellmont gave me your name, Mr. Clements."

"How is Jack?"

"He's fine. I'm a private investigator, and I have a few questions I'd like to ask you."

"About me?" Jason Clements said sharply.

"No, not at all. I'm doing a little background work on some people, and one of them is a man I think you might know—Trevor Fountaine."

The slight pause alerted Dani that something was wrong. "Oh, sure," Clements said carefully. "I know Fountaine."

"What can you tell me about him?"

"Pretty good actor."

"I'd like to have a little more information than that."

"Can you tell me what this is about? Is he in some kind of trouble?"

"No, not really. It's a routine investigation. I'm looking into the backgrounds of quite a few people. He's just one of them."

Dani listened to the man on the other end of the line. All she had to go on was the sound of his voice. He had a New England accent, which meant almost nothing, but he spoke as one accustomed to being listened to. "I can tell you this about him—he's ambitious."

"Well, so are we all."

"Not like him."

"Can you be a little more specific?"

Again the slight hesitation and then finally, as if he'd made up his mind, Clements asked, "Is this call being recorded?"

"No, sir, it's not. This is all strictly confidential. I'm just trying to get a feeling for these people."

"Well, let me put it this way—he'd do anything to get back in the loop."

"Back in the loop?"

"Sure. He was the biggest thing in Hollywood for a while. Now he's lost it. Off the record again, Miss Ross, he's a dangerous man in some ways. The suspicion is he's on drugs. I'm not saying that's true, you understand."

Dani knew Clements was covering his tracks. She was certain too that Trevor was indeed an addict.

"He's got a temper too. When he's high, he'll do anything."

"Would he do anything illegal?"

Again the pregnant silence. "If he thought he could get by with it, I'd say yes. His first wife divorced him because he beat her up really bad. There's a violent streak in that man that most people don't see. I don't like him, Miss Ross. I've worked with him in the past, but I never will again."

"Thank you very much, Mr. Clements."

Quickly Clements added, "If you have to put some heat on him, don't do it alone. Always have somebody with you."

"Thank you again. I'll remember that." Dropping the phone gently into its cradle, Dani leaned back and narrowed her eyes. *A high temper, on drugs, ambitious. That's a bad combination.* She sat for a while thinking about it all, then got up and left the office after telling Angie she'd be back soon.

She went at once to Maris Nolan's home and tried to think of some reason for her visit. What she actually wanted to do was get a little deeper into the real Trevor Fountaine—and the real Maris Nolan for that matter.

The door opened, and the twins stood staring up at her. "Hello, girls," she said. "Is your mother here?"

"Yes," Anne said quickly. "Come on in."

"You'd better tell her I'm here. She might be busy."

"She's not busy," Anne said with certainty.

"Nevertheless, I'd appreciate it if you'd tell her I'm here."

At that moment Maris appeared. She was wearing a white linen suit with a light blue silk blouse. The jacket had long sleeves and was short in length, coming only to her waist. It had a small collar trimmed in light blue piping and had light blue buttons running down the front. The skirt came down to her ankles, and she had on a pair of light blue satin shoes with the highest heels Dani had ever seen.

"Hello, Miss Ross. Is something wrong?"

"Not really. I just needed to get a few more details, and I thought you might be able to help me."

"Of course. Come in. "

Gayle looked up at Dani and said, "Do you have any little girls?"

"No, I don't."

"Any little boys?"

Dani laughed. "No. I'm not married yet, so I haven't started my family."

"Oh," Gayle said with disappointment. "I thought if you had some, you might bring them by and let them play with us."

"Girls, we're busy. Go play with your new game."

Maris said, "Come on out to the balcony. I was just having some sweet tea. Would you care for some?"

"That would be nice."

Dani stepped onto the balcony and waited for Maris to come out with the tea.

"This is very good. On a hot day like this it really hits the spot."

Maris Nolan watched Dani carefully, sizing her up. Dani was accustomed to this, and it didn't trouble her. She was impressed with Maris Nolan's appearance, for the woman had a sensuous quality that would come across well on the stage or on film, Dani was sure.

"I think I told you that I used to put up pictures of you out of *Vogue*. I thought I'd grow up to be a model." Dani laughed. "But that never happened."

"Did you try?" Maris said with interest. "You're a very beautiful woman."

"No, I never tried. I got interested in other things. I've read a little bit about it though. It must be a difficult life."

"Harder than most people know." Maris nodded. She began talking about her experiences as a model and finally shrugged. "I was glad to get out of it."

"But you went into films, which I think would be even harder."

"I loved every minute of it."

"I saw you in *Lovely Is the Night*. I thought you were magnificent. You're probably used to hearing sugary compliments, but that's how I felt."

"Why, thank you." Maris brightened up and nodded. "I appreciate your praise. I thought that was the best thing I ever did. I was in some real stinkers."

"Why did you quit making pictures?" Actually Dani already knew this, having gotten the background from J.T., but she wanted to check the woman's reaction.

"I married J.T., and of course he insisted that I give up my career."

"What a shame! But it's not too late," Dani said. "I understand you and your fiancé are anxious to do a picture together."

"Yes," Maris said quickly, and her eyes brightened. "It will be a good one too. Trevor has his faults, but he's a fine actor. And the script is wonderful. It was written by a young screenwriter who's going to make quite a name for himself."

Something in Maris's tone touched off an alarm within Dani.

"I'm not a young girl, but Trevor and I understand each other," Maris said nervously. "Romance is fine, but it doesn't pay the bills. Trevor has ambition. He was once at the top of his profession in the theater, and he's determined to climb back."

Dani recalled the words of Jason Clements about the ambition of Trevor Fountaine and how he would do anything to regain his stature.

"There's a rumor going around," Dani said carefully, "that he's had a problem with drugs."

"Oh, everybody in Hollywood takes drugs! It's not a real problem with Trevor. Besides, he doesn't do that anymore."

The conversation was interrupted when the twins came roaring in. Maris lost her temper with them, but Dani said, "Oh, please, they're not bothering me in the least. I think they're beautiful."

"They can be hideous at times."

"Mr. Denver's very fond of them."

A crafty look came into Maris's eyes. "Yes, he is," she said. Something in her tone alarmed Dani, though she couldn't put her finger on it. She tried to add it all up as she drove back to the office.

Two very ambitious people needing a large amount of money. An ex-husband who loves the twins. A smart woman who has as much mercy as a ferret. It all adds up to something, but I'm not sure what—yet.

Seventeen

MIRACLES STILL HAPPEN

Dani leaned against the wall watching Ben Savage carefully. The sounds of the hospital were muted, but the smells were always the same. She wondered why it wasn't possible to put some sort of pleasant fragrance into a hospital instead of the acrid odor of disinfectants overlaid with a whiff of sickness. She knew, of course, that this was impossible, but as often happened, Dani's imagination caused her to drift away from the solid facts of reality.

And right now the solid fact of reality was that Ben was in poor shape. He carried no spare flesh, so any weight loss showed itself immediately, and he had definitely lost weight. The lines of strain around his eyes and mouth seemed to deepen every day. As he sat there, his eyes fixed steadily on the face of Jamie Cordova, Dani wondered *again* what sort of relationship had existed between these two. It did not seem entirely natural to her that Ben would grieve so deeply over a business associate. True, the woman had saved his life, and he had saved hers—but . . .

Dani stretched and sighed so slightly that it seemed unlikely that Ben would hear her. He did, however, and turned to say, "Why don't you go home, Dani. No sense two of us staying here."

"Oh, I don't mind. But I am worried about you, Ben."

"I'll be all right."

"No, you won't. You're not eating. You're not sleeping. You're worried sick. You can't help Jamie if you destroy yourself."

"I'll be all right," he repeated. His voice was level, but the familiar steely edge of determination told Dani there was no use arguing.

Silence again fell over the room, and from the outer reaches of the hospital came the faint sound of music.

Suddenly Savage turned and said, "I think I ought to get in touch with her ex-husband."

"She's been married?"

"Yeah. She married one of the guys on the SWAT Team—Dave Cordova."

"They got divorced?"

"Yes. A few years ago. I was sorry to hear it." Ben appeared as if he were looking back through the years. His lips scarcely moved as he murmured, "They had a good marriage, one of the best I ever saw—or at least I thought so."

"What happened, Ben?"

"I never knew. Who can tell what goes on between a man and a woman? I tried to get Dave to talk to me about it, but he never would. Neither would Jamie."

"I think maybe you *should* get in touch with him." Dani wished her motives for saying that were all unselfish.

"I kept hoping Jamie would wake up. I don't want to stir up something I shouldn't." He abruptly rose, arched his back, and did several side bends to loosen up his muscles. "I've been trying to get her to try to work things out again."

"Is that what you talk about when you go get her report?"

Ben's eyes were cool as they regarded Dani. "Yes, for the most part. What did you think we talked about?"

Dani was confused and shook her head. "Oh, I don't know, Ben . . . I guess . . . I do think you ought to call her ex-husband—he needs to know."

"I think you're right. I'll do it today."

A nurse came in, a short red-haired woman with cheerful blue eyes. She checked the equipment and studied the gauges, then turned to say, "You ought to go get some sleep, Ben."

"Maybe later, June."

June turned to Dani. "Are you his girlfriend?"

"No," Dani said, reddening slightly though she wished she hadn't. "I'm his employer."

"Well, you ought to command him to go home. He's going to make himself sick acting this way."

"I've tried, but he doesn't take orders too well."

"Men are like that, aren't they? They won't ask directions, and they won't listen when you try to talk sense to them."

Ben laughed flatly. "Will you please stop with the 'men are from Mars, women are from Venus' stuff?"

"All right. I knew it wouldn't do any good. I have a husband just like you." Suddenly her whole face crinkled with a smile. "He's mine though. Stubborn as a mule, but I love him. Make him go home if you can, miss."

As soon as the nurse left the room, Dani waited for Ben to speak. When he didn't, she said, "Ben, would you mind if I said a prayer for Jamie?"

"I'd like that."

Dani stepped forward and put her hand on the head of the injured woman. Her flesh felt cool, and her skin was smooth but pale. "Lord," Dani said in a conversational tone, "I know You are the Great Healer. We use doctors and are grateful for medicine. But, Lord, all the doctors and all the medicines in the world can't cure anybody unless You put Your hand on them. So, Lord, I ask that You put your hand on Jamie. I remember the woman who touched the hem of Your robe. She just touched Your garment. And the Bible says she was healed instantly. I'm not asking anything impossible, Lord. I'm asking You to do what is so easy for You. Heal this woman's body, root and branch. Smite every evil thing that might take away her health. Bring back her mind, her memory. Heal the bones, the flesh, and the tissues."

Dani hesitated a moment, then said, "And, Lord, I ask You to do a healing work in her marriage. I don't know what caused the divorce, but You know. So I pray that You will speak to her husband, that You will bring him here and do a healing work in their relationship. Lord, You said that two are better than one, so I pray that You would put these two back together. In the name of Jesus, Amen."

Dani was shocked to see Ben's eyes fixed firmly on her. Dani was never quite sure of what Ben thought about her brand of Christianity. He never said anything negative, and a few times he had seemed to indicate he was thinking about what she had to say. Now, however, there was something in his look that she didn't recognize. "What is it, Ben?"

"You really believe God's going to hear you?"

"I always believe that, Ben. I mean, not all of my prayers are answered—at least I don't *see* the answers. And when I pray I don't know which will be answered the way I think and which won't. So I just ask for what I believe God wants me to ask for. That's what Jesus said. 'Ask and it will be given unto you.' I really believe she's going to be all right in her body and in every other way."

"That would be good. Thanks, Dani. We need a miracle."

"And they still happen, Ben—they still happen."

◆ ◆ ◆

Dani had just emerged from the shower and slipped into a pair of pajamas when the phone rang. She looked longingly at the bed all turned back and was tempted not to answer. She hated telephones for the most part and had often said, "A telephone's supposed to be for my convenience. But most of the calls I get are calls I don't want—people wanting me to do something I don't want to do or bawling me out for not doing something I should have done."

But, habit being strong, she sat down on the bed and picked up the phone. "Dani here."

For a moment Dani couldn't understand a word the woman was saying. Basically she just heard sobs, deep-throated ones at that. "Who is this?" she said.

Finally her caller got a grip on herself. "This is Shelley—Shelley Bracken."

"What's wrong, Mrs. Bracken?"

"I have to talk to someone."

"Do you want to come in and see me tomorrow?"

"Couldn't you come tonight? I'm so afraid—I don't know what to do. I can't—"

Dani listened as the voice trailed off into a series of sobs. She knew from the slurred quality of the woman's speech that she'd been drinking. She was also aware that Shelley Bracken was usually at least partially intoxicated. She felt tempted to simply put off whatever crisis was at hand. But she also knew this was a legitimate cry for help. "All right, Mrs. Bracken. Where are you?"

"I'm—at home."

"Give me your address." Dani wrote the information down, then said, "I'll be there in about thirty minutes, maybe a little more." She hung up the phone. Quickly she dressed and left the house. As she got into her car, she noted that it was after midnight. Her eyes were drooping, for she had missed a great deal of sleep recently. But she eased the Cougar out of the driveway and soon was on the causeway. She let all the windows down to let the wind blow in her face and keep her awake. She turned on the radio and played some country music loudly, which she hated though she felt like she needed all the help she could get.

A little over thirty minutes later she pulled up in front of the two-story brick house set back off the street. Getting out of the car, she walked up the front steps, noting that the yard was not kept as well as on the neighboring properties. The flower beds had not been cared for and needed weeding. The grass was dry and needed watering.

The door opened, and Shelley Bracken stumbled as she made room for Dani to enter. "Oh, I shouldn't have called you!"

"That's all right, Mrs. Bracken." As soon as Dani stepped in, she smelled the alcohol on the woman's breath. She took in the pale face, the twisted lips, and the attempt to speak carefully as intoxicated people usually do to cover up their slurred speech.

"Come into the kitchen. Won't you have something to drink?"

"No, I don't think so." Dani watched as the woman moved across the kitchen floor, picked up a dirty glass, and, moving to the refrigerator, filled it with ice, then topped it off with water.

Dani glanced around the kitchen, noting that the house was in as poor shape as the yard. There were dirty dishes in the sink, and the floor had not been mopped in some time. Disorder was everywhere.

"Sit down, Mrs. Bracken." She practically forced the woman to sit at a small dinette suite, then waited until she had downed several quick swallows of water. "What's the matter? You must have some serious trouble to call me this late at night."

Shelley Bracken had been an attractive woman in her youth, but drink had added layers of fat that plastic surgery had not been able to keep up with. Her hands were trembling violently, and finally she whispered, "I—I have to tell somebody. I'm going crazy."

"Just take it easy, Shelley. If I may call you that?"

"Oh yes, please do."

"It helps sometimes to tell people your problems, and you can be assured it will stop with me." Pity came over Dani as she stared at the woman, so broken and obviously frightened. "Maybe I can help."

"I don't think anybody can help, but I have to tell somebody." Taking a deep breath, she shuddered, then bit her lip. "It—it's something I did a long time ago."

"Something illegal?"

"No. It was wrong, but it wasn't illegal."

"If you'd just come out and tell me what it was, you might feel much better."

"All right, I'll tell you. When J.T. and I were married, he wanted a son. But I didn't want any more children, so when I got pregnant, I didn't tell him and—" Sudden tears welled up in Shelley Bracken's eyes, and her lips trembled so violently that she couldn't control them. "I never told him what I'd done."

Suddenly Dani understood. Gently she asked, "Did you have an abortion?"

"Yes, yes, I did, and I wish before God that I hadn't!"

Dani prayed quickly for the right words to comfort the frightened woman. "We always wish we could go back and undo the wrong things we've done, but that's not always possible. In this case it's not. Have you asked God to forgive you?"

"What? Oh no, I haven't."

"That always comes first."

"But you don't know all of it. The abortionist—his name was Clyde Perkins—he came to me about two years ago. I told him my husband didn't know about the abortion. I didn't think he really knew who I was or who J.T. was, but somehow he found out that J.T. was a rich man, and—and—"

"And he wanted you to pay him to keep quiet, to keep it from your husband."

"Yes. And I've been paying him ever since. I know J.T. hates me because I continue to ask for more money. He gave me a good settlement when we were divorced, but Creighton—well, he's had bad luck with some investments. And I can't let J.T. find out about this other matter. He'd never help me again."

Dani began to talk slowly. She spoke very distinctly and clearly, and she saw that the woman was listening. "You need to do two things, Shelley. First, you have to ask God for forgiveness for what you did. The second thing is, you have to tell J.T. about all this."

"Oh no! I can't! He'll hate me. He'll cut me off forever."

"I don't think so. He's not the man he was when you were married to him. He's a believer in Jesus Christ now. He'll forgive you."

For twenty minutes Dani talked to Shelley. She pulled out the New Testament she always carried in her purse and read a few simple Scriptures—John 3:16 and Romans 10:28 and 29 and a few others showing the love of God for sinners. Finally she put her arm around the woman's shaking shoulders. "You have to trust God and cast yourself on His mercy, Shelley. There's no other way. If we pray right now together, and I pray for you, would you ask Jesus to forgive you?"

"Yes, I will. I'll do anything."

Dani prayed a short prayer. Shelley didn't say a word, but her sobs filled the room.

Dani finally concluded her prayer and said, "If you asked God to forgive you, you must go to J.T. and ask for his forgiveness as well, for you wronged him too. Will you do that?"

Shelley Bracken was a weak woman. She had never been strong, and life had caved in upon her so hard and so often that she had little hope left. But something in Dani's clear eyes and quiet voice seemed to assure her.

"All right. I'll do it."

"Good. I'll go now, but remember, God's going to see you through this."

As Dani left the house and got into her car, she wondered if she'd done the right thing. She knew J.T. had been a hard man in the past. "I only hope he knows something about forgiveness," she murmured as she drove toward home and some much-needed sleep.

◆ ◆ ◆

Ben slept lightly for a while, but a slight noise brought his head up at once. His eyes flew open, and he came to his feet. Leaning over the bed, he said, "Jamie, you're awake! Can you hear me?"

Jamie Cordova's eyes were open. Though she didn't speak for some time, Ben continued to talk to her, and finally she moistened her lips and pronounced his name. "Ben?"

"I'll be right back, Jamie."

Ten minutes later Dr. Simms entered the room. He shined a light into Jamie's eyes, checked her pulse and heart, and finally slipped the stethoscope back over his neck. "This is a wonderful development, Ben," he said. The two had spoken often and were now on a first name basis. "She's conscious, she knows us, and I think she'll get better very quickly now."

Ben grasped the doctor's hand with a grip that made the physician wince. "Hey, I need that hand!" He slapped Ben on the shoulder and said, "I'll keep a close watch on her."

"Thanks, doc."

Ben's eyes were bright as he leaned over Jamie. "How do you feel?"

"Not—not too good."

"You're going to feel a lot better real soon, Jamie." Ben pushed a strand of black hair back from her forehead. "You had me pretty scared there."

"Ben . . ."

"Yes, Jamie?"

"Dave should know—"

"I've already called him, and he's on his way. He'll be here in a few hours."

Jamie smiled. "Thanks, Ben."

Eighteen

THE MOUSETRAP

"I don't see how you drink that stuff. It doesn't have any taste at all," Ben teased.

Dani looked down at the decaf coffee she was sipping, then smiled. "You're just jealous because I have willpower and you don't. You know caffeine keeps you awake. You ought to switch over like I have."

Ben leaned back in his seat and glanced around Dani's office. His eyes rested for a moment on the portrait of the Confederate officer whose stern eyes seemed to look down on him. "I'll bet your great-great-grandfather would've drunk regular coffee. None of that sissy stuff for a rebel like him. Why can't you be more like him?"

As the two of them talked lightly for a while, Dani noticed that Ben's eyes were clear, and the stress lines were fading from his face. He was wearing a pair of tan chinos and a lime-colored T-shirt that revealed the muscles of his upper body. She glanced down and noted that although he wore scruffy moccasins, at least he had socks on, though they didn't seem to match any of the rest of his clothes. She had given up long ago on helping him improve his careless dressing habits. Finally Ben looked over his cup, his dark eyes studying her thoughtfully. "Thanks, boss."

"Thanks for what?"

"For praying for Jamie."

"You think prayer works then, do you?"

"It does for you."

Dani shrugged her shoulders. She had been anxious for Ben Savage's spiritual condition, but his face usually became a mask when she brought it up. This was one of the few times he'd commented on her beliefs. "I don't understand prayer," she said thoughtfully. "I just know that God really cares about us and answers His prayers accordingly." Sipping the coffee, she leaned forward. The sunlight from the window to her right highlighted her face. Her squarish jaw gave strength to her features, and the small mole on her right cheek served almost as a beauty mark, as with ladies in the seventeenth century.

"Did you find out anything from Jamie? About how she got hurt?"

"Yes, I did." Savage leaned forward, and a light gleamed in his dark eyes. "She'd been dating one of the workers she was suspicious of. He was always in the area where the sabotage took place, so she thought she'd see if she could come up with something. His name is Con Murphy. She was supposed to meet him and pay him for information, but she never made it. She was thrown off the ship instead."

"We have to follow up on this."

"Of course. I'll ask him a few questions."

"No rough stuff, Ben."

"I'll play it smart. We'll need this guy."

The two talked a little more, and then Dani left to go to the bank. Ben pulled his cell phone from his belt and dialed a number. "Lieutenant Sixkiller," he requested. "Ben Savage calling." He waited for a moment, his eyes thoughtful.

"This is Sixkiller. What's up, Savage?"

"I need a little help, Luke. I don't usually come running to the police, but this time I think it's best if you could give me a little hand."

◆ ◆ ◆

A loud banging at the door and a raucous voice brought Con Murphy out of a sound sleep. He sat up in the ruffled bed and looked wildly around the room. It was dark, and he switched on the light, blinking at its fierce glare. The voice came again, along with another series of blows that seemed to jar the whole apartment. "Come on, Murphy, open up!"

Murphy threw the cover back and came to his feet. He grabbed a robe and put it on, shouting, "All right, I'm coming! Don't break the door down!"

When he opened the door, he was face to face with a rather frightening figure holding out a badge. "I'm Luke Sixkiller, New Orleans Police Department. You have the right to remain silent . . ."

Murphy listened, trying to pull himself together. Sixkiller was a solid-looking individual, and his obsidian eyes had a look that Murphy didn't care for.

"What's this all about, lieutenant?"

"It's all about your going to Angola for assault and attempted murder."

"Wait a minute! What are you talkin' about? I didn't do anything."

Sixkiller put his hand on Murphy's chest and squeezed his robe together. "You threw an undercover agent off a ship. She may not survive. You'll get a long sentence out of that."

"Wait a minute! Now wait a minute!" Murphy shouted. "I don't know what you're talking about!"

"You've been going out with her. We have evidence of that. She's testified that you were supposed to meet her and take a payoff for information."

"It's her word against mine."

"It's more than that," Sixkiller said, slowly rocking the smaller man back and forth. There was a cruel pleasure in his lips as he said, "You're going to love it up at Angola. Good-lookin' guy like you will be real popular among the homosexuals up there."

"You don't have any evidence. It's just her word."

"There's more than that. She had some skin under her fingernails. I have no doubt it'll match your DNA."

"No, it won't." Relief washed across Murphy's face. "And that'll prove it wasn't me."

"Let's save ourselves a lot of time. Tell me who it was, and you're home free. If you don't . . ."

Murphy was a weak man, and the policeman's chilling threats brought sweat to his forehead. "I'm not goin' to Angola for anybody. It was Juan Martinez."

"The security chief?"

"That's right. He's the one who hired me to mess up the work."

Sixkiller listened as words tumbled out of Murphy's mouth. Ten minutes later he said, "All right, let's go down to the station."

"You have to believe me, lieutenant. It wasn't me. I wasn't near the dock that night."

"You're going to write this all up as a statement. Then we'll see what Martinez has to say."

Murphy begged and pleaded, and finally Sixkiller said, "You give me one little favor, and maybe I'll give you a break."

"Okay, okay, anything. I don't want to go to Angola, lieutenant. What do you want?"

◆ ◆ ◆

Juan Martinez slept lightly, and when the phone rang he was awake in an instant. Lifting the receiver from the cradle, he turned and looked at the young woman in bed beside him. "Go back to sleep," he told her. Then he said into the phone, "This is Martinez."

"Listen, Juan." The voice that spoke was frightened and tremulous. "The cops are after me. They came by my place and shook me down. They *arrested* me."

"Where are you now?"

"I'm out on bond. But listen, I'm skippin' town. I've got to have some dough. I'm splittin'."

"What did you tell 'em?"

"I didn't tell 'em nothin', but they're gonna try to get me for attempted murder."

Martinez's eyes narrowed to mere slits. "Stay where you are, Con. I'll bring you some money."

◆ ◆ ◆

Pulling up beside the shabby apartment building where Con Murphy lived, Martinez paused and put his hand briefly on the gun at his side. He wore his uniform, which gave him the right to wear the gun. He scanned the streets. It was almost dawn, and the streets were practically empty. Getting out of the car, he mounted the steps, went quickly to the second floor, and knocked on the third door to his left. The door opened at once, and as soon as Martinez got inside he said, "All right, tell me everything."

"Sixkiller came here last night. He arrested me."

"What did you tell him?"

"I didn't tell him anything, and I ain't goin' to. I had to put up all my money to make bond, but I'm skippin' town."

"They have no proof. They're bluffing."

"The woman had skin under her fingernails where she fought somebody, and it wasn't mine."

"They lied to you," Martinez said with a scowl.

"I can't risk it, Martinez. Just give me some dough."

Martinez looked at the man for a moment, then with a swift movement pulled his gun. "You're a bad business risk, Con. I can't let you go. You know too much. Don't take this personally—this is just business, you know?"

"Wait a minute! You can't kill me, Martinez!"

"Sorry. No hard feelings. I can't—"

At that moment Sixkiller stepped through a side door, and moving like a cat he swung and struck Martinez's gun arm. The weapon clattered to the floor, and when Martinez scrambled after it, Sixkiller kicked him in the ribs, then picked up the gun. "You have the right to remain silent," he began, then completed the litany that he recited to all suspects.

As soon as Martinez came to his feet, he muttered, "You don't have anything on me, cop."

At that moment another door opened, and Ben Savage came out with a video camera in his hand. "You've been on Candid

Camera, Juan. See that little hole in the wall right beside the picture? We have it all on tape. A grand jury's going to love you."

"I'm not saying anything," Martinez said between clenched teeth. "I have the right to make a call."

"Sure. Make your call, Juan."

"I want it in private."

"All right. Take it in the bedroom. Ben, go outside and watch the window. If he tries to run, plug him."

Martinez waited until Savage left, took a deep breath and gave Con Murphy a chilling glance, then silently stepped into the bedroom.

"You did real good, Con," Sixkiller said.

"Can I go now?"

"No. You'll still be charged with sabotage, but at least that's not as serious as attempted murder. I imagine you'll only get a few months if you have a good lawyer."

Nineteen

"TWO ARE BETTER THAN ONE"

Dani and Luke Sixkiller had arranged for a meeting with J.T. Denver. They found his son Travis there, and after greeting the two, Denver said, "Well, what have you found out? Mad Jack is the culprit, right?"

Sixkiller was wearing, as usual, a rather ornate outfit for a police officer. He was given to expensive fashions, and the light gray jacket fitted him like a glove, and the charcoal slacks had a crease like a razor's edge. The Johnston and Murphy shoes gleamed under the overhead lights, and Dani thought how strange it was that such a hard, tough man, pursuing and arresting the most violent people of the world in the streets of New Orleans, took such care about his appearance.

"We have a weak case here, Mr. Denver."

"Weak! How can that be?" J.T. Denver said, astonishment dominating his facial expression. "Cordova's willing to testify, isn't she?"

"She can testify to what she saw, but it won't sound very strong to a jury. Juan says he went to buy her off, there was a scuffle, and she fell off the scaffolding."

"What does Miss Cordova say, lieutenant?" Travis asked, his sharp eyes studying the burly policeman.

"She says that when she told him she was going to blow the whistle, he simply grabbed her and threw her off."

"We all know better than to believe Martinez's story," Dani said indignantly.

"Sure, we know better, but in court it'll be his word against hers."

"You had her telephone bugged, didn't you?" Travis asked.

"Yes. We got a recording, but nothing that we can pin on Jack Byron."

"He's smart." Denver shrugged. "Mean and smart. I'd be surprised if he left any tracks we could follow."

"But Juan admits he was hired by Byron," Dani insisted.

"That's what he says," Sixkiller nodded. "But all he's got is some phone calls when he claims he talked to Byron. How long do you think it'll take a defense attorney to break that down? Besides, Byron always works through underlings. So when you come right down to it, it'll be the word of Juan Martinez against Mad Jack Byron." Sixkiller leaned back and shrugged his burly shoulders. "Who do you think they're going to believe?"

"It won't be Martinez," Travis said. "Things just don't work that way."

J.T. commented, "At least Byron knows we suspect his shenanigans, even if we can't prove it. He wouldn't dare to do anything more now. I doubt we'll have any more trouble."

"I think you're right, Dad," Travis said. "It wouldn't be smart for him to risk more sabotage."

Dani suddenly spoke up. "Lieutenant, did Martinez confess to trying to run J.T. down in that semi?"

"No. He swears he didn't have anything to do with it, and you know, I think I believe him. Not that I think he's above lying, but he seemed surprised when we sprung it on him. He got real excited. I guess he knows one more charge might put him away for a long time."

Denver sat there quietly for a moment thinking, then said, "Well, that's that. Thank you, lieutenant. You've done a fine job."

"I don't think so," Sixkiller said. He rose to his feet and turned toward the door. Just before he left he turned back and said, "There's something wrong with all this, Mr. Denver. I hope we find out what it is. In the meantime watch your back."

When the door closed, Travis said at once, "Dad, I think you ought to keep Miss Ross on the job for a while. I'm still worried about whoever tried to get you with that semi."

J.T. Denver lifted his eyebrows. "I've sort of put that out of my mind."

"I don't think you should, Mr. Denver," Dani said quickly. "You may think I'm just looking for more work, but at least let me do a little more probing. If you lift enough rocks, you just might find a snake."

"All right, Dani. You keep looking around. But rather than spend my time fretting about what might happen, I've been working on my spiritual growth. I'm getting quite an education about churchgoing."

"How's that?" Dani asked.

"Well, I was all wrong in what I thought about church and things like that." Denver's eyes narrowed, and he shook his head. "I can't believe how arrogant I was, thinking I could handle everything on my own."

"That's not surprising," Travis commented. "You've always handled things on your own. The trouble is, there are some things we can't handle ourselves."

"I ran across a verse in Ecclesiastes last night," Denver said thoughtfully. "The one that says two are better than one." He reached over and put his hand on Travis's shoulder. "Two *are* better than one, son. I'm glad there are two of us."

Dani smiled, then left saying, "I'm going to the hospital. I'll see you later."

As she drove, she thought about how strange it was that these two men, father and son, had found each other—and even more, had developed a real affection for one another. J.T. had longed to have a son, but it was surprising to Dani that Travis had so quickly accepted J.T. as a father. *If I don't do anything else in this case, at least I've helped J.T. Denver find a family and helped Travis find a new father. Thank You, Lord.*

When she arrived at the hospital, she found Jamie Cordova sitting in a chair, with Ben nearby. The patient looked rather pale but smiled at Dani. "Hello, Miss Ross."

"Hello, Jamie. You look much better!" She shook the young woman's hand and said, "When do they say you'll be able to go home?"

"Maybe in a few days."

"Well," Dani said, "if you want a permanent job, we can always use an agent like you."

Jamie shot a glance at Ben, and when she looked back at Dani there was an odd look in her eyes and a half smile on her broad lips. "I guess I can't do that, although I thank you. I've had another offer back in Denver."

"You're not going back to work for the police department, are you?"

"No. Better than that. My husband and I are getting back together again. He came, and we talked."

"I didn't know he was here."

"Yes. He couldn't stay long because he had to get back to his job. And besides, he's fixing up a place for us. We're going to get married again. I think we can make it this time."

"Sure you can, Jamie," Ben said with a grin. He reached over and tapped her lightly on the shoulder. "You tell that big lug if he doesn't treat you right, I'll come down and put *him* in the hospital."

Jamie smiled brightly. "It's going to be different this time. You know, I thought I was dead when Martinez threw me off that ship. I've always heard that people's lives flash before their eyes when they're about to die, but all I could think of was that I haven't been fair to Dave." Tears came to her eyes, and she fumbled for a Kleenex. "It's a shame I nearly had to get my neck broken to learn what a good man I had and how foolishly I've behaved."

"Better late than never," Ben said.

The three sat there for a time, and twenty minutes later the two detectives left.

"Let's go get something to eat," Ben said.

"Eating is all you ever think about, Ben Savage."

Ben suddenly reached out, put his arm around her, and pulled her around in a half embrace. "No, it's not all I think about."

Dani laughed. "I don't want to hear your foolishness. All right, let's go get something to eat."

The two drove to the Camelia Grill, where they had strawberry waffles. As they ate, Ben said, "I guess the job with Denver is over, right, boss?"

"Well, it should be, but I'm not sure we've figured out what happened with that accident, or who was behind it."

"You want me to do some more probing?"

"No. I want to look into it myself."

The two finished their meal, and when he drove her back to the hospital, where her car was parked, he started to get out to open the door for her. She reached out and caught him and pulled him back. "I have something to confess to you," she said.

Ben was surprised at the rather odd look on Dani's face. She lowered her eyes, and he said, "I can't imagine what you have to confess. I've always thought of you as the perfect woman."

"Well, you're wrong about that, Ben."

"Well, what is it? Where's the body buried? Whatever it is, we'll make it through."

"It's not so very awful, I don't think," Dani said tentatively.

Ben suddenly grinned, relieved it wasn't as momentous as he'd feared. "Tell me what it is, and I'll make up my mind about how serious it is."

"Well, I might as well tell you." Dani seemed to be struggling, and finally she blurted out, "I was jealous of Jamie." Her face grew red, and she turned away and started to leave the car.

Ben laughed, caught her by the arm, and easily pulled her back. He put his arms around her and kissed her on the lips. It started out as a light caress but quickly became more. He had never told anyone, but Dani Ross had a way of getting him to believe in the special relationship the right man and the right woman can enjoy. For the moment he only knew that there was a sweetness and a richness in this woman that filled him and satisfied him.

"This is what we need," Dani said facetiously. "Necking in broad daylight."

"I knew you'd fallen for me."

Dani laughed abruptly. The embrace had reminded her that something within her responded to Ben Savage in a way she couldn't explain. "I just didn't want you to get tied up with the wrong woman." She left the car, and when he got out and stood beside her, he smiled. "I'll bring all my women who have been chasing me to the office for your approval."

Dani knew he was treating this lightly to make it easier on her. She looked up and said quietly, "Thanks, Ben."

He reached out, ran his hand down her cheek, and marveled at the smoothness of it. But he only said, "It's been a tough time for us, boss, but we'll be all right."

Twenty

BEN'S MISTAKE

Ben Savage had a mind that could either go as straight as an inter-state or meander and twist like the Mississippi River. He was never quite sure which of these traits qualified him to be a private detective, but he had learned to trust both types of thinking depending on the circumstances. He left *The Nancy* at noon on Thursday. He had the rest of the day off, and he planned to put everything connected with J.T. Denver completely out of his mind. As he stepped out of the small dory, he nodded to the crewman dressed in white and murmured, "Thanks a lot." The sun was bright, the sky as blue as he'd ever seen it. Only a few white clouds drifted along in the east. Ben started toward his car when he heard a voice calling him.

"Ben! Ben, wait for me!"

Turning quickly, he saw Tara Franz coming toward him. She was wearing a batik print dress with a deep scoop neckline, and her ash-blonde hair was free and blowing in the slight breeze.

"Hello, Miss Franz."

"Oh, come on now. Never mind the Miss Franz stuff." She took his arm, and her green eyes laughed at him. "Where are you going?"

"It's my day off. I think I'll go down to the hardware store. They have a new selection of sheetrock in. Care to come along?"

Tara laughed, a fine musical sound that Ben found especially pleasant.

"Your day off? It's mine too. Isn't that a coincidence? Seriously, what are you going to do?"

"I'm going up for a flight."

"A flight? You're a pilot?"

"Yep. I have an old biplane I restored. A fellow was crop-dusting with it, caught the wheels in a power wire, and flipped it. It took me two years to put the thing back together."

"Take me along. I've never ridden in a small plane before."

Ben's straightforward thinking began to waver. She was an attractive young woman, too young for him, and not someone he would ever get serious about. But then again she *was* part of the complicated scheme of things in the J.T. Denver case. He and Dani had talked for some time about looking into the lives of the Sandersons and the Franzes just as they had into Maris Nolan's and Shelley Bracken's backgrounds. *This would be a good way to find out something about that part of the family.* One part of him said, *You just want to spend some time with this gorgeous woman*, while another part said, *Maybe you can break this case.* Not knowing which motive was right he grinned, his white teeth a sharp contrast with his tan skin. Undecided, he responded, "I can't take passengers—I don't carry insurance."

"I don't care about insurance. Come on, let's go."

Ben led her to the Studebaker, which he had also restored. It was a beauty now, but it had been nothing but rust and tattered fragments of upholstery when he found it under an oak tree on a farm on a back road near Baton Rouge.

"This car is awesome! Did you restore it yourself?"

"Sure. I couldn't afford a thing like this. Get in." He plopped down behind the wheel and waited until Tara sat beside him. He started the engine, which let out a deep-throated roar. He pulled out and threaded his way through traffic to the airport. Tara talked about a great many things but didn't mention her family much. She was mostly interested in Ben Savage, it seemed. The detective avoided most of her questions, and when they arrived at the airport and got out, she smiled at him and winked. "You used to be a policeman, didn't you?"

"For a while."

"You're not giving out much information. I guess you're more used to worming information out of people than in giving it."

Savage shook his head. "Hey, this is my day off. "

Thirty minutes later the two were sitting in the cockpits of the biplane. Ben had learned that his passengers generally needed some assurance of safety, especially those who had never ridden in an open plane. So he'd rigged a two-way radio, and now as the engine split the silence he spoke to Tara, who was in the front seat. "You sure you want to do this?"

"Sure, Ben. "

He taxied the plane out to the runway, spoke to the tower, then took off. When they were in the air, Tara turned back, her eyes flashing. "It's fun, Ben," she said through the radio. "Not at all like riding in an airliner."

"That's what I say. I think everyone ought to fly at least once in an old crop-duster."

For a time Ben simply circled New Orleans, and Tara enjoyed pointing out the sights from the air. "There's the zoo," she said. "And look over there—the aquarium. Ben, this is fun! Can you loop the loop or something?"

Ben Savage performed a few rather mild acrobatics, nothing serious, and she loved it.

They followed the winding, twisting curves of the Mississippi past the cotton fields and the rice farms, swooping low from time to time so Tara could get a look at some of the mansions that hadn't been destroyed by the Civil War.

Finally they returned to the airport. As soon as they landed, Tara jumped out, her eyes sparkling. "That was so much fun, Ben! I wish I could learn to fly."

"You could. Just hire yourself a good teacher."

"Couldn't you teach me?"

"I'm not qualified to do that."

Tara leaned against him. "I bet you could teach me a lot of other things though, Ben."

There was a seductive tone in Tara's voice, and her eyes gave an open invitation. Ben couldn't deny she was a beautiful young woman, but he knew that what she was suggesting would be wrong.

"Are you hungry?" he asked, hoping to defuse the situation.

"I'm always hungry."

"Let's go down to the Quarter."

"All right."

Ben drove to the French Quarter and parked on one of the narrow streets. The two walked down Bourbon Street, filled as always with tourists. They walked past strip joints and bars that advertised female wrestling. As always, Ben was discouraged by the sight of the tourists, especially the more youthful ones, many of whom had a fascination with sinful pleasures. The next morning, Ben knew, many of them would wake up trembling and sick in a motel off the old airline highway with empty wallets and memories that would sicken them.

The two walked to Jackson Square and found a seat at the Cafe DuMonde. It was crowded, so they took one of the outside tables. They drank cafe au lait and ate sweet rolls. Across the way the twin peaks of St. Louis Cathedral reached to the pale blue sky, which was growing darker now. The clean, sweeping design somehow seemed to the detective to mock the pitiful, human derelicts passing beneath its facade.

As Tara ate, she kept asking Ben leading questions and finally discovered that he'd been an aerialist with the circus as a young man.

"Really?" Her eyes grew large. "I knew you were well-built, but you really turned somersaults way above the floor?"

"I really did."

"It looks so dangerous."

"It's not as dangerous as cutting trees."

"Oh, Ben, I don't believe that!"

"It's true." Savage nodded. He enjoyed being with the young woman. She was vivacious, lovely, sexy, and quite bright. "The most dangerous job in the United States is logging. More men get hurt and killed at that than at any other profession, including being an aerialist."

Tara suddenly laughed. "You know more useless stuff than any man I ever knew."

Ben couldn't help laughing with her. "I guess you're right about that. I don't know why, but I can always remember things that don't matter. I even remember my high school locker combination."

"What was it?"

"Right ten, left six, right fourteen."

Tara reached forward and took hold of his hands. She studied them and said, "Strong hands. I bet you do karate."

Ben laughed. "Maybe *you* ought to be the private detective, not me."

They sat at the table for a long time, and Tara grew quiet. She said she felt like ordering a margarita but knew she shouldn't because she found it too easy to drink too much. But a few minutes later she gave in to temptation and had one anyway.

She was curious that Ben would drink only Perrier water. "Don't you drink alcohol at all?"

"No."

"Why not?"

"Because I'm a drunk."

Surprise widened Tara's eyes. "You mean you're an alcoholic?"

"No, I mean I'm a drunk."

"What's the difference?"

Ben laughed suddenly. "The drunks don't have to go to the AA meetings. I found out when I was very young that I could get in big trouble with alcohol. I liked it too much. That was when I was flying for the circus. I missed a catch one time. All I'd had was two small drinks, but it was enough to throw me off."

"Did you get hurt?"

"Yes. I hit the net, bounced out, and came down on the hard ground and twisted an ankle. That was the last drink I ever took. I saw I had great potential for becoming a drunk."

He studied the girl carefully. Her face was round, and she had the smoothest skin Ben had ever seen. It made a man want to reach out and touch it. But she was studying him too, and he suddenly grew uncomfortable. *I'm thinking too much about her. It's time to change the subject.*

"Are you in school, Tara?"

"College? No. I didn't even graduate from high school. I just wasn't motivated, know what I mean?"

"I didn't do too well there myself," Ben said. "As a matter of fact, I missed most of it. I did get a GED though. I never went to college either. You don't need a degree to do a triple."

"That's what I keep telling Mom—that I don't need a high school diploma. She wants me to get a GED though."

"Your mom seems nice. You have a nice family. I like Bobby real well."

"Bobby's all right, I guess."

"He kind of reminds me of a young Jimmy Stewart."

"Yep," she agreed. "He's sort of an ineffectual fumbler."

"He must be pretty sharp or he couldn't work for your granddad."

"Oh, he's smart enough all right, but Mother runs his life." Disgust swept across her face. "He's a doormat."

"You don't think he'd do anything like trying to run your granddad down in a semi?"

Tara stared at Savage in disbelief. "Is that what you think? Is that why you brought me out here, to pump me about my family?"

"Now wait a minute! *You* invited *me*! I was just making conversation. Everybody's under suspicion who's connected with J.T."

"Well, you can scratch my father off the list. He's too squeamish. I've seen him nearly run off the road just to keep from hitting a rabbit." Tara paused for a moment, then said, "Of course, my mother could have done it."

"You don't mean that," Ben said quietly.

Tara suddenly laughed. "Of course I don't. It's ridiculous. She'd do anything to get control of granddad's money, but not that."

Ben suddenly grew uncomfortable with what was happening.

He knew he was doing exactly what she had suggested—pumping her for information. He felt like he was using this young woman, and somehow he had the feeling she'd been used enough. He said abruptly, "Let's go, if you've had enough."

"No. I want another drink."

In the hour that followed, Ben tried to talk some sense into her, but Tara insisted on going to a bar where she drank three Bloody Marys. Finally Ben took her by the arm and said, "Come on. We're getting out of here."

"Leave me alone, Ben. I can get home by myself. I'll take a cab."

Savage looked around the bar and shook his head. "Not a chance," he responded. He practically dragged her out of the bar and finally got her into the car. She said little on the way home. When he pulled up to the front of the Franz house he said, "Come on, I'll walk you to the door."

Tara turned toward him and suddenly fell against him. The street was dark except for a few streetlights, one of which cast shadows into the old Studebaker. She twisted around so she was facing him. Her arms were around his neck, and with a fierce and unexpected strength she pressed her lips against his, holding him tightly.

Aside from taking advantage of his superior strength, there was little Ben could do. The girl was weeping now, and her lips moved against his. She whispered, "I love you, Ben. Do you love me?"

Ben recognized that it was the alcohol talking, not the young lady before him. There was a wildness and a beauty to this young woman, and he knew he was teetering on the brink of a temptation he had to resist. Reaching up, he grasped her forearms and pushed her away from him. "This isn't right, Tara," he said quietly.

"What's wrong? Don't you like me?"

"That's not the point. I like you as a friend, but . . ."

Tara stared at him, and her body went lax. Ben released her, and she leaned against the passenger-side car door. Tears were running down her cheeks, and Ben realized there was a vulnerable quality in her despite all her brash flirtations. He wondered how much of it all was a front, and he regretted whatever he'd done to encourage her advances and for letting her drink too much. He of all people should have known better.

"I don't blame you for not wanting me," she sobbed. "I'm nothing but a drunk with heels."

Ben didn't know what to say or how to help. He only knew that his attitude toward her had changed. He reached out, put his hand on her shoulder, and said, "People can change." Ben believed his own words, though he didn't know how such change comes about. He wished Dani were here; she'd know what to say.

"No, they can't."

"You're wrong about that, Tara. You're a young, beautiful woman. You can become somebody. Your future doesn't have to be like your past."

Tara shook her head and suddenly turned and opened the door. Savage immediately got out and came over to take her arm. She didn't look at him as he walked her up the steps. As they reached the top, she glared at him with one of the oddest expressions he'd ever seen. "Well, I took my best shot, but you weren't buying."

Ben knew that he'd hurt this girl and that she'd been hurt before. "It's not that I don't care—just not the way you wanted." He put his arms around her and whispered, "You're going to be somebody, Tara."

"You don't know what I am."

"No, but I know what you could be."

At that moment the front door opened, and Loreen Franz stepped outside. Right behind her was Bobby Franz.

"Come into the house, Tara," Bobby said, shoving past Loreen. He stared at Ben, and for an instant the innocent, ineffectual Jimmy Stewart look was replaced by something that made the self-confident detective draw himself into a position of readiness. He had a built-in warning system about trouble, and for one brief moment he felt that this man was dangerous.

But the moment passed, and Franz lowered his eyes and took

Tara's arm. He walked into the house talking to her softly, but Loreen said, "Stay away from her! She doesn't need you."

"I'm sorry, Mrs. Franz. It's not the way it appears . . . At least not exactly."

Loreen glared at him, then whirled and stepped inside, shutting the door firmly.

Ben went back to the car, got in, and started the engine. He pulled the Studebaker away from the curve. *Fine job, Savage. You've hurt a young woman who didn't need more hurt, and now you've alienated two people you didn't need to alienate.*

◆ ◆ ◆

When Ben walked into the office the next morning, Angie immediately said, "Dani wants to see you. She's mad about something."

"What have I done now?"

"I don't know, but you'd better walk softly. You know The Look, and she's got it."

Ben knocked and stepped inside. Dani turned to face him, and her look hit him like a hammer. He knew her well enough to detect personal anger.

"What is it?" he said.

"Bobby Franz called. He said you brought their daughter home drunk last night."

Ben Savage was not one to show his emotions, but the charge drew a response from him. He averted his eyes, unable to face her. "I'm sorry, boss."

"You're *sorry*? What were you thinking, Ben?" Dani's eyes were flashing. She came over to stand directly before him. He had the feeling she wanted to reach out, take him by the shoulders, and shake him as she would a small boy. "We're trying to do an investigation here, and you're fooling around with the daughter of one of the suspects."

Savage tried to defend himself. "Look, Dani, I just happened to run into her when I got off work, and I thought I might find out something about the Franzes."

Disbelief flashed in Dani's eyes. "You don't expect me to believe that, do you, Ben?"

He had no answer, and he simply stood there for a moment, then shrugged his shoulders. "I blew it. I'm sorry."

Dani was not through, however. She spent the next five minutes explaining to him the ethics of their profession. Ben just stood there unable to answer—he knew he was guilty.

Finally she said, "Just get to work. And stay away from that girl."

Without a word Ben left, and Dani suddenly found that she was trembling. She generally had steady nerves, but something about the whole affair had disturbed her. She knew it was somehow connected with her feelings for Ben Savage, and she knew also that she'd gone too far in the way she'd handled the situation.

Angie, who came in later to take dictation, asked, "What was that all about?"

"Nothing!"

"Oh," Angie said. "My mistake. I thought it was something. You ready to dictate?"

Twenty-One

A GIFT FOR SHELLEY

The Ingram Fitness Center had been a favorite spot for Dani for some time. She went there three times a week to work out, and sometimes Ben came with her. Today, however, she was alone, and as she churned her way through the water, staying within the lap lane, it felt good to put everything aside. The water was cold but invigorating, and as she hit the end of the lane, she flipped over expertly and shoved away with all of the strength in her legs. She had always been a good swimmer, having made the team in college, and it was the one thing she could beat Ben Savage at. She suspected this was the reason he'd work out on weights with her and teach her martial arts but seldom join her in the Olympic-size pool.

The regular beat of her arms and feet as they propelled her through the water lap after lap gave her pleasure. Rhythmically turning her head to take in a fresh breath of air and then the slow release as she sped along the lane was satisfying. The best thing about it, she knew, was that as she swam she put everything out of her mind—at least everything concerning the problems at the office and at home.

She finally completed her laps and, reaching upward, propelled herself out of the pool. Her chest was heaving deeply. She never felt she'd exercised enough until she was gasping for air. Getting to her feet, she picked up a towel and began to dry her hair. In the center of the pool five or six children were splashing, yelling, and screaming. Two teen-aged girls in black suits with the logo of the Ingram Fitness Center were watching them carefully and occasionally shouted instructions to not be so rough. They looked to be about sixteen and were carrying on a conversation as they kept the kids from drowning each other. Dani wondered what problems they might be facing. Trying to think back to when she was that age, she remembered that she figured then that her biggest problem was that she had a zit. She smiled as she thought about how much easier a zit was to treat than some of the problems that came along later in her life.

Moving along the edge of the pool, she made her way back to the dressing room where she took off her suit, grabbed her soap, and plunged into the shower. She started out with cold water, then warmed it slowly until finally it was as hot as she could stand it. When she was finished, she rubbed herself down fiercely with a woolly, white towel. One thing she liked about Ingram was that they furnished the thickest, fluffiest towels of any fitness center in town.

As she left the fitness center, the assistant manager, a tall blond fellow with intent blue eyes, grinned at her. "Good workout, Dani?"

"Very good, Tim."

"How about that date?"

"Ask me when you get to be as old as I am."

"Hey, I'm eighteen! And by the time I get to be your age you'll be older."

"That's right. Eat your heart out, Tim."

Dani smiled, knowing Tim had no problems with female companionship. Almost always there was a group of young girls looking at him adoringly and vying for his attention.

As she drove to the docks, she avoided taxi drivers who always paid little attention to anyone and expected people to get out of their way. The tourist season was on, and the tourists apparently thought they were immortal, for they walked across the streets without even looking.

When Dani reached the docks, she looked out over the bay

and saw it was one of those days when she wished she had nothing to do but get on a boat and sail around, just enjoying the salt air, the warm breeze, and the brilliant yellow sun reflecting onto the blue-green water. "Someday," she muttered, "I'm going to become a beach bum." As she said this, she stopped and shook her head. "I'll never own a boat like *The Nancy* though."

Coming aboard, she found J.T. out on the fantail getting a tan. She smiled as she stepped up beside him. "Those are some impressive bruises you have there, Mr. Denver."

"Oh, Dani, sit down. And I've told you a hundred times, call me J.T."

"I don't call men by their initials. Or at least only when I know their real names." She sat down and leaned back in one of the deck chairs.

J.T. sent a white-clad busboy off for some sweet tea and stretched carefully. "Why don't you use initials?"

"Because I think men are hiding something. Your name is probably Jazreal Timgonious."

Denver laughed. "It's not that bad."

"What is your real name?"

Denver gave her an odd look. "Jonathan Travis Denver."

Dani again found it touching that Nancy had named her child after Travis even though she never expected to be with him. She saw that Denver was reading her thoughts and smiled at him. "You're glad to have a son, aren't you, Travis, Sr.?"

He smiled back, and there was a light of sheer joy in his eyes. "It's what I've always wanted, Dani. And I couldn't have asked for a better son than Travis." He frowned then and shook his head. "Of course I missed his growing up. That'll always be a grief to me."

"Well, you can make it up now. You two have grown close very quickly."

"I've never seen a young man like him. He's sharp, Dani. He could be a great success in business."

"It looks like his mind has turned more toward foreign missions—helping people in other countries."

"True, and there's nothing wrong with that. That takes money, and I have the money. I plan to establish a corporation—the Agape Foundation. I'll bet you know what that means."

"Yes. It means 'love.'"

"Right." J.T. suddenly turned to her and shook his head with wonder. "I've missed so much, Dani. So much!"

"It's not too late. You're still a relatively young man. What will the Agape Foundation do?"

"Oh, all kinds of things. For one thing there's well drilling."

"Well drilling! You're going to drill wells?"

"Sure," J.T. Denver said eagerly. "In some of the villages in Central America the average people don't have any water. I noticed when I was there that you'd see people at all hours of the day and night trudging along with a big five-gallon bucket in each hand. I asked about it, and they said they had to take their buckets to where there was a spring or a river or where a friend had a well. That's pretty tough going."

"Who will you drill wells for?"

"First of all for the pastors of the churches. The people would have to come to him to get water for their needs. Then he'll be able to give them something else—the Gospel."

Dani sat back, sipped her tea, and listened with interest while J.T. described with obvious relish how he was going to get several well-drilling rigs, so he and hopefully Travis could go overseas and drill wells. He ended by saying, "It'll be hard work, and you can't believe how much government paper you have to go through just to get permission to do things for people. But we're going to do it. Nancy is excited about it too."

Dani listened with enjoyment as one of the richest men in America talked about how much fun it was going to be to put on old clothes and eat foods he might normally avoid and sleep on a cotton pad mattress. She had never seen such a change in a man, and finally she said, "I'm glad for you, Travis."

"I'm grateful to God for what He's done in my life. I was headed down the wrong way, Dani. I see that now. I thought I could run my life the same way I handle business, but this Christian life isn't a one man or a one woman thing, is it?"

"No, it's not. The Body of Christ is tied together by the blood of the cross."

The two fell silent then, watching the gulls as they squawked and begged for food. On shore a long-legged blue heron stalked majestically through the water. His head darted down, and he came up with a fish. Expertly he flipped it in the air, caught it, and swallowed it head first.

"Travis, there's something I have to talk to you about."

"What is it?"

"Well, you may think I'm interfering with your personal business, and maybe I am . . ."

"Well, that's all right. Just tell me what's on your mind."

"It's about Shelley. I think she needs something."

"What is it? Does she need more money?"

"No, it's not that." Dani hesitated, then said, "She wants your forgiveness, Travis. And I think if you'd give it to her, it would make a different woman out of her."

"Forgiveness for what?" Denver asked.

"I can't tell you."

"Why not?"

"It's not mine to say, and she's afraid to talk to you. But I think you ought to go to her. That would please me very much, and I think it would be good for you too."

"Her life is a mess, isn't it?"

"Yes, it is."

"I don't know what to do about Creighton. I've done everything I can in a material way. But you know, until a man changes in his heart, you can give him all the help you can, but it won't turn him around."

"I know. That's part of her problem too. Will you go see her?"

"Sure. I'll do it today."

♦ ♦ ♦

Shelley had only had two drinks by eleven o'clock. She didn't know why, but she had gotten up feeling depressed, again. After dressing and having a bowl of cereal for breakfast, she sat on the couch drinking coffee, with no inclination to do anything else.

The doorbell rang. Carrying the coffee cup, she went to the door and opened it, then stood stock-still.

"Why, J.T.! What are you doing here?"

"Just wanted to stop by for a little visit, Shelley. May I come in?"

Shelley was wearing a blue pantsuit, and her hair was a mess. She always tried to look her best when she saw J.T. Why, she never quite understood. Perhaps if she were honest, she would say it had something to do with getting more money from him. It was the first time he'd come to her place since the divorce, and she was so confused she could hardly speak.

"Nice place you have here, Shelley," Denver said.

"Would you like some coffee?"

"That would be nice."

"Come out on the balcony. We'll sit there."

J.T. followed her to the kitchen, and then the two went to a balcony with a wrought-iron dinette suite with dark red cushions. He sat down, looked across the bay, and said, "You always liked being near the water."

"This is a nice place."

Denver talked to her about herself, asking how she was, and finally said, "I don't know how to say this, Shelley, but Dani came to me this morning. She told me there might be something you want to tell me."

"I can't. I can't tell you." Shelley's face darkened, and she put her face in her hands. Her shoulders shook with her sobbing, and J.T. felt a sudden rush of pity.

"It's all right," he said. He reached over and put his hand on her shoulder, patting it. "It can't be all that bad."

"Yes, it is. It's the worst thing I've ever done in my life, J.T. You'll hate me."

Denver sat there waiting, puzzled, unable to think of anything this woman had done that could be so awful. He waited until her sobs subsided, then moved his chair closer to her.

"Shelley," he said, "we've had some harsh words for each other in the past. I wish I could take them back . . . But I want you to know one thing: If there's anything I can do for you, I'll do it."

Raising her tear-stained face, Shelley's lips trembled. "I have to tell you something—something that happened when we were married." Her face twisted, and tears ran down her cheeks. Groping in her pocket, she found a tissue and then said, "I may as well tell you, though I know you'll hate me."

"I promise you I won't."

Taking courage from his words, Shelly said, "When we were married I got pregnant, and I never told you."

Instantly J.T. realized what she was going to say. She couldn't seem to form the words, and as she struggled, pity grew in his heart for her. This was a new thing for him. He had been a hard man, but since he had given his heart to God, his life had changed in ways he found strange and mysterious. "You had an abortion, didn't you, Shelley?"

"Yes, I did, and I can't forget it."

J.T. waited for a moment, then said, "Shelley, I'm sorry it happened, and I wish you hadn't done that, but I'm not angry with you."

"You're not?" Shelley was shocked. Her eyes flew open, and she said, "I—I thought you'd hate me!"

"I think I would have if I hadn't found the Lord, but having Jesus in my life makes a difference. It's something I wish you'd think about, Shelley."

"Me?" Shelley was shocked. "Me become a Christian? Why, I couldn't be—not after all I've done. God couldn't forgive me now."

"Why not? Shelley, you and I made a mistake in getting married, and especially in the ways we treated each other. We hurt each other and broke God's laws. But your life isn't over."

"But I had an abortion. I know lots of women do it, but my folks were Catholic—my mother anyway, and she grilled it into me that abortion is a terrible sin—unforgivable. And the doctor who did the abortion has been blackmailing me—threatening to tell you."

"We'll put a stop to that," J.T. said quickly. "It shouldn't be too hard to put him away. I'll put Lieutenant Sixkiller onto it. I can guess how this has been a burden on you, Shelley. I know abortion is a sin, but it's no different from any other sin. I did some things, some that you know about, that were horrible. I was vicious in business. I destroyed some men completely, as much as if I'd put a gun to their heads." J.T.'s voice fell quiet, and he said, "But it's not too late for you."

"I wouldn't know what to do with myself. I wouldn't know how to start."

"I found a very good church recently—Dani's church. I think it would be good if you started going. You and Creighton."

"Creighton would never go to church."

"You never know what a man will do, or a woman either." J.T. smiled and said, "I forgive you readily, Shelley. But you need to ask God's forgiveness too."

"I don't know how to pray."

"I don't think God expects any eloquence. Just ask Him to forgive you for everything and to make you brand-new in your heart."

The two sat there for a long time. Shelley didn't know how to take this man. The man she had been married to had been hard, demanding, and unforgiving. But there was a gentleness in J.T. Denver now, and she was amazed. His kindness came as such a shock that she could barely speak for a long time. Finally she found herself saying, "All right, I'll do as you say. I'll pray, and I'll go to church. But I don't think Creighton will."

"Well, Creighton's having a bad time with his life, and I wasn't the best stepfather to him, so I guess I'm partly to blame. I'll try to talk to him."

"Oh, thank you, J.T.!"

"Well, I'll be going now, but ask Creighton to come to the ship. We'll see if we can't get him started on something a little better than what he's had."

Shelley rose quickly and showed him out. As soon as he left, she walked over to the couch and sat down. She was trembling and couldn't believe what had happened. The day passed slowly, and she couldn't stop thinking about how wonderful it was to not have to pay blackmail anymore.

About two o'clock that same day Creighton came in, and by that time she had better control of herself.

"Creighton," she said with excitement, "J.T. was here. He's such a different person now. He wants you to come by and see him. He says he'll help you."

Creighton shook his head, and bitterness distorted his face. "He doesn't care anything about us, Mother."

"Yes, he does."

"Look, I might as well tell you—I'm in hock up to my ears with some pretty bad men. If I don't pay them, they'll break my knees— or worse."

"So go see J.T."

"I wish that semi had killed him!" Creighton spat out.

"No, don't say that! Don't say that!"

"But that's what I think! You can see what's going to happen, can't you? He's going to marry that Livingston woman and adopt Travis as his heir. They've already talked to the lawyers about it. Do you know what will happen to you, to me? We'll be left out in the cold. He'll change the will, and we'll get nothing."

"But, Creighton, J.T. is a new man."

"I don't believe it."

"Will you just go see him?"

"Yeah, I'll go see him, but it won't do any good." Creighton turned and left the room, his back stiff. As soon as he was gone,

Shelley Bracken did something she hadn't done for years. Going to her bedroom, she fell on her knees and began to cry out to God for forgiveness and new life in her soul. She stayed there for a long time, praying for herself and for her son. The words J.T. had spoken to her had sounded strange, but the longer she prayed, the more she felt that somehow there was light and help for her and for Creighton.

Twenty-Two

THE SECOND TIME AROUND

The clouds over the Gulf were white and fleecy, more glistening than any lamb's wool. The sky itself was a brilliant blue canopy. Beneath it a white boat gently bobbed up and down on the swells. But the two men who sat at the rear of the boat were hardly aware of the motion. A third man sat silently behind the wheel. From time to time he looked up and nodded.

"They're just not biting today, Dad," Travis said. He reeled his line in, checked the bait, and, swinging his line out, released the catch that let the heavy weight carry the bait to the bottom. When it hit bottom he took four turns on the reel and leaned against the rail, studying the aqua waters surrounding them. "There's something really peaceful about being out here like this," he murmured.

Denver smiled. They'd been fishing all morning and had caught only a few snappers of legal size. But they had talked a great deal. Denver was fascinated by his son's mind, finding it penetrating, imaginative, exceptionally so for such a young man. The fishing trip had been his idea, and now as J.T. stood there soaking up the sun, he said, "I feel the same way, Travis. When you get out here where it's quiet and there's nothing but the water, the waves, and the breeze, it makes you think about just staying out here."

"But we can't do that." Travis grinned. He had his shirt off, and his golden tan was spread evenly over his upper body. His teeth gleamed white against his bronze face, and he lifted the line several times as if to entice a fish. "You like the action so much, I'm surprised to hear you say that."

"Yes, I like the action, but a man gets tired of that. This is the sort of thing I'd like to do more of. Maybe your mother would come out with us next time."

"Maybe. She likes to fish. But she said she wanted to go shopping."

Without warning Travis's pole suddenly dipped, and he yelled, "Hey, I got one! A keeper, I'll bet!"

The next thirty minutes were a pleasure for the two men. The fish Travis had snared was too big simply to haul aboard by brute strength. He lifted the rod as he struggled against the heavy weight, then quickly took a couple more turns on the reel. "I've never had one this big, Dad. He must be a monster!"

"Hang on to him, young fella!" the boat's captain said, grinning. "Don't let him get the best of ya!"

Denver stood back and watched. He fished a camera out of his duffel bag and took several shots of the young man as he struggled, the rod bent nearly double.

Finally the fish surfaced, and the captain came scrambling back. His eyes grew wide. "We'll have to have a gaff for that one." He snatched up a pole with a hook on the end and leaned over. "Careful now. Be a shame to lose him."

"What is it?" Travis gasped. "I've never caught a fish this big."

"It's an amberjack, and a big 'un, too. Best eatin' on the coast, I do believe."

The captain bent over, the hook poised. "Got him!" he said. Soon the fish was thrashing around on the floor of the small boat.

"Look at the size of that thing!" Travis gasped.

"That's one fine fish! It'll feed you for a long time," the captain announced.

"Congratulations, son. That's bigger than anything I've ever caught out here. You think it might be a record, captain?"

"I don't know. We'll weigh him when we get back. It's mighty big though. Fine fish!"

Travis said, "Let's go in. Anything else we do would be an anti-climax after that."

"I guess you're right." The captain nodded. He went to the cabin, started up the diesel engine, and turned the ship around in a long, smooth, sweeping curve. As the boat headed back toward the bay, the men admired the fish.

"I'm glad you caught that one, Travis. We'll get a good picture of it and have it enlarged."

"We can never eat that much fish," the young man said. "I wonder what we can do with it."

J.T. suggested, "Well, we could give some of it to the hands down at the shipyard."

"That'd be great, Dad," Travis agreed, grinning.

The two were quiet for a while, but J.T. seemed restless. He walked back and forth on the boat, balancing with the rolling of the small craft, and finally sat down beside Travis. "I have to talk to you about something."

"What is it, Dad?"

"Well, I don't know how this is going to sound to you, but—" He turned and faced Travis squarely. "I'd like to marry your mother." He hesitated, then cleared his throat. "Will that be . . . Do you think that would be all right?"

Travis laughed loudly and slapped his father on the shoulder. "I've been wondering if your intentions were honorable." His eyes made it clear he was teasing.

"I missed out on the best thing I could have ever had. The money and all that comes with it has left me empty. Muhammad Ali said, 'I had the world, and it wasn't nothin'.' I know what he meant. For years I've been going at top speed piling up money, and it's nothin'. I've loved your mother all my life. I'd buried it deep within myself, but as soon as I saw her, it all came rushing back. I was a fool, son, to let her get away. But if she'll have me, I'd like to try to make it up to her."

"Take a shot, Dad," Travis said. He smiled and said, "Sometimes things go better the second time around."

♦ ♦ ♦

The sound of the doorbell startled Nancy. She had been dozing on the couch after a hard morning's shopping. She had laid down to read but quickly dropped off to sleep. She sat up, slipped her shoes on, and went to the door.

When she opened it, she said, "Why, hello, J.T."

"Hi, Nancy. Can I come in?"

"Of course." She stepped back, and when he entered the room she shut the door. "How about some coffee?"

"Well, maybe later."

"Did you catch any fish?"

Denver grinned. "Travis did. The biggest amberjack I've ever seen. Just five pounds under the world's record."

"Oh, how wonderful!"

"Yes. I took lots of pictures of it. We kept some of the fish too. We'll have it for supper tonight. Most of it we divided among the people at the shipyard. Everybody likes fresh amberjack."

"I don't believe I've ever eaten it."

"Best fish on the coast, I think."

Nancy said, "Let's sit on the balcony."

They went outside and sat down at the small table. Nancy insisted on fixing coffee, and soon the two were drinking the fragrant brew. Nancy noticed that J.T. seemed rather nervous, and finally she said, "I know you very well. Something's on your mind. Well, out with it. What is it?"

For a moment J.T. struggled with his thoughts. Then he said, "I have something for you."

"Oh? What is it?"

Reaching into his pocket, Denver came out with a small, velvet-covered box. He handed it to her and said nothing.

Nancy gave him a quick look, then took the box and opened it. When the lid flew back, she gasped involuntarily. What she was looking at was the largest solitaire diamond ring she had ever seen. She stared at it, then looked up and waited for him to speak.

"I guess you know I love you, Nancy," Denver said simply. "I've talked this over with Travis." He laughed nervously. "I guess I asked his permission to ask you to marry me."

Nancy looked at the ring and said, "Why . . . I couldn't wear this, Travis."

"Why not?" Denver was taken by surprise. He noted, however, that she didn't refuse his proposal but merely spoke of the ring.

"I'd feel out of place wearing such an expensive stone."

J.T. took the ring back and swallowed. "I'm sorry. I meant it for the best. I do love you, Nancy." He put the ring back in his pocket, then reached out and took her hand. "Could you possibly care for me after all I've done to you?"

Nancy Livingston smiled suddenly. She was a direct woman, and over the short period of time since J.T. had come back into her life she'd thought much about this. His attention to her had been unmistakable, and she'd known for a long time that this moment was coming. She'd prayed about it too, and although she'd said nothing to anyone she was prepared for the moment.

"Yes, I do care for you, J.T. I guess I always have."

J.T. reached out and pulled her closer. He kissed her fully on the lips, then put his arms around her and held her close. "I feel like—I feel like I've been given a great gift. Travis said things can be better the second time around, and that's what I want for us."

Nancy put her arms around him, held him tightly for a moment, then released him and said, "But I can't live your lifestyle, Travis."

Denver knew what she meant. "Then I'll change my lifestyle. I've hated it for a long time anyway."

"What will you do? I know you. You can't sit still."

"I've been thinking about this a lot, and praying about it." Denver grinned then. "Sounds funny when I talk about praying. I'm brand-new at it. But I've been asking God what I could do, and here's what I think God wants of me. I've thought so much about what you and Travis have been doing in different places around the world for people. So what I want to do is to take the money I've made and set up a corporation—the Agape Foundation. Then you and Travis and I can go wherever we see a need, maybe in Central America where the hurricanes have left so many destitute. I could go down and help with that. I don't know much about such things, but you and Travis can teach me."

"Is this really what you want, Travis?" Nancy asked quietly.

"You know it is. I'm excited about it. I can't wait to get down there and get a well-drilling rig and go where people need help and carry supplies out there. And I have another idea. You'll especially like this one."

"What is it?"

"Why don't we load up *The Nancy* with supplies—blankets, food, medical supplies, building materials, anything we think is needed—and sail down to Central America. Then we can rent trucks and take everything to the interior, wherever people need help the most."

Nancy's eyes sparkled. Her lips parted with wonder. "That would be wonderful! I'd like nothing better."

"Would you consider letting it be a honeymoon trip?"

Nancy suddenly laughed. "You are a pistol, Travis Denver! But the answer is yes. We'll get married the day before we leave."

The two talked for a long time, and finally Denver stood up. "I'd better get going. There's lots to do. Give me a time limit. I'll talk with Travis, and then we'll all three get together and decide what supplies would be the best to take."

She followed him to the door, and he turned around slowly and put his arms around her. "They say you can't go home again," he murmured. "But that's what I feel like—like I've come home again."

"I feel the same way."

He studied her carefully. Her face was serene, but it grew prettier as he watched her. He drew her close, and his lips fell on hers. For a time they stood there. Finally she drew back saying, "You go your way now, and I'll think about our honeymoon."

J.T. Denver hugged her and left. As he did, he found that his heart was light, and a joy ran through him that he thought he'd left behind forever. It shocked him to realize that you don't have to be eighteen years old to be madly in love.

♦ ♦ ♦

In the days that followed Nancy's agreement to marry him, J.T. was often reminded of a saying attributed to Mark Twain: "It's easier to get a fish hook in than it is to get it out."

His life was tangled and complicated, made so by his multiple marriages. He knew now that he had never loved any of the three women he had married, but he also knew he was somehow responsible to them even though they no longer had a legal claim on him.

For several days he said nothing to anyone else but just made his plans. But finally he set out to do what he could to clarify the matter with his ex-wives. He went first to Vivian along with her daughter Loreen and Bobby, Vivian's son-in-law. It was a difficult meeting, and he could see as he explained his plan that they were all bitterly disappointed.

"I know you won't really understand this," he said finally. "I don't understand it all myself. I just know I'm trying to live my life God's way for the first time in my life. I've asked Nancy to marry me, and she's agreed. She, Travis, and I will be involved in our new venture."

The three listened as he explained his plan to devote all his energy and money to mission work, and Loreen finally said, "But what about us?"

"I'm going to be in this full-time, Loreen. But it's going to be a big undertaking—we can't do it all ourselves. If you and Bobby want to join in, maybe you could help with the book work."

Bobby said practically nothing, but after Denver left, he said heavily, "Well, that's that."

"He's got to be stopped!" Loreen snapped. Vivian nodded. She'd been married to the man for only a few years, but she'd never understood him. "I'll tell you, he's lost his mind!"

"We can get him committed," Loreen suggested.

Bobby said, "You'll never make that stand up." He acted as if he'd been given a paralyzing blow and couldn't get his mind clear. Loreen looked at him with surprise. "What's the matter with you, Bobby?"

"We've lost everything!" he mumbled. "We've lost it all."

"Not yet," Loreen said. "I'm going to talk to a lawyer. There must be something that can be done."

◆ ◆ ◆

Denver's meeting with Maris and Trevor was much easier. He went through his explanation again and finally said, "I know you're disappointed, but there's one thing I can do for you. It'll be about the last because all my money will be tied up in the foundation." He turned to Trevor and said, "I'm going to get the financing together for you to do this picture."

"Very good!" Trevor beamed.

Denver held up his hand. "But you have to understand, this will be the last thing I'll be able to help you with. Of course," he added quickly, "I've set up separate trust funds for Anne and Gayle. You won't have to worry about their college education."

"We won't have to worry about anything," Maris said. Relief was in her face, and she added quickly, "This picture's going to be a hit. It's the beginning of great things."

"I hope so, Maris." He wanted to add a warning that Hollywood was one of the most treacherous places in the world to work. Reputations and fortunes were lost there every day. He saw, however, that they wouldn't take his comments seriously; so he left and went on his final errand.

◆ ◆ ◆

"I think it's good, J.T.," Shelley said. Her eyes were clear, and it was the first time in many years that J.T. had seen her this late in the day without the effects of drinking. She was smiling, and her voice was clear as she said, "It's just wonderful, and I wish I could help."

"Well, maybe you can. I could take you down to Central America with us. You could lay bricks." His eyes teased, but not entirely.

Shelley shook her head. "I wouldn't be any good at that, but I have felt so much better since we prayed. And Dani's been a great help. She introduced me to the pastor of the church, and I've joined a class of women about my age. My life has changed."

"What about Creighton?"

A cloud came across Shelley's face. "I don't know what to do with him, J.T."

"I'll have a talk with him, just like I promised."

"Would you really?"

"Yes. I'll do the best I can."

He left and later that day found Creighton at his apartment. He seemed somewhat the worse for wear. His eyes were bleary, and he obviously was not at his best.

"I won't stay long, Creighton. You know I'm going to marry Nancy . . ." He explained carefully what his plan was, going into detail about the foundation. But Creighton was unresponsive.

"What's all that to me? I don't know what to do, J.T. I'm in such deep trouble."

"Gambling debts?"

"Yes. To Trumps Lamont."

"I've heard he's a dangerous man to welsh on."

"To tell the truth, I'm scared."

Denver hesitated, then said, "I'll tell you what I'll do, Creighton. I'll pay off your gambling debts this time, but that's it. If you're willing to work, you can work for the foundation. You'd be doing hard work in Central America, maybe in Europe." He had little hope that the young man would respond.

"That's not for me, but thanks for paying off my debt."

"How much is it?" Denver's eyes opened wide at the amount named, but he instantly wrote out a check. "All right. Be sure you pay him off. And, Creighton, I hope you don't mind my direct-ness, but you're a fool if you gamble with him or anyone else again. It's time to make big changes in your life."

"Yes, well . . . thanks."

J.T. noted that Creighton didn't say he would take his advice. He tried one more time. "I have lots of contacts, Creighton. You have brains. You're young. You could go far in just about anything you tried, but you've never really tried."

"So now I get the sermon, eh?"

"No sermon. I just want to make it clear that my money will be tied up in a foundation. I won't be able to reach in and get it like I can now. Doing a thing like this won't be possible later."

"Don't worry, I won't come asking you for anything else."

"You need to watch over your mother too, Creighton. She needs all the encouragement she can get."

"Of course. I'll do that."

Denver left Creighton's apartment feeling defeated. He felt good about Shelley, but he didn't see any bright future for Creighton. Nor did he think Maris and Trevor would survive in the world of Hollywood. He was worried about Vivian too, considering that she was such a helpless woman. Loreen was smart, and so was her hus-band Bobby, but they had leaned on him for a long time. Now they'd have to make it on their own.

Twenty-Three

DANI REAPS A HARVEST

The wedding of J.T. Denver and Nancy Livingston took place in the church that Dani had led them into. It was not, however, a large wedding. In fact, Nancy had taken a firm stand on this. "It's a new beginning, and this is a very private matter. I don't want to be in *People* magazine."

J.T. had been quick to agree. "You're right. I've had enough publicity to last me for a lifetime. It's going to be bad enough when the media folk find out how my life has changed direction."

Dani attended the wedding ceremony and was one of the first to go forward and embrace Nancy. She whispered to her, "You're going to have a good life together."

J.T. gave Dani a hug and said, "I can't tell you how much I appreciate all you've done for me, Dani. Before I get all my money tied up, I want you to know that I sent an extra bonus to the Ross Investigation Agency."

After they left the church, the small group went at once to *The Nancy*. When they arrived at the dock, Dani, who had not been at the ship for several days, was somewhat shocked. The dock was piled high with blankets, packages, and boxes of all sorts. She wandered along the stacks noting canned food, dried beans, spaghetti, and many other food items besides an impressive array of medical supplies. She and Ben hurriedly made their way through the men who were busily loading the supplies onto the ship.

"I bet the designer of *The Nancy* never thought it'd be used for a supply ship." Ben dodged a man with a hand truck piled high with cases of beans. They stopped long enough to watch him store it in a stateroom packed to the ceiling. The man wiped his brow and said, "A nice boat like this, and he's makin' a scow out of it. He must be crazy! Rich people are always crazy, I say."

Dani laughed and said, "I don't know about that. I think he's doing a very fine thing." She gazed at the huge piles of materials and supplies, then said, "Ben, did I tell you that J.T. and Nancy have decided to fly down to Nicaragua instead of going on *The Nancy*?"

"No. Why are they doing that?"

"It was young Travis's idea. He thinks they need some time alone, to get to know each other again. He talked them into leasing a plane and letting him fly them down there."

"He's a pilot?"

"Yes, and a good one."

"Pretty romantic," Savage commented. "You think it will work out, this marriage?"

"Yes, I'm sure of it. J.T. missed his way when he was a young man, but now God is giving him a second chance."

The two wandered around the ship, noting that every square inch of *The Nancy* was being filled with all sorts of supplies. "Look here—cases of dolls and toys," Ben said with interest. "What's that for?"

"I think that must be some of Nancy's doing. She was telling me the other day that the children over there, even under the best of circumstances, don't have anything to play with."

"She's a sweet lady."

"Yes, she is."

"She's going to have her hands full with J.T. Denver though. I know he's on the glory road and all that, but he has more energy than any man I ever saw."

"Well, he'll use it for Jesus Christ now, and that's good news."

Ben suddenly grinned. "I think you're right. I like to see a man go whole hog at anything. If I ever became a Christian, do you think God could use a thug like me?"

"Yes, He could, Ben," Dani said, suddenly growing very serious.

Savage couldn't bring himself to meet her gaze. He cleared his throat and, thinking of a convenient distraction, said, "I saw Shelley Bracken and her son getting on, and then Maris and her family. What's all this about?"

"J.T. told me he was going to have one last meeting with his ex-wives. I don't know what he's got planned, but the ship's leaving in two days. I think he just wants to tie up all the loose ends that he can."

"Three wives and all the kids. Sounds like a sultan meeting with his harem."

"Don't say anything like that to Mr. Denver. He's carrying a great deal of regret and guilt about these marriages. I've told him he can't go through life rebuking himself—he just has to start where he is and go on from there."

"I don't think they're going to be a very happy group. They're losing their meal ticket. Especially Creighton."

"Things might be looking up for him. His mother's had a change of heart."

"Well, I hope she passes it along to the son. He needs it."

The two wandered around with interest, and Dani remarked once that she wished she could go on a mission trip like this.

"Why don't we go?" Savage said.

"You wouldn't do that."

"Sure, I would, if you went."

Regretfully Dani said, "Right now we have some cases that need to be resolved."

She looked at her watch and said, "Nancy asked us to attend the meeting. I guess she needs a little support being in the room with so many of her predecessors."

The two made their way to J.T.'s large stateroom, which was already occupied by the ex-wives and their families.

Dani nodded and smiled to Nancy, then went to sit beside her. Nancy had taken a seat as far away from the center of the room as she could. "I wish I didn't have to be here, but J.T. wanted me to."

"Where's your son?"

"He said he'd just as soon not sit in on this. He's helping with the loading."

Savage moved along the wall, wondering what he was doing here. It didn't seem like his bodyguarding skills were needed any longer. But out of long habit his eyes studied the faces of those in the room. In some ways Vivian Sanderson looked more like Bette Davis than ever. Her hair was dyed too red, she wore too much makeup, and she was smoking like a chimney. During the investigation he'd found out she was a compulsive gambler, and he'd also learned that Loreen and Bobby Franz had financial problems. He studied Loreen and thought, *She's a hard woman. I'll bet she gives Bobby a tough time.* His glance shifted to Bobby, and he saw that the young man was sitting bolt upright in a chair. His face was pale, and he gripped his hands together. *He's scared*, Ben thought. *I guess he's never really been out on his own before, and he's got a whale of a challenge with that wife and that mother-in-law.*

His glance shifted to Shelley Bracken, who looked much better than she had on any previous occasion. She was wearing a dress made of pale green silk that was sleeveless and had a scooped neckline and wore a matching jacket. The dress fell below her knees, where shiny stockings covered her legs and pale green shoes finished her look. There was a glow about her that surprised Ben. Her son, however, was obviously not happy. There was a hardness about Creighton Bracken, and Ben Savage, who had bumped up against hard men most of his life, was wary. *There's the one I think most bears watching.* He had suspected for some time that Creighton was behind the accident that had almost killed J.T. Denver. But there was no way he could prove it.

Across the room, slightly separated from the others, Maris Nolan and her fiancé Trevor sat close together. She seemed tense, and the twin girls were for some reason quiet for once. Ben noted that Maris kept glancing at J.T., and there was something in her expression he couldn't define. However, Trevor seemed at ease.

There had been a murmur of talk in the room, but when J.T.

stood up, it all stopped, as if a signal had been given. He said quickly, "I appreciate you all coming." He hesitated momentarily, then shook his head. "This is an awkward moment for us all, I'm sure. I won't make a long speech. Nancy and Travis and I will be leaving in two days, and we may be gone for quite a while. I don't know exactly how long. But Nancy came to me a few days ago and made a proposal. That's why you're all here."

He looked around at the group and said, "I suppose every person would like to go back and change some things, but that's impossible. But as Nancy told me, the one thing I can do is to help you all financially."

Immediately each of the women perked up. Bobby Franz straightened up too, and his eyes widened. They all waited expectantly, and J.T. said, "I've decided to do what I can before I tie up all my money in the foundation. So this will be a gift to you from my wife Nancy. I gave all three ex-wives what I thought was a generous settlement when we were divorced. I'm going to follow Nancy's advice and give you that same amount now."

Immediately Shelley said, "Oh, J.T., that's so sweet of you!" Her face glowed, and she looked as if she wanted to run over and kiss him, but she restrained herself.

"I must say that's very nice of you," Maris said.

"Furthermore, although I don't have much confidence in your picture, Trevor, I'm going to finance it just as I promised."

J.T. turned to Creighton and said, "I know you've had some financial problems, Creighton, in addition to the one we discussed privately earlier. So I'm opening an account for you, aside from the one I'm giving your mother. She'll be paid regularly out of her fund, but she won't be able to withdraw any money from it." All understood the rest of the arrangement though it remained unspoken: *And neither will you.* "Creighton, I'm also going to pay off your debts, and I'll help you with any sort of *reasonable* project you want to start. What I want you to do, Creighton, is to get a new life."

Creighton swallowed hard. "Well, thanks. That's most generous of you."

"I hope you'll make responsible choices and do well, which you will if you include God in your plans."

Turning to Vivian, Loreen, and Bobby, who were sitting together, he said, "Bobby, you've worked hard for me, and I want you and Loreen to do well. If you want to start some sort of business, I'll be glad to help you."

Bobby swallowed hard and said, "Well, that's nice of you. We all appreciate it."

Loreen and Vivian gave their thanks, and then J.T. said, "Now remember, this is the last time I can assist you. I know you've always been aware I was there if you were in real trouble. But the way the foundation will be set up, I won't be able to take funds out of it for private reasons. We're giving all this to the Lord, and I hope that all of you will find the Lord as I have."

Turning to Nancy, J.T. smiled warmly. "Well, did I do it right?"

"Yes." Nancy looked around the room and said quietly, "I wish you all well, and my prayers are with you."

The group filed out then, but J.T. stopped Dani as she was about to leave with Ben beside her. "Thanks, you two."

Dani answered for them. "Well, maybe we'll be making a trip with you one day. A mission trip, I mean. Ben said he'd like to go."

"We can always use a pair of good private detectives when we're digging a foundation for a church building," Nancy said, her eyes sparkling. She was relieved, Dani could tell, that the ordeal was over, and J.T. also seemed to be very lighthearted.

As they left the room, Dani said, "Stories do have happy endings once in a while."

Ben said, "Well, it's not over yet."

"You're such a gloomy gus, Ben! Why not admit it's a happy ending? They love each other, and they're going to do a great work for God. And now J.T. has a son he can pour himself into."

"I guess you're right, boss. I've read too many modern novels where everybody ends up dead or miserable or at least unhappy. What say we go out and celebrate?"

"By doing what?"

"We could go to a wrestling match."

"You're crazy! I wouldn't sit through one of those things for a million dollars."

"In that case let's go to my apartment, and I'll entertain you with card tricks."

"No thanks. But you can buy me a steak at Antoine's."

"There goes my Christmas bonus," Savage said, grinning. As the two left, both felt they'd closed the door on the J.T. Denver case. And both were wrong.

◆ ◆ ◆

"I need to talk to you, Miss Ross."

"Why, of course." Taking the phone call in her office, Dani recognized the voice of Allison St. John and noted that she sounded fearful.

"I'll come over at once, unless you want to come to the office."

"No, I think you'd better come here."

"All right, Allison. I'll be there in thirty minutes."

It took forty minutes because the traffic was heavy. As soon as she entered, she saw that Allison was troubled.

"Where are the children?"

"Oh, they're at the playground. I wanted to talk to you alone, Dani."

"What is it? Is there a problem?"

Allison wrung her hands for a moment, then said, "I've been so happy with the church, and you've done so much for me and the kids. And I love my new job." Dani had managed to find Allison a fine job with full benefits. "I can't thank you enough."

"I was glad to do it. So what's the trouble?"

A quick streak of fear crossed Allison's face, and she straightened up. "I haven't been telling you the truth about that accident."

"Allison, did you see something you didn't report?"

"Yes. The police talked to me, and they wanted me to make a full report. But before I did, I got a call from a man. At first I thought he was from the police, but when I told him what I saw, he said I could never tell them. He offered me money to keep quiet. And when I refused he said . . . he said he'd hurt my kids if I told anyone."

"I wish you'd told me this earlier, Allison."

"I was so afraid, Dani. I didn't know who he was, and I didn't have the money to run and hide."

Dani took Allison's arm and led her over to the couch. They sat down, and Dani talked to her soothingly for a time, though her mind was racing. Finally she said, "What did you see?"

"I was right behind Mr. Denver's car. I could see everything. This truck pulled out of the other lane and headed straight for him. I knew there wasn't a chance of survival if that small car Mr. Denver was driving was hit by that big semi."

"Did you see the driver of the truck?"

"No, but I saw what kind of truck it was."

"What was it, Allison?"

"It was a Pilgrim truck."

"The big rental firm?"

"Yes. You know the ones—they're all white with that pilgrim logo. I tried to see the driver, and then I tried to get the license number, but it all happened so fast. I was afraid Mr. Denver had been killed anyway, with his car rolling over the way it did."

"I'm glad you told me this, Allison."

"Dani, I'm afraid something will happen to me or my children."

"Don't worry. I think the danger is over. But I'll have one of my operatives keep an eye on your place for a few days anyway, just to be sure."

Relief swept across Allison's face, and she said, "I've felt so awful, especially since we've gotten so close and we started attending the church and all."

"You won't see my man, but he'll be around, protecting you all."

Dani left at once and drove to the office. She found Ben sitting on Angie Park's desk and said, "Come into the office, Ben."

"Sounds official," he remarked.

As soon as he was inside, she closed the door and told him what she'd learned.

"You want me to watch Allison's apartment?"

"No, I'll send Beau to do that. What we have to do is run down who was driving that truck."

"It's a big outfit. They have trucks coming and going all over the place."

"I have a feeling that whoever rented that truck did so right here in New Orleans."

"He'd be stupid to rent it around here, Dani."

"We have to find out. Let's get the phone book and find out how many Pilgrim rental agencies there are."

They studied the Yellow Pages for a few minutes, then divided up the rental offices. There were six of them in New Orleans, and Dani said, "You take these three, and I'll take the others."

"Okay, boss. You have any ideas about who's behind this?"

"I still think it's some member of the family, just as I always have. And here's another thought—J.T. hasn't changed his will yet. If he were to be killed before he can do so, I think the ex-wives are in for even more money than he's giving them now. So we have to run this down in a hurry."

"All right. If you find out anything, call me on your cell phone."

"You do the same."

Dani and Ben left at once, Dani leaving instructions with Angie that she'd be back as soon as she could.

The first two Pilgrim offices that Dani checked were quite willing to show her the rental records for that day.

At the second location she was told, "Not many people rent the big semis. Mostly people who want to move themselves, but they have to be able to handle a big truck."

The speaker was a large man named Max Simpson. He was wearing a white shirt with Pilgrim written over the breast pocket and a picture of a pilgrim wearing a tall hat with a wide brim and carrying a musket. "What do you want to know all this stuff for, miss?"

"Oh, just trying to run down a report."

"Well, sorry I can't help you."

Dani left, and as she headed toward the third Pilgrim office, she called Ben. "Did you get anything yet?"

"Not a thing, boss. Struck out all three times."

"Well, I have one more. If that doesn't work, we'll have to go outside the state."

"That would make it a lot harder for us to find out who the guilty party is, boss."

"I'll meet you back at the office as soon as I can."

"Call me if you learn anything."

Dani hung up the phone, then drove to the final Pilgrim office. It was actually outside New Orleans, in a nearby town. When she entered the place she discovered that the manager was a woman.

"Hello. Can I help you?" The woman was tall and had blonde hair. She was rather attractive though overweight.

"My name's Dani Ross. I'm a private investigator." She showed her license.

"Hey, a real private detective. My name's Suzy Martin."

"Miss Martin, I'm trying to trace a truck that was rented." She named the date and the time, and the woman's fingers scurried over the computer keyboard. "Let's see. Yes, we rented two semis that day."

Instantly Dani said, "Were you here when they were rented?"

"Sure. I rented both of them myself."

"Did you know either of the people?"

"I knew one of them. I should. He's my brother-in-law. He moved his wife and family to Arizona. They won't like it there, I told him. Nothing but cactus and sand."

"What about the other truck?"

"I didn't know the man. Let me pull the paper on it."

She fumbled through a file, pulled out a long yellow sheet, and studied it. "I don't guess there's anything wrong with letting you see this."

Dani stared at the name—John Johnson. He had given a New Orleans address. "Do you remember anything about him?"

"Not much."

"Would you know him if you saw him again?"

"I might. I have a good memory for faces."

Dani pulled out the small envelope in her purse. She had brought pictures of Juan Martinez and also of the family members of J.T. Denver. She handed them all over, and the woman at once put her finger on one. "This is him."

"Are you sure? It's very important."

"I never forget a face. That's him."

"Hmm . . . Bobby Franz. Thanks very much." Dani took a deep breath. "Hang onto that record. It'll be very important."

As she left the office, Dani dialed Ben's number. But she got the hated sound—"The person you have dialed is out of your area."

"Oh, great!" Dani said. "Well, I'll just have to catch him later."

She drove quickly back toward New Orleans, her mind working overtime. She thought about going to see Luke Sixkiller, but she had to be absolutely sure. "Ben will know what to do. I'll talk to him before I do anything."

THE KILLER

As Dani headed for the bay, she tried several times to get ahold of Ben, but there was apparently some sort of malfunction, and she couldn't make the connection with the cell phone. Finally she punched in the office number, and when Angie answered, she said, "Is Ben there?"

"No." Angie sounded startled.

"If he comes or calls in, tell him to meet me at the shipyard. I'll be waiting outside the ferry."

"All right, Miss Ross. I'll take care of it."

Dani hesitated, then dialed another number. Since she couldn't talk with Ben, she needed to get some other reinforcements.

"New Orleans Police Department. How may I direct your call?"

"Lieutenant Sixkiller please."

"Just a moment."

The phone buzzed in Dani's ear, and she swerved to move around a pickup truck with a Confederate flag flying proudly from the antenna. Across the back window she could see a thirty-thirty rifle, and as she passed, a huge, bearded man waved at her grinning toothlessly.

"This is Homicide. How can I help you?"

"I need to speak with Lieutenant Sixkiller."

"I'm sorry, ma'am, he's not here."

"Can you give me a number where he might be?"

"No, but I can give your number to him."

"All right. This is Dani Ross—983-4271. "

"Right, Miss Ross. I'll pass this on to him."

By the time Dani reached the docks, it was growing dark. She could see that the workday was over on the ferry, which now rose high in the sky, almost finished as far as she could tell. J.T. Denver had told her the work was going well and that he was assured of getting the contract.

She parked in front of the dock and watched carefully for a while. On the seat beside her lay a copy of a magazine called *The Robb Report*. The subtitle said "For the Affluent." Interested in the very, very rich and the way they think, she leafed through the magazine, at the same time keeping a close watch on the walk leading up to the ferry. The magazine mostly advertised expensive watches she'd never heard of—Hublot, Girard-Perrigaux, Ulysse Nardin. There were also numerous ads for guard dogs, mostly German shepherds. Part of the magazine listed real estate, and out of curiosity she studied the ads. One lake house on Cobin's Island in Canada had 4,400 square feet and listed for a mere 1,450,000 dollars.

But of course that's Canadian dollars, she joked. *A real bargain.* She played a little game with herself, picking out where she'd like to live, finally selecting a house outside Austin, Texas. It was listed for 4,650,000 dollars, and Dani studied it for a while, wondering what kind of people would spend that much money on a house. She had known that J.T. had that kind of money, but she couldn't really imagine what that would be like.

Quite a few cars were listed too, and she picked a 1999 Lamborghini Diablo Roadster. It was a flaming red, and she had the feeling she wouldn't even be able to afford the insurance on such a vehicle.

She began to grow nervous and wondered what she should do. She had long suspected, along with Ben Savage, that someone in the family had been behind the attempt on J.T. Denver's life, and now she had the evidence.

Granted, it was only *attempted* murder, but once she set in motion the events that were sure to follow, someone would be put in jail. She thought of talking to J.T. and almost decided to do so.

"I might as well at least go aboard and see who's here."

As she crossed the gangplank, she met a young man looking to be no more than seventeen. He was wearing a security guard's outfit.

"Hello, miss. Sorry, but we're closed for the day."

"I'd like to see Mr. Franz. My name's Dani Ross."

"I think he's in his office, but he doesn't like visitors after closing time."

Dani showed him her license and said, "I'm sure he won't mind. I'm working for Mr. Denver."

"Oh, yes, ma'am. I heard about that. I guess it's all right then. You go right ahead."

Dani flashed him a smile, then made her way on board. She didn't know what she was looking for exactly. She walked the whole length of the ferry and finally climbed the stairs that led to the top deck. Some perverse instinct moved her to come to the place where Jamie Cordova had nearly met her death. She stood there for a time wondering what to do. She tried Ben's number but again couldn't make the connection.

She left the ferry, said good night to the guard, and started back toward her car. Something caused her to turn back, and she glanced at Bobby Franz's office. All the other buildings were dark, but a light was still burning there.

"Maybe I should talk to Bobby and Loreen," she murmured. "Maybe there's a way to handle this without bringing everything into the open."

She made her way back and knocked on the door. When there was no answer, she opened it. The light was on, but no one was there. Quickly she stepped inside and closed the door. For a moment she just stood there, then moved over to the desk. Not knowing what she was looking for, she began scanning the materials on and in the desk. She found nothing and shook her head. "This is silly," she murmured. "What did I expect to find here?" She turned to leave when suddenly the door opened, and Bobby Franz stepped inside. His eyes were half closed as he shut the door behind him and turned the lock. "Hello, Miss Ross."

"Hello, Mr. Franz."

"What are you doing here?"

Dani hesitated. There was an odd expression in his eye, a glinty, dazed look. She suspected he'd been either drinking or taking some kind of drug. The pupils, she saw, were very small. "I just stopped by to talk to you and your wife."

"She's already gone home, so now it's just you and me."

Rather than feeling afraid, Dani felt she had to try to help this man. There'd always been something pitiful about him. He was insecure and saddled with a nagging wife and a domineering mother-in-law. Everybody spoke well of him but despairingly.

Taking a deep breath, she said, "Mr. Franz, I want to try to help you."

"Help me? In what way?"

Dani hesitated, then said, "Mr. Franz, you've done a terrible thing, but it's not too late to make amends."

"What terrible thing is that?"

Dani let her arms fall to her side, then quickly touched the small of her back. The .38 she sometimes carried there was in place, making her feel a little more secure. "I know what you did." He didn't move, and his expression scarcely changed. She went on, "I have proof that you rented the Pilgrim semi that nearly killed Mr. Denver."

For an instant, shock widened Bobby Franz's eyes, and then he began to tremble. "All right," he said, "I hired the truck. That doesn't prove anything. I wasn't driving it."

"I don't think that matters. If you rented it, no matter who drove it, you'll have to answer for what happened."

Bobby stood silently, and Dani could see that his mind was racing wildly. He moved a trembling hand through his thinning hair and shook his head. "I must have been crazy. I don't know what I was thinking." He moved around the room restlessly, then turned to her and held his hands out. "I didn't want to do it, but Vivian kept talking about how if he was dead, we'd have all that money and we wouldn't have to kowtow to him."

"Was Loreen in on it?"

"No. She didn't know anything about it. She treats me like a dog, but she's always respected her father. It was Vivian—she's the one who came up with the idea. Now I'll have to pay for it."

"Bobby, let's go talk to Mr. Denver. He's a changed man—more forgiving than in the past."

Franz laughed shakily. "I know what he'll do. He'll throw me to the wolves."

"I don't think he'll do that. There's more to J.T. Denver than you realize."

Bobby Franz said, "I want to show you something."

"What is it?"

"This." Suddenly Franz plunged his hand into a filing cabinet, and the overhead light reflected off the metal in his hand—a pistol with a silencer on it. He shut the drawer, then said, "I'm sorry you learned what you did. It's too bad for you."

"Think before you do anything rash, Mr. Franz. Don't make things worse for yourself."

"Just walk over to that wall and put your hands on it."

Dani looked at the gun and at Franz's hands and thought perhaps she could talk her way out of this, but when she looked at his eyes, she knew she'd better do what he said. She walked to the wall and placed her hands on it. He ran his hand across her back.

"I thought you might have a little toy like this," Franz said as he pulled the .38 out. He stuck it in his belt. "Too bad. Too bad."

Dani regretted that she hadn't talked with Ben or Luke Sixkiller. She knew what the man had done but hadn't realized he was so unbalanced. He had always been nervous and insecure, perhaps because of drugs, but now there was a malevolent purpose in his eyes, and she knew he would do whatever he thought necessary to protect himself.

"Why did you do it, Mr. Franz?"

"Because he always put me down. I did all the work, and he just threw me a few bones." His voice was bitter, but the weapon in his hand was steady. "Now he's married that woman and taken Travis as his son. What chance does that leave for any of the rest of us?"

"But he's made generous arrangements for all of you. Besides, if you go to him and just tell him you made a mistake, admit what you've done, I don't think he'll take it to the police."

An insane-sounding laugh echoed across the room. "I don't need to do that because after tomorrow there won't be a problem."

Dani stared at Bobby, hoping he didn't mean what she thought he meant. Finally she said, "What are you talking about?"

"By tomorrow noon at the very latest all my problems will be over. We'll have all the money we need then." He shrugged and said, "Too bad I have to share my portion with my wife and mother-in-law. I hate to think of that sorry Creighton getting his full share."

Dani felt a great uneasiness. "What have you done?"

"Oh, it's simple enough. He had to die, that's all there is to it. He's already made out a new will, but it hasn't been made legal yet, so it won't matter. He's leaving on a plane in the morning at ten o'clock. I have a friend who specializes in little things like this, the same man who drove the truck. That airplane will never make it to Central America. It'll go down somewhere over the Gulf, and there won't be enough left for anybody to find."

"You put a bomb on the airplane?"

"Yes—and the radio will malfunction too. I didn't want to do it, but he forced me into it. I went to the old man and told him he couldn't leave us out like this, but he refused to listen."

"You can't do this, Bobby."

"Bobby. That's what everybody calls me. You called me Mr. Franz earlier, but I'm just plain, little old Bobby to everybody else. But I won't be after tomorrow. I'll be Mr. Franz."

Dani saw that the man would not listen to reason. The drugs or whatever made that impossible, and she began desperately to think of a way to get his weapon away from him.

"You have to let me go."

"I'm afraid not. Lie down on the floor facedown."

Dani lay down fully expecting to be shot. But instead of hearing a shot, she heard a drawer being opened. Then her hands were pulled behind her, and she felt wire tighten around her wrists.

The same treatment was given to her ankles, and she could barely move as the wire cut into her ankles and wrists. He rolled her over and said, "I'm gonna gag you and leave you here, but I'll be back for you. We're going to take a little boat ride, but only one of us will be coming back." He giggled maliciously. He removed some duct tape from the filing cabinet and tore off a strip. He firmly pressed it over her mouth. "So long. I'll be back as soon as I can get the boat. It'll take a while, but you won't be going anywhere, will you?"

Franz looked around the room, turned the light out, and then stepped outside. Dani heard the lock engage, and the room was plunged into almost utter darkness. A little light entered around the blinds but not enough to see by. She was grateful he hadn't taped her eyes, but that was a small favor.

She struggled to a kneeling position and awkwardly moved over to the phone. She tried to scrape the mouth tape off against her shoulder but couldn't. She knocked the phone off with her head and tried to press the 0 with her nose, succeeding on the fifth try.

She put her head down to the receiver as a voice said, "How may I help you?"

Dani groaned and grunted but couldn't get any words out.

"May I help you please?"

Dani again tried to speak but couldn't. Finally the connection was broken. Desperately Dani tried again, getting an operator four times but unable to speak each time.

In the darkness she couldn't see the keys but tried blindly to dial a number. Once a voice answered, "Jackson Bowling Alley." Dani tried to scream, but nothing came out. "What is it? Is anybody there? What do you want?" Dani could've wept when the connection ended with a loud bang.

Her neck was aching as she thrust her shoulder onto the desktop and awkwardly stood to her feet. She hopped to the door and tried to open it with her hands but couldn't move the dead bolt, several inches over the doorknob, which itself was higher than her waist. Her hands were going numb.

I've got to find something to stand on. Staggering around the room, she crashed into a chair and fell, striking her temple on the edge of the desk. She felt the blood seep from her head, and pain knifed through her.

She finally worked her way to her feet again and found a straight chair and, grasping it behind her with her hands, managed to drag it back to the door, then tried to figure out how to climb onto it. Unable to use her hands or her feet, she got onto it on her knees but could go no further. She gave a desperate lunge, and the chair fell over backwards, toppling her onto the floor. She lay there helplessly and finally realized there was no way she could escape this prison. And when Franz came back, he would kill her.

Lying there in the darkness, Dani knew that unless a miracle took place she would soon be dead. She could hear the sound of her own heart. Outside a foghorn boomed somewhere down the coast, and far overhead she could hear a plane flying over.

Lord, if I can't get out of here, all three people in that plane will die. I'm helpless, but I know that You're not helpless. Lord, send somebody to set me free.

♦ ♦ ♦

The night was fading. Dani couldn't see a clock, but she knew she must've been bound for at least five or six hours, maybe longer. She was exhausted and had no feeling left in her hands or feet. Franz had made sure the wire was tight, cutting off the circulation. She made no other attempts to escape; there was nothing else she could do.

From outside she could hear cars and boats starting up. She'd prayed for hours, and she expected Franz to come back at any moment. In fact, she was surprised that he'd been away so long.

As she lay there exhausted and discouraged, she heard the sound of footsteps. They stopped in front of the door, and her whole body tensed. She expected to hear a key turn, but instead there was a knock. "Dani, are you in there?"

It was Ben Savage!

Feeling new hope, Dani rolled across the floor, right into the chair she'd knocked over. She heard Ben call out again, and then there was only a frightening silence. She rolled to the door, then raised her legs and struck the door with the heels of her shoes. She kicked again and again.

Finally she heard Ben say, "Back away from the door."

Dani could do no more than roll to one side. She heard Ben picking the lock. Suddenly the door swung open, and the radiance of nearby streetlights flooded in.

"Dani," Ben whispered. She felt his hands working on the wire. Suddenly her hands were free, and with a sob of relief she tried to rub her wrists. The wire was taken from her ankles as well, and then she was in Ben's arms. He was kneeling beside her. "Dani, are you all right?" he whispered. Then he saw the tape. "This'll hurt," he said. He pulled the tape off with a yank, and Dani gasped at the pain, though she knew it would've been worse if he'd pulled it off slowly. Her mouth was dry, and she tried to speak. "Here. Let me get some water," Ben offered. He carried her to the desk chair and set her down. He filled a cup from a nearby water dispenser and gave it to her. She drank all of it, and while he got another, she said, "Ben, we have to get to the airport—right away!"

He gave her the water and watched her gulp it down. She tried to stand to her feet, but her legs were weak. "Bobby Franz is going to kill them all. He's put a bomb on the airplane."

"Where is he?"

"I don't know. He went to get a boat. He was going to take me away and kill me, but he didn't come back. We can worry about him later. Help me to the car."

Ben didn't waste any time but just swept her up in his arms

and carried her out of the office. As they approached her Cougar, she realized it was locked. "My purse—it's in the office."

"You wait here."

Savage left her leaning against the car, and Dani stood there unsteadily, feeling nauseated. When Ben came back and unlocked the door, he had to help her get into the car.

"How are your hands and feet?"

"They're starting to feel prickly, but they'll be all right," she said. "How'd you find me, Ben?"

"I called the office this morning, and Angie said you were looking for me. I couldn't get you on the phone, so I went to that Pilgrim place, the last one you went to, and they told me what you'd learned. So I knew it was Franz. I had hoped you'd wait for me."

"I should have."

Savage started the car and drove away at high speed.

"We have to stop that plane from taking off."

"I'll call the airport." Ben drove with one hand and dialed with the other. When he got the airport on the line, it took five minutes to get through to someone who knew what was happening. He listened, then said, "Thanks."

He turned to Dani, his face sober. "They've already taken off."

"Ben, they'll all be killed."

Ben Savage shook his head. "No, they won't."

"But how can we get in touch with them? Franz told me he had the radio sabotaged—we can't communicate with them."

"We have a chance, boss. It's a small chance, but it's the only game in town."

He punched the airport number again. "I want to rent a plane, and it has to be warmed up and ready when I get there." He gave his credit card information. "We'll work out the details and the flight plan later. This is a matter of life and death. You can check with Lieutenant Sixkiller of Homicide."

He dialed another number and said, "Lieutenant Sixkiller please."

He waited for a moment and said, "Luke, I found her. Bobby

Franz is the guy we want. He's loose somewhere." He listened hard for a moment, then said, "Well, that's poetic justice." He turned to Dani. "Franz was picked up for drunk driving, and they found drugs in his car. He's in jail now on a narcotics charge."

"That'll be the least of his problems, I'm afraid."

"You're right. Meet us at the airport, Luke. They may give us some static, but with you there . . ." He briefly explained the situation, then said, "We're going to try to catch them." He listened again for a moment and said, "I don't know, but we have to try."

He turned the phone off, stuck it in his pocket, and raced down the road at top speed.

Twenty-Five

"IT'S A BIG SKY"

As soon as Savage piled out of the Cougar, he saw Sixkiller who came forward at once. "What is all this?" he demanded.

"Dani's been hurt. Will you take care of her while I see about the plane? She'll tell you all about it."

"What's wrong with her?" Sixkiller said, alarm flashing in his obsidian eyes.

"She has a bad cut on her temple, and her wrists and ankles are numb from tight wires. Do what you can."

Sixkiller stepped to the car at once and leaned down. "How's it going, doll?" he said, his eyes taking in the wan features. Dani was pale, and blood had stained her blouse and was matted in her hair.

"Come on inside. We'll have a medic check you out."

"No time for that," Dani said.

Sixkiller led her inside the airport, ignoring the curious glances. The burly lieutenant was known to some of them, and no one questioned him. He demanded and got a private room for him and Dani.

"We can't take much time, Luke," she said. "We have to get after them."

"Well, you need to get that cut looked at. It may need a stitch or two."

"That'll have to wait."

The door opened, and a tall, slender, young man of some thirty years walked through. "A little trouble here?" he said pleasantly. He had a flat Texas drawl. "I'm Dr. Mitchell."

"The lady got a bruise here and some cuts on her wrists and ankles."

"Let me take a look." Setting down his black bag, he looked first at Dani's head.

"How'd you get here so quickly?" Dani said.

"I'm waiting for a plane, and they asked for a doctor over the loudspeaker. This needs a little antiseptic, but no stitches, I'd say."

He cleaned the cut quickly and efficiently, put a bandage on Dani's temple, then examined the cuts the wire had made. He put antiseptic on them as well and said, "How'd you get these?"

"I did it, doc," Sixkiller said grinning. "I'm holding her captive until she agrees to marry me."

"Oh, Luke, stop that! Thank you so much, doctor. I got in some trouble, and a friend got me out of it."

As soon as the doctor left, Dani stood up and said, "Come on, we have to find Ben. Wait a minute! I need some paper and a big marking pencil."

"What for?"

"The radio on their plane is out. We'll have to show them a message in the window."

Sixkiller found the business office, where he commandeered a large roll of white paper and several black markers. "Come on," he said. "Are you sure you're up to this?"

"Yes. I'll have to be."

They found Ben standing beside a four-seater Cessna arguing with one of the managers of the airport.

"I can't let you take a plane until you've filed the flight plan."

"It's all right. This is an emergency." Sixkiller moved between Ben and the manager and flashed his badge. "We'll talk about it when we get back. Is this thing ready to go?"

"Yes, lieutenant."

Ben grinned, then climbed into the plane. Sixkiller easily picked Dani up and placed her inside. Then he got into the seat behind them. He pulled the door shut, and Ben said tersely, "Fasten your seat belts! This is going to be a quick takeoff."

He began taxiing toward the runway and, picking up the microphone, said, "Cessna 120 to tower. I'm taking off."

The voice jumped in and said, "You can't. There's another plane ahead of you."

"This is an emergency. Sorry." Ben shut off the protesting voice, grasped the stick, and shoved the throttle forward. The plane shot down the runway, passing several startled pilots who were waiting to take off.

As the Cessna left the ground at a sharp angle, Sixkiller said, "They're going to love you for this."

Ben made no reply. He was working the radio again. Dani and Sixkiller listened as he called the tower at the Navy's Pensacola Air Station. "This is Ben Savage, and I have Lieutenant Sixkiller of the New Orleans Police Department. This is an emergency. There's a plane flying over the Gulf with a bomb aboard and set to go off."

He gave the general location, and the voice answered, "We have a squadron of jets in the area. Keep on this channel so you can direct them."

"Right," Ben said. "Thanks a lot."

"Did you get a copy of their flight plan?" Sixkiller asked.

"Yes. It's pretty simple. They're headed straight across the Gulf. The first stop is Nicaragua."

"Will we be able to find them, Ben?" Dani asked.

"It's a big sky, Dani," he answered, his voice tight and his face tense. He shoved the throttle forward as they reached the right altitude. "I just hope Travis follows the flight plan."

"I'm betting he will," Dani said. "He's a very careful pilot, from what his mother told me."

"So what's the deal with Bobby Franz?" Sixkiller wanted to know.

Dani was silent for a moment, then sighed. "I guess it's time to tell you everything. He's the one who hired the truck that tried to run Denver down."

"But who is he?"

"He's J.T.'s son-in-law. Married to a daughter from a previous marriage."

She went on to tell how she had come to confront Franz. When she mentioned she'd gone alone, Sixkiller said, "Nice how you let the police know. We always appreciate cooperation like that."

"I'm sorry. I did call your office, but you weren't in."

"And you couldn't wait?"

"I know I should have. I made a mistake."

"I suggest that you not do that again," Sixkiller said sharply.

"He's right. Don't do it again, boss. It's too hard on my nerves."

The morning sun lit up the Gulf. It was a brilliant day, and all three of them searched the sky in every direction. Clouds were forming, and Ben said worriedly, "I don't know whether he'll go over them or fly under them."

"What would you do?"

"I'd stay under them."

"Better go with that then."

" I'll tell the jets to check over. They can cover a lot more ground than I can."

They flew on for a while but sighted nothing. "I don't know what speed they'll be flying at. This crate's not too fast, but we ought to be about even with them pretty soon."

"Seems kind of unlikely that we'll find them," Sixkiller said dubiously. "I never did like airplanes."

There was a silence for a time. Finally Dani said, "God will have to help us, Ben, but He's done it before, hasn't He?"

Five minutes later the radio crackled loudly. "Navy to Savage! Navy to Savage!"

"Savage here, Navy."

"We just spotted the plane," a jet pilot announced.

"What's your location?"

Savage listened, then said, "Stay with him. Can one of you guys come to our location and lead us to the plane?"

"Will do, Savage."

"Well, we have a chance anyhow," Ben said as he hung up the speaker.

"If they can find us, that is," Sixkiller mumbled pessimistically.

"They'll find us, Luke. I'm sure of it," Dani said.

No more than five or six minutes later, they saw a Navy fighter streaking toward them. It circled them with ease, then pulled up beside them. The fighter pilot grinned at them, moved closer, and waved his hand as if to say, "This way."

Ben waved back at him, then followed the jet, which had to fly at a much slower speed than usual to allow the Cessna to keep up.

"Wish we knew what time that bomb's set for. It might go off anytime," Sixkiller said.

"I believe God is with us, and with them," Dani said. "He can protect us."

It seemed like a long time, but finally Ben said, "There it is." He pointed forward and above their heads at a white plane with a jet slightly in front of it.

"I bet they wonder what that jet's doing," Ben said. "With no radio they're bound to be out of their minds."

Dani had been writing on the pieces of paper. "Ben, you'll have to get close enough for them to read what I've written."

"No problem." Ben pulled the plane up beside the white plane, and Travis gave him a startled look. "They see us. Show your message, Dani."

Dani had printed large letters on the biggest sheets that would fit in the window, and she said, "Give them to me one at a time, Luke."

"Okay."

Dani picked up the first paper—B—and held it there for a few seconds. When she lowered it, she saw Travis nod. She held up the other sheets one at a time, spelling out the message, "Bomb aboard."

Dani said, "They understand! I can see J.T. moving around, and Nancy too."

"Now they have to find it, and that won't be easy. It might even be in with the engine," the police officer commented.

"I don't think so. The flight pre-op would have taken care of that," Ben said. "It's inside—I'd bet on it. Probably under a seat or in a bag."

"Maybe you'd better move away a little bit, Ben," Sixkiller said a little nervously. "We're so close that if that thing goes off, it'll get us too."

Reluctantly Ben edged away, though not far enough to suit Sixkiller. But he said no more. Jets were flanking them on their right and left.

Suddenly Dani said, "Look!" They all saw a window slide open, and a brown bag fell out. They all watched it, hypnotized as it fell toward the blue water below. Just moments after it hit, there was a tremendous explosion and a huge geyser of water.

Sixkiller cleared his throat nervously. "Well," he said, "I wouldn't want to come any closer than that."

Dani saw Denver and Nancy waving at them. Dani motioned back and said, "All right, Ben, let's lead them home."

As they wheeled and turned, the jets followed. Ben picked up the microphone and said, "Savage to Navy."

"Come in, Savage. We read you."

"Well done, Navy. You saved three lives there."

"Call us anytime. We never close." The jets waggled their wings, turned upward, and with a majestic, sweeping curve headed back down the Gulf.

Dani watched them go and said, "Don't they call some of their planes Blue Angels?"

"Those weren't Blue Angels. Wrong kind of planes," Ben said. Then he grinned at the two. "But I guess they were close enough to angels for us."

Twenty-Six

WHEN THE GOING GETS
TOUGH . . .

Silence filled the office with an almost palpable air. It seemed to hang in the darkened corners and move across the ceiling. The only light in the room was a faint, pale glow that emanated from somewhere outside, perhaps one of the streetlights. The beams seemed to filter through the window even though the drapes were drawn, making a faint, squarish outline as they fell upon the carpet.

Dani sat in her chair, her hands folded and her head bowed. The silence of the office troubled her, a disturbing change from the music she always kept going on the stereo. Usually in the next room Angie was speaking over the phone or was talking with clients waiting to see Dani. But none of that could be heard now.

Until Dani heard a sudden sound—men's voices singing something outside. She couldn't understand the words of the song, but there was a rollicking quality to it that caused her to feel tense. She was not in a rollicking mood.

Angie had tried several times to penetrate the gloom that her employer had manifested during the last few hours of the day but without success. Finally Dani ordered her to leave. Angie did so, feeling troubled at the absence of her boss's usual cheerfulness.

Hours afterward, Dani locked the doors and turned the lights out in the outer office. She then returned to her own office, sat down in a chair, and turned off all the lights except for a small one on her desk. For a time she simply sat doing nothing and finally pulled out a Bible she kept in her top right-hand drawer, then peered into it silently for some time. Finally she put the Bible back and simply sat with her hands folded and her head bowed. She turned the light out so that darkness fell like a cloak over the room. She tried to pray, but it was one of those times when her prayers seemed to go no further than the ceiling. The words came slowly, laboriously, only with great effort. Finally she fell silent, and her mind started to wander—mostly over the intricacies of the Denver case. The case was solved, and everything had worked out, and yet parts of what had happened troubled her. She felt that the agency hadn't done as fine a job as it should have. True, nothing had happened to Denver, but he had almost been killed, and Nancy and Travis with him.

A slight sound caught her attention, and she straightened up. It sounded as if the door to the outer office was being opened. She hesitated, then reached into the central drawer of her desk and pulled out the Lady Detective .38 that she'd so disliked. But Savage had insisted that she buy it, and he'd also prevailed upon her to go out several times for target practice. She knew she would never become a marksman, considering that she had no talent or inclination in that direction. She went to stand beside the door. If it swung open and someone entered, she was ready.

She heard several more sounds and then the sound of the outer door closing, followed by a distinct clicking sound. Dani lifted the .38, wondering if she'd really be able to make herself use it. She'd never shot at anyone, but Ben had told her that a time might come when she would have to use it.

Who could it be? she wondered. Several cases involving the agency had made some people angry at her, and at least two men had made threats against her life. But both of them, as far as she knew, were still in prison, though convicts did sometimes escape.

Catching her breath, Dani saw the doorknob turn. She raised the gun and held her breath, willing herself to be totally silent. A shadow, darker than the shadows in her office, approached. Her eyes were accustomed to the darkness, and she saw that it was a man.

"Stay right there or I'll shoot!"

The intruder stopped, and Dani saw him turn toward her. "I mean it! I'll shoot if you don't stand perfectly still!"

"There ain't nobody here but us feebleminded detectives, boss lady."

Dani angrily lowered the gun. "Ben Savage, you fool! What do you think you're doing!"

Ben reached out and threw the switch, flooding the room with light. Dani's eyes blinked; then she shut them and turned away from him in disgust. Going back to the desk she opened the drawer, put the .38 away, and slammed the drawer shut.

"You forgot to take the safety off," Ben said casually.

"I don't want to talk to you! Please leave!" Despite Ben's role in rescuing J.T. and the others, Dani was still peeved at him for his foolish behavior with Tara Franz.

He was wearing his usual outfit—a pair of worn jeans, a white T-shirt that outlined the firm muscles of his upper body, and a tattered New Orleans Saints cap over his dark hair. "Well," he said coming closer and standing across the desk from her, "I've come here to worm my way back into your good graces."

"You'd better get started then," Dani said. "You've got a lot of explaining to do, especially about your behavior with Tara. I hope you don't think your better deeds made up for that."

"I know it, boss. I was wrong to try to get something out of Tara the way I did. I thought I might find out something about her family, and it backfired on me. I'm sorry."

The words had practically no effect on Dani. She glared at Savage and nodded briefly. "All right, you've apologized. I forgive you. Now go home."

Savage made no move to leave. He went over to the green leather chair pushed against the wall under a picture of horses anxious to jump over fences. "That fellow didn't know how to draw horses."

Dani glared at him with even more venom. "What do you want now?"

"Why are you sitting here in the dark?" Savage asked pleasantly. "Your eyes troubling you?"

"Yes, they are."

"I don't believe that. You're lying to me, and I'm going to get the truth out of you." Ben's eyes crinkled as he added, "After all, I'm a trained investigator. Bobby Franz is in custody, we got to J.T., Nancy, and Travis in time, but you're obviously unhappy. Now, out with it. What's wrong, boss?"

Dani rose from behind the desk and went over to the window. Throwing the curtains back, she stared outside without speaking. It was a foggy night following a rain, and the musky smell of the wet streets came to her clearly. Halos had appeared around the street-lights, giving them a ghostly air. Although it was late for most people—11 P.M.—the Quarter was just getting started. The streets below were not jammed as during the earlier hours, but there was still fairly heavy traffic.

She stood there so long that Ben came to stand behind her. "You have a case of the mulligrubs, boss?"

Despite herself Dani smiled slightly. "Mulligrubs? What's that?"

"Oh, being down in the mouth, I guess you might call it. Grief, overwhelming grief, aggravation, wishing you were in Hawaii or the North Pole—anywhere but where you are. That's the mulligrubs."

"Does it include not wanting to talk to anybody?"

"Oh, yes. That's a certain symptom. Come sit down by Dr. Savage." He pulled her over to the soft leather couch on the far side of the room, shoved her gently down, and sat beside her. "Now, let me see, I would say offhand that your trouble stems from the fact that your mother didn't change your diaper soon enough when you were a baby. No? Well, let's see. You weren't fed on time and you hate your father? No? Then I can't imagine what's wrong. Those two things are the root cause of most crimes, you know. Nobody's guilty anymore. Their mama is, or their daddy."

Despite herself, Dani felt better because of Ben's foolishness. He didn't show this side of himself often, but she realized that he'd seen beneath the facade she'd put up. "I'm unhappy all right, but it wasn't because of anything my mom or dad did."

"Is it because I put the moves on Tara?"

"No!"

"That's good because I'm an innocent man."

"No, you're not!"

"Yes, I am."

"You are not."

"Am too."

Dani turned so he couldn't see her smile, but he reached out and turned her face back. "Caught you," he said. "You're grinning."

Slapping his hand, she started to get up. But he simply reached out and placed his hand on the back of her neck and pulled her back down. "What is it, boss?" he inquired softly. There was concern in his tone and in his dark eyes. He had the darkest eyes Dani had ever seen, and his hair was almost as dark. There was a toughness about him that everyone could see, but only Dani and perhaps her mother had seen the gentleness that lay not far beneath the surface.

"Oh, I don't know, Ben," she said. His hand was on the back of her neck, and it felt comforting. "It's just everything. I mean, things worked out with the Denver case, but now it seems like everything is weighing me down—the agency, my dad's health, you name it. I'm worried about Rob and Allison too. It's hard growing up these days."

"It's always been hard growing up."

"I know, but times have changed, and they have some difficult choices to make."

His grip tightened, and he said, "I know it's tough, but they're good kids. And they have good parents, and they have you. They'll make it. They may get a few bumps and bruises along the way, but they'll make it."

"Do you really think so, Ben?"

"Sure. Can't miss."

His words cheered Dani up, and she said, "I like to hear you talk like that. Tell me some more good things."

"All right. You have a fine family. That's about half the battle. They don't come any better than your folks."

"You're right. I don't know why I let myself get down like this."

Ben said suddenly, "Are you really worried about the agency?"

"That's part of it."

"But we're doing pretty well, aren't we? I mean, Denver paid us well, and we got good publicity off the Silo Case. I thought you were even thinking about taking on a new agent."

"I am, but—I'm just not sure this is what I want to do."

"Now we're getting down to it. What do you want to do?"

"That's just it. I don't know."

"Join the club. Most people don't know. I had a friend who was a professor in college. He said most students got to be seniors without knowing what they wanted to do. They chose majors out of desperation in their junior year."

"This is worse than that."

"You just don't like the job?"

"Oh, I don't know, Ben. I just don't know."

The room fell silent again, and Savage studied the woman sitting beside him. He'd always admired her inner strength, but he had to admit that he liked the outer woman too. His eyes traced her clear-cut jaw, the mouth that was too wide for real beauty but could be pretty tempting at times, the eyes with the alluring lashes.

"Why are you looking at me?"

"Just resting my eyes."

"Have you listened to one single thing I've said, Ben Savage?"

"Oh, yes. You said you're unhappy, miserable, and don't know what to do with yourself. So why don't you get married?"

The words shocked Dani. "What are you talking about?"

"I've been reading some more women's books and magazines. You need fulfillment. Get in touch with the inner you; find a man you can dominate and make him marry you. That'll keep your hands full."

"You're ridiculous!"

"I'll let you borrow the book I read that in. It'll help you, boss."

Dani knew he was just trying to cheer her up, but because of her mood the past few days she couldn't quite accept his encouragement.

"I always try to be funny when I feel something strongly," Ben said suddenly. He put his arm around her and drew her close. "I think maybe you need a good cry."

"That wouldn't help."

"Well, it works for me."

"You never cry."

"That's what you think."

Dani started to answer, but her beeper suddenly went off. She looked at it, then said, "It's somebody from the house." She went over to her desk, picked up the small phone, and dialed.

Savage watched her carefully. One moment she was just discouraged, but the next she looked downright apprehensive.

"All right. I'll meet you at the hospital."

She turned the phone off and turned to Ben. "It's Dad. He's had another heart attack."

"Which hospital?"

"Baptist."

"Come on. I'll drive you there."

◆ ◆ ◆

The two entered the hospital and went at once to the cardiac ward. Ellen Ross was standing beside Dani's brother and sister, and the three of them turned with pale faces toward Dani.

"What happened?" Dani asked quickly.

"He started having chest pains. Pretty severe," Ellen said. She was frightened and unable to conceal it. "We called 911. We haven't been here long."

"Did he pass out?"

"No. Nothing like that," Rob added. "He just had this pain in his chest. I wanted to put him in the car, but Mom said it would be better if he were in an ambulance."

"That was the right thing to do," Dani said at once. "Has the doctor said anything?"

"No. We haven't talked to anybody yet. They're working on him now."

"There's nothing we can do but wait," Allison said. She looked very young and vulnerable, and Ben stepped over and hugged her.

"It'll be okay," he said quietly.

Allison looked up and swallowed hard. "Sure it will, Ben."

They stood there not knowing what to say. Finally they sat down, with Ben close to Allison. She held on to his hand as if she were a six-year-old, and he knew she was badly frightened indeed.

Time seemed to stand still as they waited. They had exhausted all conversation; there was nothing more to say. Rob stood staring out the window. Ellen leaned toward Dani as if to draw strength from her.

Finally the door opened, and a husky man with reddish hair came to greet them. "I'm Dr. Granger. "

"I'm Mrs. Ross. These are my daughters Dani and Allison and my son Rob. "

"How is he, doctor?" Dani said.

Ben studied the doctor and thought, *He looks more like a wrestler or a biker than he does a doctor.* He gazed at the huge, strong-looking hands. A long scar started at the doctor's eyebrow and wound around his face, and Savage wondered how he had received it.

"We're going to have to do a catheterization test."

"That's dangerous, isn't it?" Ellen said.

"Not nearly as dangerous as not having one. Most times it's just routine. We put a tube in from an artery, usually in the groin, and up into the heart. Then we release dye, so we can see where the blockage is."

Ellen said, "He had that done once before. It's frightening seeing that thing in your heart."

"You can *see* it?" Ben asked.

"Yes. It's on a monitor. It sounds worse than it is."

Ben swallowed hard. Somehow this was more intimidating than the many dangers he'd faced.

"How long will it take, doctor?" Allison asked.

"We can do it rather quickly. An hour at the most. Don't worry," he said. "Your father is in good hands."

After Dr. Granger left, the waiting resumed. Rob took Allison down to the cafeteria, mostly to get her out of the waiting room. "I'll bring some coffee back," he said as he left.

"Why don't you go with him, Mother. Ben and I will stay here. Nothing's going to happen right away."

"I think I will," Ellen said at once.

When they were gone, Dani paced the floor, then came and sat down heavily beside Ben who was staring at his clasped hands. "Why does this have to happen?"

"I guess a lot of people ask that," Ben said.

"I just don't understand it. Why do bad things happen to good people?"

"That's a title of a book," Ben said.

"Did you read it?"

"No."

"Well, what do you think?"

"I don't know, Dani, but you ought to have a better handle on this than I do—your being a Christian and all."

"That's not helping me much right now," Dani said, instantly regretting it. *I can't let Ben see how frightened I am. If being a Christian means anything, it means having faith. I'm not being much of a witness right now.* "Sorry, Ben," she said and forced herself to smile.

"It's all right," Ben said. Then he quickly added, "Did I ever tell you about the time we took the circus over to Europe?"

"No."

For the next thirty minutes Ben kept her entertained with stories of circus life in Europe. She knew what he was doing and was grateful for it. When her mother, Rob, and Allison came back, all three of them listened as Ben talked rapidly.

The door swung open right in the middle of one of Ben's stories, and they all rose at once. Quickly the doctor said, "It's all right. He had one artery that was almost occluded."

"Occluded? What's that?" Allison demanded.

"Almost closed. We're going to put a shunt in there."

"A shunt? I don't know what that is," Dani said.

"Well, there was a time," Doctor Granger said, "when we would put a little balloon in there, and it would press the walls of the artery outward and free it up. There's a new technique now. We put a stainless steel sleeve in there. It's very flexible, and the artery can't close on itself again as it did sometimes with the angioplasty—that is, with the balloon."

"Is it dangerous?" Ellen asked quietly.

"Not particularly. Anytime we go inside the body there's some danger, but we've had very good success with this. You mustn't worry."

"Will it take long?"

"No. We're already in there, so I just wanted to tell you what's happening. We should be done in about thirty minutes. I'll come back as soon as it's over."

"Thank you, doctor."

♦ ♦ ♦

Ben watched the clock on the wall and wished he could invent more stories. Thirty minutes had turned out to be an hour and a half, and a very young intern had appeared at the door once saying, "We've had a little delay, but we'll soon be through."

"We'll soon be through," Dani said quietly to Ben. "That word *soon* doesn't mean anything."

"It'll be all right, boss."

"Oh, I know, Ben. Thanks for staying with us."

"Where else would I go?"

Even as he spoke, Dr. Granger came back, and one look at his face told them what they needed to know. Dani expelled a sigh of relief as he said, "He's okay. We had a little trouble getting the shunt in place. It was in a spot that's hard to work on, but he's fine now. The artery is open and clear."

"Can we see him?" Ellen asked eagerly.

"It'll be a few minutes. He'll need to stay in intensive care tonight. We like to keep a close watch on these things. You can take him home tomorrow if there's no more difficulty."

Ellen couldn't speak, and tears came to her eyes. Dani went to her and put her arms around her. "It's all right, Mom. He's going to be fine."

"Thanks, doc," Ben said. "If I ever have this trouble, you're my man."

"What kind of work do you do, Mr. Savage?"

"I'm sort of a thug," Ben said.

"He is not," Dani said indignantly. "He's a private investigator."

Granger laughed. "Let's hope neither one of us needs the other. Someone will come and take you to see your husband, Mrs. Ross."

Before long, they were taken to a room where Daniel was lying on a gurney. He took one look at them and said, "I think I look better than any of you do."

"Dan, are you all right?" Ellen said, reaching over to take his hand.

"I'm okay. The good Lord was with us—again."

Dani brushed a lock of hair back from his forehead. "You scared the life out of me."

Her father squeezed her hand. "It's all right, honey."

Allison and Rob crowded in, but soon a thin nurse with a pair of serious gray eyes said, "Sorry to break this up, but we have to get him to intensive care. Two of you can see him in four hours." She wheeled the patient off, and he waved and smiled cheerfully as he disappeared from sight.

"I'm going to stay here at the hospital," Ellen said.

"I'm staying too," Allison and Rob said simultaneously.

Dani said, "I'll take a little break. After you see him in four hours, come on home, and I'll come back for the next visit." They all agreed, and Dani walked out of the room and down the hall and took the elevator down to the main floor. She was aware that Ben was at her side, and when they stepped out of the elevator, she said, "I'll see you later, Ben."

"You sure will because I'll be right with you."

She looked and saw that he was smiling at her.

"I'm glad about your dad."

"Thanks, Ben." She hesitated and said, "I guess I ought to go home and get some sleep."

"I'll drive you."

"You don't have to do that."

"I know, but I want to."

◆ ◆ ◆

The car pulled up in front of the Ross house, and as they got out Dani said, "You can go on back to your place, Ben. There's nothing to do here."

"If I thought you'd go to bed I would—but you won't. I know you too well."

"I'm going to try to sleep."

"I'll just see to it. Come on, I'll tuck you in."

"No, you won't!"

"Just kidding."

Ben followed her inside and said, "Are you sleepy?"

"No, just tense. I know Dad's going to be all right, but I can't relax."

"In the movies they always give somebody a glass of warm milk."

"I hate warm milk," Dani said. "But I suppose we had better fix something to eat. I'll cook."

"Nope. I'll cook."

"We'll both cook."

The cooking turned out to be fun, even relaxing. Ben knew absolutely nothing about cooking, while Dani was an expert, having learned it all from her mother. She fixed eggs and bacon and on a whim made biscuits from scratch. Ben hovered around her as she made them saying, "Why do you want to make them? You can buy them already made, can't you?"

"Yes, but they taste like wallpaper paste."

"When did you ever taste wallpaper paste?"

"Well, they taste the way I think wallpaper paste would taste." Dani laughed. "There's nothing like homemade biscuits, and I have some real honey that Dad got from one of our hives."

"You raise honey? I didn't know that."

"Dad does. He keeps five hives now."

When the meal was ready, they sat down with two cups of steaming coffee, and Dani bowed her head and said, "Lord, we thank You for the food, and we thank You for healing dad. In Jesus' name, Amen."

"Amen," Ben said. He picked up one of the biscuits, split it with a knife, then put butter on it. After spreading some of the honey over it, he bit into it. His eyes flew open with surprise. "Hey, this is good!"

"Of course it's good."

Ben devoured six of the biscuits along with his eggs and a good bit of the honey.

After Dani put the dishes in the dishwasher, she said, "Ben, stay with me a while."

"Sure. That's why I came."

A warmth came over Dani. She had long known that her feelings toward Ben Savage were more than just that of a friend. Now she knew, however, that he understood this. He had read her desire not to be alone. She leaned against him and put her arms around his neck.

She felt his arms tighten around her, and she clung to him for a moment, then pulled her head back. "How much do you charge for saving damsels in distress?"

"I have special rates for good-looking broads like you. Now, you go to bed and get some sleep."

"What will you do?"

"I'll lie down on the couch. Go on now."

Dani finally felt like she could sleep, or at least relax. She smiled saying, "We have to be back there in a few hours."

"No problem."

Dani left him then and went to her room. As she stretched out, the weariness and tension caught up with her. She began to grow sleepy. *Ben Savage is a pain most of the time—but he has his moments!*

Twenty-Seven

AN IMPROPER PROPOSAL

"I still can't believe what happened." J.T. Denver rubbed the heels of his hands against his eyes. Nancy stepped closer and put her arm around him. He blinked and then returned her embrace. "I always knew Bobby was weak, but I never thought he'd do what he did."

"What will happen to him, Dani?" Nancy asked.

Despite the trauma of her father's heart problems, Dani felt she owed it to J.T. and Nancy to help them deal with their own traumas.

"He'll have to stand trial for the drug possession. It depends on your husband about the other," she answered.

"I'm not going to press charges, and I'm going to hire the best lawyers we can get."

"He's going to do time," Dani said. "There's no way out of it for possession. I don't know how long he's been taking drugs, but this is the first time he's been caught."

"We'll do the best we can for him," Nancy said quickly.

J.T. was gloomy. "I guess some of it's my fault. I should have been a little closer to Bobby. After all, he's my son-in-law, and in some ways he's a good man."

"We'll do all we can," Nancy said soothingly.

"You're going to go ahead with your trip to Central America, aren't you?"

"Oh, sure, Dani. This won't change any of that. I was just thinking," J.T. said, "how things catch up with a man or a woman."

"Yes, they do. Sometimes not in this life, but we always pay."

"I hate to think about some of the things I have to pay for."

"Wait a minute," Dani said. "You don't need to worry about
that. You'll have to educate him a little bit, Nancy."

"That's right, J.T. When you're saved, the past is all gone."

"But you still have to pay for some of the results, don't you?"

"I suppose in a way that's true," Nancy said thoughtfully. "If
you get drunk and get hit by a train and lose a leg, God will forgive
you for your drunkenness, but you'll have an artificial leg for the rest
of your life."

"But God's given you a great second chance, Travis," Dani said,
calling him unconsciously by his first name. "He's given you a fine
wife, a fine son, and a great mission for God. And don't forget, Ben
and I are going to make one of those mission trips with you just as
soon as we get things cleared away."

"How is your father doing? We've been praying for him," Nancy
said with concern.

"He's doing well. God had His hand on Him, that's for sure."

Dani watched the two as they left her office, then sat down.
She was tired to the bone and laid her head back for a time against
the smooth, black leather. "I guess the case is all over," she murmured to herself. "And it had a good ending, all in all. It could
have been much worse. Jamie could have been killed. J.T. and Nancy
and Travis could have been killed. I guess a jail sentence for one
person is a small price to pay."

She got up abruptly and went out to the outer office. "I'm going
home, Angie, and I won't be in tomorrow. Dad's out of the hospital, but we're all still keeping a close eye on him. "

"All right. I'll hold all your calls. You ought to get some sleep.
You look exhausted."

"I feel like a wet dishrag."

Dani left in time to miss the traffic jam that always tied up
New Orleans streets at rush hour. She passed over the causeway,

not enjoying the sight of the water as much as usual. When she finally pulled up in front of her house, she was surprised to see Ben's car there. She walked around the house where she found him giving a gymnastics lesson to Allison. She stood there for a moment thinking of Allison, how innocent she was and how much pain and grief might lie in her path, and breathed a prayer for her safety.

She didn't interrupt the lesson, knowing that Allison was jealous of every moment she could get with Ben. Instead Dani went into the house, where she discovered that her mother had gone out shopping for groceries. Her dad was resting. Tired, she changed her clothes, pulling on a pair of jeans and a blue and white checkered shirt and slipping her feet into her half boots. Leaving the house, she went to the stable where she found Biscuit, her quarter horse, eagerly waiting for her. "You scoundrel," she said, "I'm going to give you a workout today." She saddled him, mounted, and enjoyed a ride for the next hour. She remembered the days when she'd run the barrels and thought fleetingly, *I'd like to do that again. Maybe I'll just leave everything and go on the rodeo circuit.*

The thought amused her, and she laughed aloud. Finally, when it was growing dark, she headed back to the stable. She'd taken off the saddle and was rubbing Biscuit down when Ben entered.

"Hi, boss," he said.

"Hello, Ben. Did Allison do well?"

"Yes. She always does." Ben stood watching her groom the horse and said nothing. Finally she turned and said, "Did you ever ride, Ben? I never asked you."

"No. I'm afraid of large animals."

"That's silly! After all you did in the circus on a trapeze?"

"At least part of the time there's a safety net under you. But if that horse falls on you, where's your safety net?"

She finished rubbing Biscuit down, then put some oats into his box and slapped his flank as she left. Ben followed her outside, and when they got to the end of the stable, he said, "There's something I want to ask you."

Dani turned. "What is it, Ben?"

"I—I want you to do something."

"Do what?"

"I think this case and your father's medical emergency have sort of wiped you out. So . . . well, see, I have this beach house for a week. It's down in Orange Beach. Lots of bedrooms, more baths than anyone can use. And a fishing boat goes with it! We'll do some offshore fishing. It'll be romantic. Maybe you'll lose some of your inhibitions."

Dani stared at him unbelievingly. "Ben, just what are you asking me to do?"

"I want you to spend a week with me at the beach house. What's so complicated about that?"

Dani tried to laugh. "That's ridiculous! You know I would never do a thing like that."

"Why not?"

"Because it would be wrong. What would people think?"

"What's wrong with a little vacation?" Ben said. He stood with hands on hips, examining her critically, an inviting look in his eyes.

"Ben, I know you think I'm the world's most straitlaced Puritan, but you've known me long enough to know that I won't go off with a man to a beach house for a week."

"I think you ought to, boss," Ben said. "We could get to know each other better."

Dani suddenly grew angry. "I never imagined you'd make such an improper proposal to me!"

Ben stared at her. "An improper proposal?"

"I know what you want, and I'm not going to spend a week with you that way!"

"Hey, it's not my idea. It's J.T. Denver's beach house, and Nancy told him to offer it to us. I don't think he has a mind of his own anymore. He just does whatever she says. It's his place, and he's put it up for sale. But he gave me the keys and said we might as well get some use out of it."

"Well, I'm not going with you and that's that!"

"I didn't think you'd be so narrow-minded, boss."

"I didn't think you'd be so rude!"

"Well, I've always been rude. It's never bothered you before."

"You never asked me to go off with you for a week!"

Dani was even more angry now. She started toward the house, aware that Ben was following her. "I can't believe you'd ask a thing like that!" she muttered.

As soon as she stepped inside, Rob and Allison met her. They were both obviously excited. "Isn't it great, Dani?" Allison asked.

"Isn't what great?"

"That we're all going to that wonderful beach house to spend a week together."

Dani blinked with surprise. She was determined not to look at Ben. "What's all this about?"

"Didn't Ben tell you?" Rob said. "J.T. Denver's given us his beach house for a week, or even longer if we want. It has a boat and everything. It'll be great."

"She says she won't go," Ben said suddenly.

"Won't go! Why not?" Allison inquired, bewildered.

Dani's parents had come up to join in the conversation. Ben looked at them and said flatly, "She thought I was making an improper proposal."

"I—I—you turn everything around!"

"Well, that's what you said," Ben protested. "You said I was making 'an improper proposal.'"

"You're nothing but an old Puritan, Dani," Rob said, "and you don't have a romantic bone in your body!"

Suddenly Dani was aware that everyone was trying to hide their grins. She whirled suddenly and saw that Ben's face was expressionless, but there was mischief in his eyes.

"You're just terrible, Ben Savage!"

"I know, I know. But doesn't that just make me adorable?"

A laugh went up, and they all converged on Dani. "You really need to be liberated, Dani," Rob said, winking over her head at Ben.

"Right," the detective said, "and I'm just the one to do it."

Dani couldn't help but join in the laughter. "I hate you, Ben Savage! You treat me—" When she couldn't finish, Ben said, "I promise to repent or whatever the right word is. You have a week to work on me."

Dani Ross looked at her family and suddenly felt a surge of gratitude. "You're right, Ben. We'll all see what can be done for you."

"Now that we have the improper proposals out of the way," Dani's mother said, "supper's on the table."

They all filed inside, but Allison stayed out long enough to whisper to Ben, "I think you have her eating out of your hand."

"That woman? Never!" Ben laughed suddenly. "If anybody will be eating out of anybody's hand, it'll be me eating out of hers. Come on, let's eat."

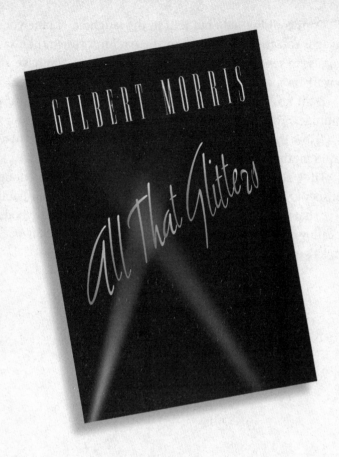

ALL THAT GLITTERS

Standing alone in her mother's empty apartment, Afton Burns is startled by the ringing phone—and the voice of her father on the other end, inviting her to join him on the set of the movie he's directing. Still suffering from the loss of her mother, Afton knows she needs to be near him and reestablish a relationship that was broken long ago. But that tinseled, movie-star world is an alien place that turns even stranger when it becomes clear that someone doesn't want this film to be completed. There is only one person Afton can trust with her heart and her life—and it's the last person anyone would expect.

THE CHRONICLES OF THE GOLDEN FRONTIER

Jennifer DeSpain's life used to be quiet and dull, but that was before a whirlwind romance and marriage—and a tragedy that left her a widow with only a defunct newspaper to her name. With hopes of a fresh start, Jennifer boldly moves her family to Nevada, where she will have to resolve the challenges of poverty, newspaper publishing, a reversal of fortune, parenting—and matters of the heart—all with the help of some colorful friends and the Lord above.

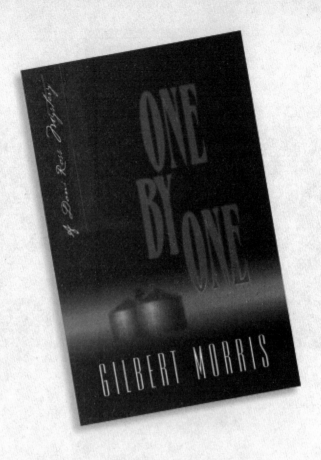

DANI ROSS MYSTERIES

Danielle Ross is a bright, attractive young woman whose plans of becoming a missionary have been put on hold. Returning home to run her ailing father's detective agency, she is immediately caught up in a sinister kidnapping case in which she becomes a victim, and later hired to protect a wealthy man from his would-be assassin. As Dani and her partner unravel each tangled web to identify the sinister minds behind the scenes, Dani also uncovers a fresh faith and a different way of understanding her new life.

BOOK 1: *One by One*   BOOK 2: *And Then There Were Two*